Doña Perfecta

Doña Perfecta

Benito Pérez Galdós

MINT EDITIONS

Doña Perfecta was first published in 1876.

This edition published by Mint Editions 2021.

ISBN 9781513290942 | E-ISBN 9781513293790

Published by Mint Editions®

MINT
EDITIONS

minteditionbooks.com

Publishing Director: Jennifer Newens
Design & Production: Rachel Lopez Metzger
Project Manager: Micaela Clark
Translated by: Mary J. Serrano
Typesetting: Westchester Publishing Services

Contents

INTRODUCTION

The very acute and lively Spanish critic who signs himself Clarín, and is known personally as Don Leopoldo Alas, says the present Spanish novel has no yesterday, but only a day-before-yesterday. It does not derive from the romantic novel which immediately preceded it, but it derives from the realistic novel which preceded that: the novel, large or little, as it was with Cervantes, Hurtado de Mendoza, Quevedo, and the masters of picaresque fiction.

Clarín dates its renascence from the political revolution of 1868, which gave Spanish literature the freedom necessary to the fiction that studies to reflect modern life, actual ideas, and current aspirations; and though its authors were few at first, "they have never been adventurous spirits, friends of Utopia, revolutionists, or impatient progressists and reformers." He thinks that the most daring, the most advanced, of the new Spanish novelists, and the best by far, is Don Benito Pérez Galdós.

I should myself have made my little exception in favor of Don Armando Palacio Valdés, but Clarín speaks with infinitely more authority, and I am certainly ready to submit when he goes on to say that Galdós is not a social or literary insurgent; that he has no political or religious prejudices; that he shuns extremes, and is charmed with prudence; that his novels do not attack the Catholic dogmas—though they deal so severely with Catholic bigotry—but the customs and ideas cherished by secular fanaticism to the injury of the Church. Because this is so evident, our critic holds, his novels are "found in the bosom of families in every corner of Spain." Their popularity among all classes in Catholic and prejudiced Spain, and not among free-thinking students merely, bears testimony to the fact that his aim and motive are understood and appreciated, although his stories are apparently so often anti-Catholic.

I

Doña Perfecta is, first of all, a story, and a great story, but it is certainly also a story that must appear at times potently, and even bitterly, anti-Catholic. Yet it would be a pity and an error to read it with the preoccupation that it was an anti-Catholic tract, for really it is not that. If the persons were changed in name and place, and modified in passion to fit a cooler air, it might equally seem an anti-Presbyterian or anti-Baptist tract; for what it shows in the light of their own hatefulness and cruelty are perversions of any religion, any creed. It is not, however, a tract at all; it deals in artistic largeness with the passion of bigotry, as it deals with the passion of love, the passion of ambition, the passion of revenge. But Galdós is Spanish and Catholic, and for him bigotry wears a Spanish and Catholic face. That is all.

Up to a certain time, I believe, Galdós wrote romantic or idealistic novels, and one of these I have read, and it tired me very much. It was called "Marianela," and it surprised me the more because I was already acquainted with his later work, which is all realistic. But one does not turn realist in a single night, and although the change in Galdós was rapid it was not quite a lightning change; perhaps because it was not merely an outward change, but artistically a change of heart. His acceptance in his quality of realist was much more instant than his conversion, and vastly wider; for we are told by the critic whom I have been quoting that Galdós's earlier efforts, which he called *Episodios Nacionales,* never had the vogue which his realistic novels have enjoyed.

These were, indeed, tendencious, if I may Anglicize a very necessary word from the Spanish *tendencioso.* That is, they dealt with very obvious problems, and had very distinct and poignant significations, at least in the case of "Doña Perfecta," "Leon Roch," and "Gloria." In still later novels, Emilia Pardo-Bazan thinks, he has comprehended that "the novel of today must take note of the ambient truth, and realize the beautiful with freedom and independence." This valiant lady, in the campaign for realism which she made under the title of "La Cuestión Palpitante"—one of the best and strongest books on the subject—counts him first among Spanish realists, as Clarín counts him first among Spanish novelists. "With a certain fundamental humanity," she says, "a certain magisterial simplicity in his creations, with the natural tendency of his clear intelligence toward the truth, and with the frankness of his observation, the great novelist was always disposed to pass over to realism with arms and munitions; but his æsthetic inclinations were idealistic, and only in his latest works has he adopted the method of the modern novel, fathomed more and more the human heart, and broken once for all with the picturesque and with the typical personages, to embrace the earth we tread."

For her, as I confess for me, "Doña Perfecta" is not realistic enough—

realistic as it is; for realism at its best is not tendencious. It does not seek to grapple with human problems, but is richly content with portraying human experiences; and I think Señora Pardo-Bazan is right in regarding "Doña Perfecta" as transitional, and of a period when the author had not yet assimilated in its fullest meaning the faith he had imbibed.

II

YET IT IS A GREAT novel, as I said; and perhaps because it is transitional it will please the greater number who never really arrive anywhere, and who like to find themselves in good company *en route*. It is so far like life that it is full of significations which pass beyond the persons and actions involved, and envelop the reader, as if he too were a character of the book, or rather as if its persons were men and women of this thinking, feeling, and breathing world, and he must recognize their experiences as veritable facts. From the first moment to the last it is like some passage of actual events in which you cannot withhold your compassion, your abhorrence, your admiration, anymore than if they took place within your personal knowledge. Where they transcend all facts of your personal knowledge, you do not accuse them of improbability, for you feel their potentiality in yourself, and easily account for them in the alien circumstance. I am not saying that the story has no faults; it has several. There are tags of romanticism fluttering about it here and there; and at times the author permits himself certain old-fashioned literary airs and poses and artifices, which you simply wonder at. It is in spite of these, and with all these defects, that it is so great and beautiful a book.

III

WHAT SEEMS TO BE SO very admirable in the management of the story is the author's success in keeping his own counsel. This may seem a very easy thing; but, if the reader will think over the novelists of his acquaintance, he will find that it is at least very uncommon. They mostly give themselves away almost from the beginning, either by their anxiety to hide what is coming, or their vanity in hinting what great things they have in store for the reader. Galdós does neither the one nor the other. He makes it his business to tell the story as it grows; to let the characters unfold themselves in speech and action; to permit the events to happen unheralded. He does not prophesy their course, he does not forecast the weather even for twenty-four hours; the atmosphere becomes slowly, slowly, but with occasional lifts and reliefs, of such a brooding breathlessness, of such a deepening density, that you feel the wild passion-storm nearer and nearer at hand, till it bursts at last; and then you are astonished that you had not foreseen it yourself from the first moment.

Next to this excellent method, which I count the supreme characteristic of the book merely because it represents the whole, and the other facts are in the nature of parts, is the masterly conception of the characters. They are each typical of a certain side of human nature, as most of our personal friends and enemies are; but not exclusively of this side or that. They are each of mixed motives, mixed qualities; none of them is quite a monster; though those who are badly mixed do such monstrous things.

Pepe Rey, who is such a good fellow—so kind, and brave, and upright, and generous, so fine a mind, and so high a soul—is tactless and imprudent; he even condescends to the thought of intrigue; and though he rejects his plots at last, his nature has once harbored deceit. Don Inocencio, the priest, whose control of Doña Perfecta's conscience has vitiated the very springs of goodness in her, is by no means bad, aside from his purposes. He loves his sister and her son tenderly, and wishes to provide for them by the marriage which Pepe's presence threatens to prevent. The nephew, though selfish and little, has moments of almost being a good fellow; the sister, though she is really such a lamb of meekness, becomes a cat, and scratches Don Inocencio dreadfully when he weakens in his design against Pepe.

Rosario, one of the sweetest and purest images of girlhood that I know in fiction, abandons herself with equal passion to the love she feels for her cousin Pepe, and to the love she feels for her mother, Doña Perfecta. She is ready to fly with him, and yet she betrays him to her mother's pitiless hate.

But it is Doña Perfecta herself who is the transcendent figure, the most powerful creation of the book. In her, bigotry and its fellow-vice, hypocrisy, have done their perfect work, until she comes near to being a devil, and really does a devil's deeds. Yet even she is not without some extenuating traits. Her bigotry springs from her conscience, and she is truly devoted to her daughter's eternal welfare; she is of such a native frankness that at a certain point she tears aside her mask of dissimulation and lets Pepe see all the ugliness of her perverted soul. She is wonderfully managed. At what moment does she begin to hate him, and to wish to undo her own work in making a match between him and her daughter? I could defy anyone to say. All one knows is that at one moment she adores her brother's son, and at another she abhors him, and has already subtly entered upon her efforts to thwart the affection she has invited in him for her daughter.

Caballuco, what shall I say of Caballuco? He seems altogether bad, but the author lets one imagine that this cruel, this ruthless brute must have somewhere about him traits of lovableness, of leniency, though he never lets one see them. His gratitude to Doña Perfecta, even his murderous devotion, is not altogether bad; and he is certainly worse than nature made him, when wrought upon by her fury and the suggestion of Don Inocencio. The scene where they work him up to rebellion and assassination is a compendium of the history of intolerance; as the mean little conceited city of Orbajosa is the microcosm of bigoted and reactionary Spain.

IV

I HAVE CALLED, OR HALF-CALLED, this book tendencious; but in a certain larger view it is not so. It is the eternal interest of passion working upon passion, not the temporary interest of condition antagonizing condition, which renders "Doña Perfecta" so poignantly interesting, and which makes its tragedy immense. But there is hope as well as despair in such a tragedy. There is the strange support of a bereavement in it, the consolation of feeling that for those who have suffered unto death, nothing can harm them more; that even for those who have inflicted their suffering this peace will soon come.

"Is Pérez Galdós a pessimist?" asks the critic Clarín. "No, certainly; but if he is not, why does he paint us sorrows that seem inconsolable? Is it from love of paradox? Is it to show that his genius, which can do so much, can paint the shadow lovelier than the light? Nothing of this. Nothing that is not serious, honest, and noble, is to be found in this novelist. Are they pessimistic, those ballads of the North, that always end with vague resonances of woe? Are they pessimists, those singers of our own land, who surprise us with tears in the midst of laughter? Is Nature pessimistic, who is so sad at nightfall that it seems as if day were dying forever? . . . The sadness of art, like that of nature, is a form of hope. Why is Christianity so artistic? Because it is the religion of sadness."

W. D. HOWELLS

I

Villahorrenda! Five Minutes!

When the down train No. 65—of what line it is unnecessary to say—stopped at the little station between kilometres 171 and 172, almost all the second- and third-class passengers remained in the cars, yawning or asleep, for the penetrating cold of the early morning did not invite to a walk on the unsheltered platform. The only first-class passenger on the train alighted quickly, and addressing a group of the employés asked them if this was the Villahorrenda station.

"We are in Villahorrenda," answered the conductor, whose voice was drowned by the cackling of the hens which were at that moment being lifted into the freight car. "I forgot to call you, Señor de Rey. I think they are waiting for you at the station with the beasts."

"Why, how terribly cold it is here!" said the traveller, drawing his cloak more closely about him. "Is there no place in the station where I could rest for a while, and get warm, before undertaking a journey on horseback through this frozen country?"

Before he had finished speaking the conductor, called away by the urgent duties of his position, went off, leaving our unknown cavalier's question unanswered. The latter saw that another employé was coming toward him, holding a lantern in his right hand, that swung back and forth as he walked, casting the light on the platform of the station in a series of zigzags, like those described by the shower from a watering-pot.

"Is there a restaurant or a bedroom in the station of Villahorrenda?" said the traveller to the man with the lantern.

"There is nothing here," answered the latter brusquely, running toward the men who were putting the freight on board the cars, and assailing them with such a volley of oaths, blasphemies, and abusive epithets that the very chickens, scandalized by his brutality, protested against it from their baskets.

"The best thing I can do is to get away from this place as quickly as possible," said the gentleman to himself. "The conductor said that the beasts were here."

Just as he had come to this conclusion he felt a thin hand pulling him gently and respectfully by the cloak. He turned round and saw a figure enveloped in a gray cloak, out of whose voluminous folds peeped the shrivelled and astute countenance of a Castilian peasant. He looked at the ungainly figure, which reminded one of the black poplar among trees; he observed the shrewd eyes that shone from beneath the wide brim of the old velvet hat; the sinewy brown hand that grasped a green switch, and the broad foot that, with every movement, made the iron spur jingle.

"Are you Señor Don José de Rey?" asked the peasant, raising his hand to his hat.

"Yes; and you, I take it," answered the traveller joyfully, "are Doña Perfecta's servant, who have come to the station to meet me and show me the way to Orbajosa?"

"The same. Whenever you are ready to start. The pony runs like the wind. And Señor Don José, I am sure, is a good rider. For what comes by race—"

"Which is the way out?" asked the traveller, with impatience. "Come, let us start, señor—What is your name?"

"My name is Pedro Lucas," answered the man of the gray cloak, again making a motion to take off his hat; "but they call me Uncle Licurgo. Where is the young gentleman's baggage?"

"There it is—there under the clock. There are three pieces—two portmanteaus and a box of books for Señor Don Cayetano. Here is the check."

A moment later cavalier and squire found themselves behind the barracks called a depot, and facing a road which, starting at this point, disappeared among the neighboring hills, on whose naked slopes could be vaguely distinguished the miserable hamlet of Villahorrenda. There were three animals to carry the men and the luggage. A not ill-looking nag was destined for the cavalier; Uncle Licurgo was to ride a venerable hack, somewhat loose in the joints, but sure-footed; and the mule, which was to be led by a stout country boy of active limbs and fiery blood, was to carry the luggage.

Before the caravan had put itself in motion the train had started, and was now creeping along the road with the lazy deliberation of a way train, awakening, as it receded in the distance, deep subterranean echoes. As it entered the tunnel at kilometre 172, the steam issued from the steam whistle with a shriek that resounded through the air.

BENITO PÉREZ GALDÓS

From the dark mouth of the tunnel came volumes of whitish smoke, a succession of shrill screams like the blasts of a trumpet followed, and at the sound of its stentorian voice villages, towns, the whole surrounding country awoke. Here a cock began to crow, further on another. Day was beginning to dawn.

II

A Journey in the Heart of Spain

When they had proceeded some distance on their way and had left behind them the hovels of Villahorrenda, the traveller, who was young and handsome, spoke thus:

"Tell me, Señor Solon—"

"Licurgo, at your service."

"Señor Licurgo, I mean. But I was right in giving you the name of a wise legislator of antiquity. Excuse the mistake. But to come to the point. Tell me, how is my aunt?"

"As handsome as ever," answered the peasant, pushing his beast forward a little. "Time seems to stand still with Señora Doña Perfecta. They say that God gives long life to the good, and if that is so that angel of the Lord ought to live a thousand years. If all the blessings that are showered on her in this world were feathers, the señora would need no other wings to go up to heaven with."

"And my cousin, Señorita Rosario?"

"The señora over again!" said the peasant. "What more can I tell you of Doña Rosarito but that she is the living image of her mother? You will have a treasure, Señor Don José, if it is true, as I hear, that you have come to be married to her. She will be a worthy mate for you, and the young lady will have nothing to complain of, either. Between Pedro and Pedro the difference is not very great."

"And Señor Don Cayetano?"

"Buried in his books as usual. He has a library bigger than the cathedral; and he roots up the earth, besides, searching for stones covered with fantastical scrawls, that were written, they say, by the Moors."

"How soon shall we reach Orbajosa?"

"By nine o'clock, God willing. How delighted the señora will be when she sees her nephew! And yesterday, Señorita Rosario was putting the room you are to have in order. As they have never seen you, both mother and daughter think of nothing else but what Señor Don José is like, or is not like. The time has now come for letters to be silent and tongues to talk. The young lady will see her cousin and all will be joy and merry-making. If God wills, all will end happily, as the saying is."

BENITO PÉREZ GALDÓS

"As neither my aunt nor my cousin has yet seen me," said the traveller smiling, "it is not wise to make plans."

"That's true; for that reason it was said that the bay horse is of one mind and he who saddles him of another," answered the peasant. "But the face does not lie. What a jewel you are getting! and she, what a handsome man!"

The young man did not hear Uncle Licurgo's last words, for he was preoccupied with his own thoughts. Arrived at a bend in the road, the peasant turned his horse's head in another direction, saying:

"We must follow this path now. The bridge is broken, and the river can only be forded at the Hill of the Lilies."

"The Hill of the Lilies," repeated the cavalier, emerging from his revery. "How abundant beautiful names are in these unattractive localities! Since I have been travelling in this part of the country the terrible irony of the names is a constant surprise to me. Some place that is remarkable for its barren aspect and the desolate sadness of the landscape is called Valleameno.* Some wretched mud-walled village stretched on a barren plain and proclaiming its poverty in diverse ways has the insolence to call itself Villarica;† and some arid and stony ravine, where not even the thistles can find nourishment, calls itself, nevertheless, Valdeflores.‡ That hill in front of us is the Hill of the Lilies? But where, in Heaven's name, are the lilies? I see nothing but stones and withered grass. Call it Hill of Desolation, and you will be right. With the exception of Villahorrenda, whose appearance corresponds with its name, all is irony here. Beautiful words, a prosaic and mean reality. The blind would be happy in this country, which for the tongue is a Paradise and for the eyes a hell."

Señor Licurgo either did not hear the young man's words, or, hearing, he paid no attention to them. When they had forded the river, which, turbid and impetuous, hurried on with impatient haste, as if fleeing from its own banks, the peasant pointed with outstretched arm to some barren and extensive fields that were to be seen on the left, and said:

"Those are the Poplars of Bustamante."

"My lands!" exclaimed the traveller joyfully, gazing at the melancholy fields illumined by the early morning light. "For the first time, I see the

---

* Pleasant Valley.
† Rich Town.
‡ Vale of Flowers.

patrimony which I inherited from my mother. The poor woman used to praise this country so extravagantly, and tell me so many marvellous things about it when I was a child, that I thought that to be here was to be in heaven. Fruits, flowers, game, large and small; mountains, lakes, rivers, romantic streams, pastoral hills, all were to be found in the Poplars of Bustamante; in this favored land, the best and most beautiful on the the earth. But what is to be said? The people of this place live in their imaginations. If I had been brought here in my youth, when I shared the ideas and the enthusiasm of my dear mother, I suppose that I, too, would have been enchanted with these bare hills, these arid or marshy plains, these dilapidated farmhouses, these rickety norias, whose buckets drip water enough to sprinkle half a dozen cabbages, this wretched and barren desolation that surrounds me."

"It is the best land in the country," said Señor Licurgo; "and, for the chick-pea, there is no other like it."

"I am delighted to hear it, for since they came into my possession these famous lands have never brought me a penny."

The wise legislator of Sparta scratched his ear and gave a sigh.

"But I have been told," continued the young man, "that some of the neighboring proprietors have put their ploughs in these estates of mine, and that, little by little, they are filching them from me. Here there are neither landmarks nor boundaries, nor real ownership, Señor Licurgo."

The peasant, after a pause, during which his subtle intellect seemed to be occupied in profound disquisitions, expressed himself as follows:

"Uncle Paso Largo, whom, for his great foresight, we call the Philosopher, set his plough in the Poplars, above the hermitage, and, bit by bit, he has gobbled up six fanegas."

"What an incomparable school!" exclaimed the young man, smiling. "I wager that he has not been the only—philosopher?"

"It is a true saying that one should talk only about what one knows, and that if there is food in the dove-cote, doves won't be wanting. But you, Señor Don José, can apply to your own case the saying that the eye of the master fattens the ox, and now that you are here, try and recover your property."

"Perhaps that would not be so easy, Señor Licurgo," returned the young man, just as they were entering a path bordered on either side by wheat-fields, whose luxuriance and early ripeness gladdened the eye. "This field appears to be better cultivated. I see that all is not dreariness and misery in the Poplars."

BENITO PÉREZ GALDÓS

The peasant assumed a melancholy look, and, affecting something of disdain for the fields that had been praised by the traveller, said in the humblest of tones:

"Señor, this is mine."

"I beg your pardon," replied the gentleman quickly; "now I was going to put my sickle in your field. Apparently the philosophy of this place is contagious."

They now descended into a canebrake, which formed the bed of a shallow and stagnant brook, and, crossing it, they entered a field full of stones and without the slightest trace of vegetation.

"This ground is very bad," said the young man, turning round to look at his companion and guide, who had remained a little behind. "You will hardly be able to derive any profit from it, for it is all mud and sand."

Licurgo, full of humility, answered:

"This is yours."

"I see that all the poor land is mine," declared the young man, laughing good-humoredly.

As they were thus conversing, they turned again into the high-road. The morning sunshine, pouring joyously through all the gates and balconies of the Spanish horizon, had now inundated the fields with brilliant light. The wide sky, undimmed by a single cloud, seemed to grow wider and to recede further from the earth, in order to contemplate it, and rejoice in the contemplation, from a greater height. The desolate, treeless land, straw-colored at intervals, at intervals of the color of chalk, and all cut up into triangles and quadrilaterals, yellow or black, gray or pale green, bore a fanciful resemblance to a beggar's cloak spread out in the sun. On that miserable cloak Christianity and Islamism had fought with each other epic battles. Glorious fields, in truth, but the combats of the past had left them hideous!

"I think we shall have a scorching day, Señor Licurgo," said the young man, loosening his cloak a little. "What a dreary road! Not a single tree to be seen, as far as the eye can reach. Here everything is in contradiction. The irony does not cease. Why, when there are no poplars here, either large or small, should this be called The Poplars?"

Uncle Licurgo did not answer this question because he was listening with his whole soul to certain sounds which were suddenly heard in the distance, and with an uneasy air he stopped his beast, while he explored the road and the distant hills with a gloomy look.

"What is the matter?" asked the traveller, stopping his horse also.

"Do you carry arms, Don José?"

"A revolver—ah! now I understand. Are there robbers about?"

"Perhaps," answered the peasant, with visible apprehension. "I think I heard a shot."

"We shall soon see. Forward!" said the young man, putting spurs to his nag. "They are not very terrible, I dare say."

"Keep quiet, Señor Don José," exclaimed the peasant, stopping him. "Those people are worse than Satan himself. The other day they murdered two gentlemen who were on their way to take the train. Let us leave off jesting. Gasparón el Fuerte, Pepito Chispillas, Merengue, and Ahorca Suegras shall not see my face while I live. Let us turn into the path."

"Forward, Señor Licurgo!"

"Back, Señor Don José," replied the peasant, in distressed accents. "You don't know what kind of people those are. They are the same men who stole the chalice, the Virgin's crown, and two candlesticks from the church of the Carmen last month; they are the men who robbed the Madrid train two years ago."

Don José, hearing these alarming antecedents, felt his courage begin to give way.

"Do you see that great high hill in the distance? Well, that is where those rascals hide themselves; there in some caves which they call the Retreat of the Cavaliers."

"Of the Cavaliers?"

"Yes, señor. They come down to the high-road when the Civil Guards are not watching, and rob all they can. Do you see a cross beyond the bend of the road? Well, that was erected in remembrance of the death of the Alcalde of Villahorrenda, whom they murdered there at the time of the elections."

"Yes, I see the cross."

"There is an old house there, in which they hide themselves to wait for the carriers. They call that place The Pleasaunce."

"The Pleasaunce?"

"If all the people who have been murdered and robbed there were to be restored they would form an army."

While they were thus talking shots were again heard, this time nearer than before, which made the valiant hearts of the travellers quake a little, but not that of the country lad, who, jumping about for joy, asked Señor Licurgo's permission to go forward to watch the conflict which was taking place so near them. Observing the courage of the boy Don José felt a little ashamed of having been frightened, or at least a little disturbed, by the proximity of the robbers, and cried, putting spurs to his nag:

"We will all go forward, then. Perhaps we may be able to lend assistance to the unlucky travellers who find themselves in so perilous a situation, and give a lesson besides to those cavaliers."

The peasant endeavored to convince the young man of the rashness of his purpose, as well as of the profitlessness of his generous design, since those who had been robbed were robbed and perhaps dead also, and not in a condition to need the assistance of anyone.

The gentleman insisted, in spite of these sage counsels; the peasant reiterated his objections more strongly than before; when the appearance of two or three carters, coming quietly down the road driving a wagon, put an end to the controversy. The danger could not be very great when these men were coming along so unconcernedly, singing merry songs; and such was in fact the case, for the shots, according to what the carters said, had not been fired by the robbers, but by the Civil Guards, who desired in this way to prevent the escape of half a dozen thieves whom they were taking, bound together, to the town jail.

"Yes, I know now what it was," said Licurgo, pointing to a light cloud of smoke which was to be seen some distance off, to the right of the road. "They have peppered them there. That happens every other day."

The young man did not understand.

"I assure you, Señor Don José," added the Lacedæmonian legislator, with energy, "that it was very well done; for it is of no use to try those rascals. The judge cross-questions them a little and then lets them go. If at the end of a trial dragged out for half a dozen years one of them is sent to jail, at the moment least expected he escapes, and returns to the Retreat of the Cavaliers. That is the best thing to do—shoot them! Take them to prison, and when you are passing a suitable place—Ah, dog, so you want to escape, do you? pum! pum! The indictment is drawn up, the witnesses summoned, the trial ended, the sentence pronounced—all in a minute. It is a true saying that the fox is very cunning, but he who catches him is more cunning still."

"Forward, then, and let us ride faster, for this road, besides being a long one, is not at all a pleasant one," said Rey.

As they passed The Pleasaunce, they saw, a little in from the road, the guards who a few minutes before had executed the strange sentence with which the reader has been made acquainted. The country boy was inconsolable because they rode on and he was not allowed to get a nearer view of the palpitating bodies of the robbers, which could be distinguished forming a horrible group in the distance. But they had not proceeded twenty paces when they heard the sound of a horse galloping after them at so rapid a pace that he gained upon them every moment. Our traveller turned round and saw a man, or rather a Centaur, for the most perfect harmony imaginable existed between horse and rider. The latter was of a robust and plethoric constitution, with large fiery eyes, rugged features, and a black mustache. He was of middle age and had a general air of rudeness and aggressiveness, with indications of strength in his whole person. He was mounted on a superb horse with a muscular chest, like the horses of the Parthenon, caparisoned in the picturesque fashion of the country, and carrying on the crupper a great leather bag on the cover of which was to be seen, in large letters, the word Mail.

"Hello! Goodday, Señor Caballuco," said Licurgo, saluting the horseman when the latter had come up with them. "How is it that we got so far ahead of you? But you will arrive before us, if you set your mind to it."

"I will rest a little," answered Señor Caballuco, adapting his horse's pace to that of our travellers' beasts, and attentively observing the most distinguished of the three, "since there is such good company."

"This gentleman," said Licurgo, smiling, "is the nephew of Doña Perfecta."

"Ah! at your service, señor."

The two men saluted each other, it being noticeable that Caballuco performed his civilities with an expression of haughtiness and superiority that revealed, at the very least, a consciousness of great importance, and of a high standing in the district. When the arrogant horseman rode aside to stop and talk for a moment with two Civil Guards who passed them on the road, the traveller asked his guide:

"Who is that odd character?"

"Who should it be? Caballuco."

"And who is Caballuco?"

"What! Have you never heard of Caballuco?" said the countryman, amazed at the crass ignorance of Doña Perfecta's nephew. "He is a very brave man, a fine rider, and the best connoisseur of horses in all the surrounding country. We think a great deal of him in Orbajosa; and he

　　　　　　　　　BENITO PÉREZ GALDÓS

is well worthy of it. Just as you see him, he is a power in the place, and the governor of the province takes off his hat to him."

"When there is an election!"

"And the Governor of Madrid writes official letters to him with a great many titles in the superscription. He throws the bar like a St. Christopher, and he can manage every kind of weapon as easily as we manage our fingers. When there was market inspection here, they could never get the best of him, and shots were to be heard every night at the city gates. He has a following that is worth any money, for they are ready for anything. He is good to the poor, and any stranger who should come here and attempt to touch so much as a hair of the head of any native of Orbajosa would have him to settle with. It is very seldom that soldiers come here from Madrid, but whenever they do come, not a day passes without blood being shed, for Caballuco would pick a quarrel with them, if not for one thing for another. At present it seems that he is fallen into poverty and he is employed to carry the mail. But he is trying hard to persuade the Town Council to have a market-inspector's office here again and to put him in charge of it. I don't know how it is that you have never heard him mentioned in Madrid, for he is the son of a famous Caballuco who was in the last rebellion, and who was himself the son of another Caballuco, who was also in the rebellion of that day. And as there is a rumor now that there is going to be another insurrection—for the whole country is in a ferment—we are afraid that Caballuco will join that also, following in the illustrious footsteps of his father and his grandfather, who, to our glory be it said, were born in our city."

Our traveller was surprised to see the species of knight-errantry that still existed in the regions which he had come to visit, but he had no opportunity to put further questions, for the man who was the object of them now joined them, saying with an expression of ill-humor:

"The Civil Guard despatched three. I have already told the commander to be careful what he is about. Tomorrow we will speak to the governor of the province, and I—"

"Are you going to X.?"

"No; but the governor is coming here, Señor Licurgo; do you know that they are going to send us a couple of regiments to Orbajosa?"

"Yes," said the traveller quickly, with a smile. "I heard it said in Madrid that there was some fear of a rising in this place. It is well to be prepared for what may happen."

"They talk nothing but nonsense in Madrid," exclaimed the Centaur violently, accompanying his affirmation with a string of tongue-blistering vocables. "In Madrid there is nothing but rascality. What do they send us soldiers for? To squeeze more contributions out of us and a couple of conscriptions afterward. By all that's holy! if there isn't a rising there ought to be. So you"—he ended, looking banteringly at the young man—"so you are Doña Perfecta's nephew?"

This abrupt question and the insolent glance of the bravo annoyed the young man.

"Yes, señor, at your service."

"I am a friend of the señora's, and I love her as I do the apple of my eye," said Caballuco. "As you are going to Orbajosa we shall see each other there."

And without another word he put spurs to his horse, which, setting off at a gallop, soon disappeared in a cloud of dust.

After half an hour's ride, during which neither Señor Don José nor Señor Licurgo manifested much disposition to talk, the travellers came in sight of an ancient-looking town seated on the slope of a hill, from the midst of whose closely clustered houses arose many dark towers, and, on a height above it, the ruins of a dilapidated castle. Its base was formed by a mass of shapeless walls, of mud hovels, gray and dusty looking as the soil, together with some fragments of turreted walls, in whose shelter about a thousand humble huts raised their miserable adobe fronts, like anæmic and hungry faces demanding an alms from the passerby. A shallow river surrounded the town, like a girdle of tin, refreshing, in its course, several gardens, the only vegetation that cheered the eye. People were going into and coming out of the town, on horseback and on foot, and the human movement, although not great, gave some appearance of life to that great dwelling-place whose architectural aspect was rather that of ruin and death than of progress and life. The innumerable and repulsive-looking beggars who dragged themselves on either side of the road, asking the obolus from the passerby, presented a pitiful spectacle. It would be impossible to see beings more in harmony with, or better suited to the fissures of that sepulchre in which a city was not only buried but gone to decay. As our travellers approached the town, a discordant peal of bells gave token, with their expressive sound, that that mummy had still a soul.

It was called Orbajosa, a city that figures, not in the Chaldean or Coptic geography, but in that of Spain, with 7324 inhabitants, a town-hall, an episcopal seat, a court-house, a seminary, a stock farm, a high school, and other official prerogatives.

"The bells are ringing for high mass in the cathedral," said Uncle Licurgo. "We have arrived sooner than I expected."

"The appearance of your native city," said the young man, examining the panorama spread out before him, "could not be more disagreeable. The historic city of Orbajosa, whose name is no doubt a corruption of Urbs Augusta, looks like a great dunghill."

"All that can be seen from here is the suburbs," said the guide, in an offended tone. "When you enter the Calle Real and the Calle del Condestable, you will see handsome buildings, like the cathedral."

"I don't want to speak ill of Orbajosa before seeing it," said the young man. "And you must not take what I have said as a mark of contempt, for whether humble and mean, or stately and handsome, that city will always be very dear to me, not only because it is my mother's native place, but because there are persons living in it whom I love without seeing them. Let us enter the august city, then."

They were now ascending a road on the outskirts of the town, and passing close to the walls of the gardens.

"Do you see that great house at the end of this large garden whose wall we are now passing?" said Uncle Licurgo, pointing to a massive, whitewashed wall belonging to the only dwelling in view which had the appearance of a cheerful and comfortable habitation.

"Yes; that is my aunt's house?"

"Exactly so! What we are looking at is the rear of the house. The front faces the Calle del Condestable, and it has five iron balconies that look like five castles. The fine garden behind the wall belongs to the house, and if you rise up in your stirrups you will be able to see it all from here."

"Why, we are at the house, then!" cried the young man. "Can we not enter from here?"

"There is a little door but the señora had it condemned."

The young man raised himself in his stirrups and, stretching his neck as far as he could, looked over the wall.

"I can see the whole of the garden," he said. "There, under the trees, there is a woman, a girl, a young lady."

"That is Señorita Rosario," answered Licurgo.

And at the same time he also raised himself in his stirrups to look over the wall.

"Eh! Senorita Rosario!" he cried, making energetic signs with his right hand. "Here we are; I have brought your cousin with me."

"She has seen us," said the young man, stretching out his neck as far as was possible. "But if I am not mistaken, there is an ecclesiastic with her—a priest."

"That is the Penitentiary," answered the countryman, with naturalness.

"My cousin has seen us—she has left the priest, and is running toward the house. She is beautiful."

"As the sun!"

"She has turned redder than a cherry. Come, come, Señor Licurgo."

III

Pepe Rey

Before proceeding further, it will be well to tell who Pepe Rey was, and what were the affairs which had brought him to Orbajosa.

When Brigadier Rey died in 1841, his two children, Juan and Perfecta, had just married: the latter the richest land-owner of Orbajosa, the former a young girl of the same city. The husband of Perfecta was called Don Manuel Maria José de Polentinos, and the wife of Juan, Maria Polentinos; but although they had the same surname, their relationship was somewhat distant and not very easy to make out. Juan Rey was a distinguished jurisconsult who had been graduated in Seville and had practised law in that city for thirty years with no less honor than profit. In 1845, he was left a widower with a son who was old enough to play mischievous pranks; he would sometimes amuse himself by constructing viaducts, mounds, ponds, dikes, and trenches of earth, in the yard of the house, and then flooding those fragile works with water. His father let him do so, saying, "You will be an engineer."

Perfecta and Juan had ceased to see each other from the time of their marriage, because the sister had gone to Madrid with her husband, the wealthy Polentinos, who was as rich as he was extravagant. Play and women had so completely enslaved Manuel Maria José that he would have dissipated all his fortune, if death had not been beforehand with him and carried him off before he had had time to squander it. In a night of orgy the life of the rich provincial, who had been sucked so voraciously by the leeches of the capital and the insatiable vampire of play, came to a sudden termination. His sole heir was a daughter a few months old. With the death of Perfecta's husband the terrors of the family were at an end, but the great struggle began. The house of Polentinos was ruined; the estates were in danger of being seized by the money-lenders; all was in confusion: enormous debts, lamentable management in Orbajosa, discredit and ruin in Madrid.

Perfecta sent for her brother, who, coming to the distressed widow's assistance, displayed so much diligence and skill that in a short time the greater part of the dangers that threatened her had disappeared. He began by obliging his sister to live in Orbajosa, managing herself her vast estates, while he faced the formidable pressure of the creditors in Madrid. Little by little the house freed itself from the enormous burden of its debts, for the excellent Don Juan Rey, who had the best way in the world for managing such matters, pleaded in the court, made settlements with the principal creditors and arranged to pay them by instalments, the result of this skilful management being that the rich patrimony of Polentinos was saved from ruin and might continue, for many years to come, to bestow splendor and glory on that illustrious family.

Perfecta's gratitude was so profound that in writing to her brother from Orbajosa, where she determined to reside until her daughter should be grown up, she said to him, among other affectionate things: "You have been more than a brother to me, more than a father to my daughter. How can either of us ever repay you for services so great? Ah, my dear brother? from the moment in which my daughter can reason and pronounce a name I will teach her to bless yours. My gratitude will end only with my life. Your unworthy sister regrets only that she can find no opportunity of showing you how much she loves you and of recompensing you in a manner suited to the greatness of your soul and the boundless goodness of your heart."

At the time when these words were written Rosarito was two years old. Pepe Rey, shut up in a school in Seville, was making lines on paper, occupied in proving that "the sum of all the interior angles of any polygon is equal to twice as many right angles, wanting four, as the figure has sides." These vexatious commonplaces of the school kept him very busy. Year after year passed. The boy grew up, still continuing to make lines. At last, he made one which is called "From Tarragona to Montblanch." His first serious toy was the bridge, 120 metres in length, over the River Francoli.

During all this time Doña Perfecta continued to live in Orbajosa. As her brother never left Seville, several years passed without their seeing each other. A quarterly letter, as punctually written as it was punctually answered, kept in communication these two hearts, whose affection neither time nor distance could cool. In 1870, when Don Juan Rey, satisfied with having fulfilled his mission in society, retired from it and went to live in his fine house in Puerto Real, Pepe, who had been employed for several years in the works of various rich building companies, set out on a tour through Germany and England, for the purpose of study. His father's fortune (as large as it is possible for a fortune which has only an honorable law-office for its source to be in Spain), permitted him to free himself in a short time from the yoke of material labor. A man of exalted ideas and with an ardent love for science, he found his purest enjoyment in the observation and study of the marvels by means of which the genius of the age furthers at the same time the culture and material comfort and the moral progress of man.

On returning from his tour his father informed him that he had an important project to communicate to him. Pepe supposed that it concerned some bridge, dockyard, or, at the least, the draining of some marsh, but Don Juan soon dispelled his error, disclosing to him his plan in the following words:

"This is March, and Perfecta's quarterly letter has not failed to come. Read it, my dear boy, and if you can agree to what that holy and exemplary woman, my dear sister, says in it, you will give me the greatest happiness I could desire in my old age. If the plan does not please you, reject it without hesitation, for, although your refusal would grieve me, there is not in it the shadow of constraint on my part. It would be unworthy of us both that it should be realized through the coercion of an obstinate father. You are free either to accept or to reject it, and if there is in your mind the slightest repugnance to it, arising either from your inclinations or from any other cause, I do not wish you to do violence to your feelings on my account."

Pepe laid the letter on the table after he had glanced through it, and said quietly:

"My aunt wishes me to marry Rosario!"

"She writes accepting joyfully my idea," said his father, with emotion. "For the idea was mine. Yes, it is a long time, a very long time since it occurred to me; but I did not wish to say anything to you until I knew what my sister might think about it. As you see, Perfecta receives my plan with joy; she says that she too had thought of it, but that she did not venture to mention it to me, because you are—you have seen what she says—because you are a young man of very exceptional merit and her daughter is a country girl, without either a brilliant education or worldly attractions. Those are her words. My poor sister! How good she is! I see that you are not displeased; I see that this project of mine, resembling a little the officious prevision of the fathers of former times who married their children without consulting their wishes in the matter, and making generally inconsiderate and unwise matches, does not seem absurd to you. God grant that this may be, as it seems to promise, one of the happiest. It is true that you have never seen your cousin, but we are both aware of her virtue, of her discretion, of her modest and noble simplicity. That nothing may be wanting, she is even beautiful. My opinion is," he added gayly, "that you should at once start for that out-of-the-way episcopal city, that Urbs Augusta, and there, in the presence of my sister and her charming Rosarito, decide whether the latter is to be something more to me or not, than my niece."

Pepe took up the letter again and read it through carefully. His countenance expressed neither joy nor sorrow. He might have been examining some plan for the junction of two railroads.

"In truth," said Don Juan, "in that remote Orbajosa, where, by the way, you have some land that you might take a look at now, life passes with the tranquillity and the sweetness of an idyl. What patriarchal customs? What noble simplicity! What rural and Virgilian peace! If, instead of being a mathematician, you were a Latinist, you would repeat, as you enter it, the *ergo tua rura manebunt*. What an admirable place in which to commune with one's own soul and to prepare one's self for good works. There all is kindness and goodness; there the deceit and hypocrisy of our great cities are unknown; there the holy inclinations which the turmoil of modern life stifles spring into being again; there dormant faith reawakens and one feels within the breast an impulse, vague but keen, like the impatience of youth, that from the depths of the soul cries out: 'I wish to live!'"

A few days after this conference Pepe left Puerto Real. He had refused, some months before, a commission from the government to survey, in its mineralogical aspects, the basin of the River Nahara, in the valley of Orbajosa; but the plans to which the conference above recorded gave rise, caused him to say to himself: "It will be as well to make use of the time. Heaven only knows how long this courtship may last, or what hours of weariness it may bring with it." He went, then, to Madrid, solicited the commission to explore the basin of the Nahara, which he obtained without difficulty, although he did not belong officially to the mining corps, set out shortly afterward, and, after a second change of trains, the mixed train No. 65 bore him, as we have seen, to the loving arms of Uncle Licurgo.

The age of our hero was about thirty-four years. He was of a robust constitution, of athletic build, and so admirably proportioned and of so commanding an appearance that, if he had worn a uniform, he would have presented the most martial air and figure that it is possible to imagine. His hair and beard were blond in color, but in his countenance there was none of the phlegmatic imperturbability of the Saxon, but, on the contrary, so much animation that his eyes, although they were not black, seemed to be so. His figure would have served as a perfect and beautiful model for a statue, on the pedestal of which the sculptor might engrave the words: "Intellect, strength." If not in visible characters, he bore them vaguely expressed in the brilliancy of his glance, in the potent attraction with which his person was peculiarly endowed, and in the sympathy which his cordial manners inspired.

He was not very talkative—only persons of inconstant ideas and unstable judgment are prone to verbosity. His profound moral sense made him sparing of words in the disputes in which the men of the day are prone to engage on any and every subject, but in polite conversation he displayed an eloquence full of wit and intelligence, emanating always from good sense and a temperate and just appreciation of worldly matters. He had no toleration for those sophistries, and mystifications, and quibbles of the understanding with which persons of intelligence, imbued with affected culture, sometimes amuse themselves; and in defence of the truth Pepe Rey employed at times, and not always with moderation, the weapon of ridicule. This was almost a defect in the eyes of many people who esteemed him, for our hero thus appeared wanting in respect for a multitude of things commonly accepted and believed. It must be acknowledged, although it may lessen him in the opinion of many, that Rey did not share the mild toleration of the compliant age which has invented strange disguises of words and of acts to conceal what to the general eye might be disagreeable.

Such was the man, whatever slanderous tongues may say to the contrary, whom Uncle Licurgo introduced into Orbajosa just as the cathedral bells were ringing for high mass. When, looking over the garden wall, they saw the young girl and the Penitentiary, and then the flight of the former toward the house, they put spurs to their beasts and entered the Calle Real, where a great many idlers stood still to gaze at the traveller, as if he were a stranger and an intruder in the patriarchal city. Turning presently to the right, and riding in the direction of the cathedral, whose massive bulk dominated the town, they entered the Calle del Condestable, in which, being narrow and paved, the hoofs of the animals clattered noisily, alarming the people of the neighborhood, who came to the windows and to the balconies to satisfy their curiosity.

Shutters opened with a grating sound and various faces, almost all feminine, appeared above and below. By the time Pepe Rey had reached the threshold of the house of Polentinos many and diverse comments had been already made on his person.

IV

The Arrival of the Cousin

When Rosarito left him so abruptly the Penitentiary looked toward the garden wall, and seeing the faces of Licurgo and his companion, said to himself:

"So the prodigy is already here, then."

He remained thoughtful for some moments, his cloak, grasped with both hands, folded over his abdomen, his eyes fixed on the ground, his gold-rimmed spectacles slipping gently toward the point of his nose, his under-lip moist and projecting, and his iron-gray eyebrows gathered in a slight frown. He was a pious and holy man, of uncommon learning and of irreproachable clerical habits, a little past his sixtieth year, affable in his manners, courteous and kind, and greatly addicted to giving advice and counsel to both men and women. For many years past he had been master of Latin and rhetoric in the Institute, which noble profession had supplied him with a large fund of quotations from Horace and of florid metaphors, which he employed with wit and opportuneness. Nothing more need be said regarding this personage, but that, as soon as he heard the trot of the animals approaching the Calle del Condestable, he arranged the folds of his cloak, straightened his hat, which was not altogether correctly placed upon his venerable head, and, walking toward the house, murmured:

"Let us go and see this paragon."

Meanwhile Pepe was alighting from his nag, and Doña Perfecta, her face bathed in tears and barely able to utter a few trembling words, the sincere expression of her affection, was receiving him at the gate itself in her loving arms.

"Pepe—but how tall you are! And with a beard. Why, it seems only yesterday that I held you in my lap. And now you are a man, a grown-up man. Well, well! How the years pass! This is my daughter Rosario."

As she said this they reached the parlor on the ground floor, which was generally used as a reception-room, and Doña Perfecta presented her daughter to Pepe.

Rosario was a girl of a delicate and fragile appearance, that revealed a tendency to pensive melancholy. In her delicate and pure countenance there was something of the soft, pearly pallor which most novelists attribute to their heroines, and without which sentimental varnish it appears that no Enriquieta or Julia can be interesting. But what chiefly distinguished Rosario was that her face expressed so much sweetness and modesty that the absence of the perfections it lacked was not observed. This is not to say that she was plain; but, on the other hand, it is true that it would be an exaggeration to call her beautiful in the strictest meaning of the word. The real beauty of Doña Perfecta's daughter consisted in a species of transparency, different from that of pearl, alabaster, marble, or any of the other substances used in descriptions of the human countenance; a species of transparency through which the inmost depths of her soul were clearly visible; depths not cavernous and gloomy, like those of the sea, but like those of a clear and placid river. But the material was wanting there for a complete personality. The channel was wanting, the banks were wanting. The vast wealth of her spirit overflowed, threatening to wash away the narrow borders. When her cousin saluted her she blushed crimson, and uttered only a few unintelligible words.

"You must be fainting with hunger," said Doña Perfecta to her nephew. "You shall have your breakfast at once."

"With your permission," responded the traveller, "I will first go and get rid of the dust of the journey."

"That is a sensible idea," said the señora. "Rosario, take your cousin to the room that we have prepared for him. Don't delay, nephew. I am going to give the necessary orders."

Rosario took her cousin to a handsome apartment situated on the ground floor. The moment he entered it Pepe recognized in all the details of the room the diligent and loving hand of a woman. All was arranged with perfect taste, and the purity and freshness of everything in this charming nest invited to repose. The guest observed minute details that made him smile.

"Here is the bell," said Rosario, taking in her hand the bell-rope, the tassel of which hung over the head of the bed. "All you have to do is to stretch out your hand. The writing-table is placed so that you will have the light from the left. See, in this basket you can throw the waste papers. Do you smoke?"

"Unfortunately, yes," responded Pepe Rey.

"Well, then, you can throw the ends of your cigars here," she said, touching with the tip of her shoe a utensil of gilt-brass filled with sand.

BENITO PÉREZ GALDÓS

"There is nothing uglier than to see the floor covered with cigar-ends. Here is the washstand. For your clothes you have a wardrobe and a bureau. I think this is a bad place for the watch-case; it would be better beside the bed. If the light annoys you, all you have to do is to lower the shade with this cord; see, this way."

The engineer was enchanted.

Rosarito opened one of the windows.

"Look," she said, "this window opens into the garden. The sun comes in here in the afternoon. Here we have hung the cage of a canary that sings as if he was crazy. If his singing disturbs you we will take it away."

She opened another window on the opposite side of the room.

"This other window," she continued, "looks out on the street. Look; from here you can see the cathedral; it is very handsome, and full of beautiful things. A great many English people come to see it. Don't open both windows at the same time, because draughts are very bad."

"My dear cousin," said Pepe, his soul inundated with an inexplicable joy; "in all that is before my eyes I see an angel's hand that can be only yours. What a beautiful room this is! It seems to me as if I had lived in it all my life. It invites to peace."

Rosarito made no answer to these affectionate expressions, and left the room, smiling.

"Make no delay," she said from the door; "the dining-room too is down stairs—in the centre of this hall."

Uncle Licurgo came in with the luggage. Pepe rewarded him with a liberality to which the countryman was not accustomed, and the latter, after humbly thanking the engineer, raised his hand to his head with a hesitating movement, and in an embarrassed tone, and mumbling his words, he said hesitatingly:

"When will it be most convenient for me to speak to Señor Don José about a—a little matter of business?"

"A little matter of business? At once," responded Pepe, opening one of his trunks.

"This is not a suitable time," said the countryman. "When Señor Don José has rested it will be time enough. There are more days than sausages, as the saying is; and after one day comes another. Rest now, Señor Don José. Whenever you want to take a ride—the nag is not bad. Well, goodday, Señor Don José. I am much obliged to you. Ah! I had forgotten," he added, returning a few moments later. "If you have any message for the municipal judge—I am going now to speak to him about our little affair."

"Give him my compliments," said Pepe gayly, no better way of getting rid of the Spartan legislator occurring to him.

"Goodbye, then, Señor Don José."

"Goodbye."

The engineer had not yet taken his clothes out of the trunk when for the third time the shrewd eyes and the crafty face of Uncle Licurgo appeared in the door-way.

"I beg your pardon, Señor Don José," he said, displaying his brilliantly white teeth in an affected smile, "but—I wanted to say that if you wish to settle the matter by means of friendly arbitrations— Although, as the saying is, 'Ask other people's opinion of something that concerns only yourself, and some will say it is white and others black.'"

"Will you get away from here, man?"

"I say that, because I hate the law. I don't want to have anything to do with the law. Well, goodbye, again, Señor Don José. God give you long life to help the poor!"

"Goodbye, man, goodbye."

Pepe turned the key in the lock of the door, saying to himself:

"The people of this town appear to be very litigious."

V

Will there be Dissension?

A little later Pepe made his appearance in the dining-room.

"If you eat a hearty breakfast," said Doña Perfecta to him, in affectionate accents, "you will have no appetite for dinner. We dine here at one. Perhaps you may not like the customs of the country."

"I am enchanted with them, aunt."

"Say, then, which you prefer—to eat a hearty breakfast now, or to take something light, and keep your appetite for dinner."

"I prefer to take something light now, in order to have the pleasure of dining with you. But not even if I had found anything to eat in Villahorrenda, would I have eaten anything at this early hour."

"Of course, I need not tell you that you are to treat us with perfect frankness. You may give your orders here as if you were in your own house."

"Thanks, aunt."

"But how like your father you are!" said the señora, regarding the young man, as he ate, with real delight. "I can fancy I am looking now at my dear brother Juan. He sat just as you are sitting and ate as you are eating. In your expression, especially, you are as like as two drops of water."

Pepe began his frugal breakfast. The words, as well as the manner and the expression, of his aunt and cousin inspired him with so much confidence that he already felt as if he were in his own house.

"Do you know what Rosario was saying to me this morning?" said Doña Perfecta, looking at her nephew. "Well, she was saying that, as a man accustomed to the luxuries and the etiquette of the capital and to foreign ways, you would not be able to put up with the somewhat rustic simplicity and the lack of ceremony of our manner of life; for here everything is very plain."

"What a mistake!" responded Pepe, looking at his cousin. "No one abhors more than I do the falseness and the hypocrisy of what is called high society. Believe me, I have long wished to give myself a complete bath in nature, as someone has said; to live far from the turmoil of existence in the solitude and quiet of the country. I long for the tranquillity of a life without strife, without anxieties; neither envying nor envied, as the poet has said. For a long time my studies at first, and my work afterward, prevented me from taking the rest which I need, and which my mind and my body both require; but ever since I entered this house, my dear aunt, my dear cousin, I have felt myself surrounded by the peaceful atmosphere which I have longed for. You must not talk to me, then, of society, either high or low; or of the world, either great or small, for I would willingly exchange them all for this peaceful retreat."

While he was thus speaking, the glass door which led from the dining-room into the garden was obscured by the interposition between it and the light of a dark body. The glasses of a pair of spectacles, catching a sunbeam, sent forth a fugitive gleam; the latch creaked, the door opened, and the Penitentiary gravely entered the room. He saluted those present, taking off his broad-brimmed hat and bowing until its brim touched the floor.

"It is the Señor Penitentiary, of our holy cathedral," said Doña Perfecta: "a person whom we all esteem greatly, and whose friend you will, I hope, be. Take a seat, Señor Don Inocencio."

Pepe shook hands with the venerable canon, and both sat down.

"If you are accustomed to smoke after meals, pray do so," said Doña Perfecta amiably; "and the Señor Penitentiary also."

The worthy Don Inocencio drew from under his cassock a large leather cigar-case, which showed unmistakable signs of long use, opened it, and took from it two long cigarettes, one of which he offered to our friend. Rosario took a match from a little leaf-shaped matchbox, which the Spaniards ironically call a wagon, and the engineer and the canon were soon puffing their smoke over each other.

"And what does Señor Don José think of our dear city of Orbajosa?" asked the canon, shutting his left eye tightly, according to his habit when he smoked.

"I have not yet been able to form any idea of the town," said Pepe. "From the little I have seen of it, however, I think that half a dozen large capitalists disposed to invest their money here, a pair of intelligent heads to direct the work of renovating the place, and a couple of thousands of active hands to carry it out, would not be a bad thing for Orbajosa. Coming from the entrance to the town to the door of this house, I saw more than a hundred beggars. The greater part of them are healthy, and even robust men. It is a pitiable army, the sight of which oppresses the heart."

"That is what charity is for," declared Don Inocencio. "Apart from that, Orbajosa is not a poor town. You are already aware that the best garlic in all Spain is produced here. There are more than twenty rich families living among us."

"It is true," said Doña Perfecta, "that the last few years have been wretched, owing to the drought; but even so, the granaries are not empty, and several thousands of strings of garlic were recently carried to market."

"During the many years that I have lived in Orbajosa," said the priest, with a frown, "I have seen innumerable persons come here from the capital, some brought by the electoral hurly-burly, others to visit some abandoned site, or to see the antiquities of the cathedral, and they all talk to us about English ploughs and threshing-machines and water-power and banks, and I don't know how many other absurdities. The burden of their song is that this place is very backward, and that it could be improved. Let them keep away from us, in the devil's name! We are well enough as we are, without the gentlemen from the capital visiting us; a great deal better off without hearing that continual clamor about our poverty and the grandeurs and the wonders of other places. The fool in his own house is wiser than the wise man in another's. Is it not so, Señor Don José? Of course, you mustn't imagine, even remotely, that I say this on your account. Not at all! Of course not! I know that we have before us one of the most eminent young men of modern Spain, a man who would be able to transform into fertile lands our arid wastes. And I am not at all angry because you sing us the same old song about the English ploughs and arboriculture and silviculture. Not in the least. Men of such great, such very great merit, may be excused for the contempt which they manifest for our littleness. No, no, my friend; no, no, Señor Don José! you are entitled to say anything you please, even to tell us that we are not much better than Kaffirs."

This philippic, concluded in a marked tone of irony, and all of it impertinent enough, did not please the young man; but he refrained from manifesting the slightest annoyance and continued the conversation, endeavoring to avoid as far as possible the subjects in which the oversensitive patriotism of the canon might find cause of offence. The latter rose when Doña Perfecta began to speak to her nephew about family matters, and took a few turns about the room.

This was a spacious and well-lighted apartment, the walls of which were covered with an old-fashioned paper whose flowers and branches, although faded, preserved their original pattern, thanks to the cleanliness which reigned in each and every part of the dwelling. The clock, from the case of which hung, uncovered, the apparently motionless weights and the voluble pendulum, perpetually repeating. No, no, occupied, with its variegated dial, the most prominent place among the solid pieces of furniture of the dining-room, the adornment of the walls being completed by a series of French engravings representing the exploits of the conqueror of Mexico, with prolix explanations at the foot of each concerning a Ferdinand Cortez, and a Donna Marine, as little true to nature as were the figures delineated by the ignorant artist. In the space between the two glass doors which communicated with the garden was an apparatus of brass, which it is not necessary to describe further than to say that it served to support a parrot, which maintained itself on it with the air of gravity and circumspection peculiar to those animals, taking note of everything that went on. The hard and ironical expression of the parrot tribe, their green coats, their red caps, their yellow boots, and, finally, the hoarse, mocking words which they generally utter, give them a strange and repulsive aspect, half serious, half-comic. There is in their air an indescribable something of the stiffness of diplomats. At times they remind one of buffoons, and they always resemble those absurdly conceited people who, in their desire to appear very superior, look like caricatures.

The Penitentiary was very fond of the parrot. When he left Doña Perfecta and Rosario conversing with the traveller, he went over to the bird, and, allowing it to bite his forefinger with the greatest good humor, said to it:

"Rascal, knave, why don't you talk? You would be of little account if you weren't a prater. The world of birds, as well as men, is full of praters."

Then, with his own venerable hand, he took some peas from the dish beside him, and gave them to the bird to eat. The parrot began to call to the maid, asking her for some chocolate, and its words diverted the two ladies and the young man from a conversation which could not have been very engrossing.

VI

In Which it is Seen that Disagreement May Arise When Least Expected

Suddenly Don Cayetano Polentinos, Doña Perfecta's brother-in-law, appeared at the door, and entering the room with outstretched arms, cried:

"Let me embrace you, my dear Don José."

They embraced each other cordially. Don Cayetano and Pepe were already acquainted with each other, for the eminent scholar and bibliophile was in the habit of taking a trip to Madrid whenever an executor's sale of the stock of some dealer in old books was advertised. Don Cayetano was tall and thin, of middle age, although constant study or ill-health had given him a worn appearance; he expressed himself with a refined correctness which became him admirably, and he was affectionate and amiable in his manners, at times to excess. With respect to his vast learning, what can be said but that he was a real prodigy? In Madrid his name was always mentioned with respect, and if Don Cayetano had lived in the capital, he could not have escaped becoming a member, in spite of his modesty, of every academy in it, past, present, and to come. But he was fond of quiet and retirement, and the place which vanity occupies in the souls of others, a pure passion for books, a love of solitary and secluded study, without any other aim or incentive than the books and the study themselves, occupied in his.

He had formed in Orbajosa one of the finest libraries that is to be found in all Spain, and among his books he passed long hours of the day and of the night, compiling, classifying, taking notes, and selecting various sorts of precious information, or composing, perhaps, some hitherto unheard-of and undreamed-of work, worthy of so great a mind. His habits were patriarchal; he ate little, drank less, and his only dissipations consisted of a luncheon in the Alamillos on very great occasions, and daily walks to a place called Mundogrande, where were often disinterred from the accumulated dust of twenty centuries, medals, bits of architecture, and occasionally an amphora or cubicularia of inestimable value.

Don Cayetano and Doña Perfecta lived in such perfect harmony that the peace of Paradise was not to be compared to it. They never disagreed. It is true that Don Cayetano never interfered in the affairs of the house nor Doña Perfecta in those of the library, except to have it swept and dusted every Saturday, regarding with religious respect the books and papers that were in use on the table or anywhere else in the room.

After the questions and answers proper to the occasion had been interchanged Don Cayetano said:

"I have already looked at the books. I am very sorry that you did not bring me the edition of 1527. I shall have to make a journey to Madrid myself. Are you going to remain with us long? The longer the better, my dear Pepe. How glad I am to have you here! Between us both we will arrange a part of my library and make an index of the writers on the Art of Horsemanship. It is not always one has at hand a man of your talents. You shall see my library. You can take your fill of reading there—as often as you like. You will see marvels, real marvels, inestimable treasures, rare works that no one but myself has a copy of. But I think it must be time for dinner, is it not, José? Is it not, Perfecta? Is it not, Rosarito? Is it not, Señor Don Inocencio? Today you are doubly a Penitentiary—I mean because you will accompany us in doing penance."

The canon bowed and smiled, manifesting his pleased acquiescence. The dinner was substantial, and in all the dishes there was noticeable the excessive abundance of country banquets, realized at the expense of variety. There was enough to surfeit twice as many persons as sat down to table. The conversation turned on various subjects.

"You must visit our cathedral as soon as possible," said the canon. "There are few cathedrals like ours, Señor Don José! But of course you, who have seen so many wonders in foreign countries, will find nothing remarkable in our old church. We poor provincials of Orbajosa, however, think it divine. Master Lopez of Berganza, one of the prebendaries of the cathedral, called it in the sixteenth century *pulchra augustissima*. But perhaps for a man of your learning it would possess no merit, and some market constructed of iron would seem more beautiful."

The ironical remarks of the wily canon annoyed Pepe Rey more and more every moment, but, determined to control himself and to conceal his anger, he answered only with vague words. Doña Perfecta then took up the theme and said playfully:

BENITO PÉREZ GALDÓS

"Take care, Pepito; I warn you that if you speak ill of our holy church we shall cease to be friends. You know a great deal, you are a man eminent for your knowledge on every subject, but if you are going to discover that that grand edifice is not the eighth wonder of the world you will do well to keep your knowledge to yourself and leave us in our ignorance."

"Far from thinking that the building is not handsome," responded Pepe, "the little I have seen of its exterior has seemed to me of imposing beauty. So that there is no need for you to be alarmed, aunt. And I am very far from being a savant."

"Softly; softly," said the canon, extending his hand and giving his mouth a truce from eating in order to talk. "Stop there—don't come now pretending modesty, Señor Don José; we are too well aware of your great merit, of the high reputation you enjoy and the important part you play wherever you are, for that. Men like you are not to be met with everyday. But now that I have extolled your merits in this way—"

He stopped to eat a mouthful, and when his tongue was once more at liberty he continued thus:

"Now that I have extolled your merits in this way, permit me to express a different opinion with the frankness which belongs to my character. Yes, Señor Don José, yes, Señor Don Cayetano; yes, señora and señorita, science, as the moderns study and propagate it, is the death of sentiment and of every sweet illusion. Under its influence the life of the spirit declines, everything is reduced to fixed rules, and even the sublime charms of nature disappear. Science destroys the marvellous in the arts, as well as faith in the soul. Science says that everything is a lie, and would reduce everything to figures and lines, not only *maria ac terras*, where we are, but *cælumque profundum*, where God is. The wonderful visions of the soul, its mystic raptures, even the inspiration of the poets, are all a lie. The heart is a sponge; the brain, a place for breeding maggots."

Everyone laughed, while the canon took a draught of wine.

"Come, now, will Señor Don José deny," continued the ecclesiastic, "that science, as it is taught and propagated today, is fast making of the world and of the human race a great machine?"

"That depends," said Don Cayetano. "Everything has its *pro* and its *contra*."

"Take some more salad, Señor Penitentiary," said Doña Perfecta; "it is just as you like it—with a good deal of mustard."

Pepe Rey was not fond of engaging in useless discussions; he was not a pedant, nor did he desire to make a display of his learning, and still less did he wish to do so in the presence of women, and in a private re-union; but the importunate and aggressive verbosity of the canon required, in his opinion, a corrective. To flatter his vanity by agreeing with his views would, he thought, be a bad way to give it to him, and he determined therefore to express only such opinions as should be most directly opposed to those of the sarcastic Penitentiary and most offensive to him.

"So you wish to amuse yourself at my expense," he said to himself. "Wait, and you will see what a fine dance I will lead you."

Then he said aloud:

"All that the Señor Penitentiary has said ironically is the truth. But it is not our fault if science overturns day after day the vain idols of the past: its superstitions, its sophisms, its innumerable fables—beautiful, some of them, ridiculous others—for in the vineyard of the Lord grow both good fruit and bad. The world of illusions, which is, as we might say, a second world, is tumbling about us in ruins. Mysticism in religion, routine in science, mannerism in art, are falling, as the Pagan gods fell, amid jests. Farewell, foolish dreams! the human race is awakening and its eyes behold the light. Its vain sentimentalism, its mysticism, its fevers, its hallucination, its delirium are passing away, and he who was before sick is now well and takes an ineffable delight in the just appreciation of things. Imagination, the terrible madwoman, who was the mistress of the house, has become the servant. Look around you, Señor Penitentiary, and you will see the admirable aggregation of truths which has taken the place of fable. The sky is not a vault; the stars are not little lamps; the moon is not a sportive huntress, but an opaque mass of stone; the sun is not a gayly adorned and vagabond charioteer but a fixed fire; Scylla and Charybdis are not nymphs but sunken rocks; the sirens are seals; and in the order of personages, Mercury is Manzanedo; Mars is a clean-shaven old man, the Count von Moltke; Nestor may be a gentleman in an overcoat, who is called M. Thiers; Orpheus is Verdi; Vulcan is Krupp; Apollo is any poet. Do you wish more? Well, then, Jupiter, a god who, if he were living now, would deserve to be put in jail, does not launch the thunderbolt, but the thunderbolt falls when electricity wills it. There is no Parnassus; there is no Olympus; there is no Stygian lake; nor are there any other Elysian Fields than those of Paris. There is no other descent to hell than the descents of Geology, and this traveller, everytime he returns from it, declares that there are no damned souls in the centre of the earth. There are no other ascents to heaven than those of Astronomy, and she, on her return, declares that she has not seen the six or seven circles of which Dante and the mystical dreamers of the Middle Ages speak. She finds only stars and distances, lines, vast spaces, and nothing more. There are now no false computations of the age of the earth, for paleontology and prehistoric research have counted the teeth of this skull in which we live and discovered its true age. Fable, whether it be called paganism or Christian idealism, exists no longer, and imagination plays only a secondary part. All the miracles possible are such as I work, whenever I desire to do so, in my laboratory, with my Bunsen pile, a conducting wire, and a magnetized needle. There are now no other multiplications of loaves and fishes than those which Industry makes, with her moulds and her machines, and those of the printing press, which imitates Nature, taking from a single type millions of copies. In short, my dear canon, orders have been given to put on the retired list all the absurdities, lies, illusions, dreams, sentimentalities, and prejudices which darken the understanding of man. Let us rejoice at the fact."

When Pepe finished speaking, a furtive smile played upon the canon's lips and his eyes were extraordinarily animated. Don Cayetano busied himself in giving various forms—now rhomboidal, now prismatic—to a little ball of bread. But Doña Perfecta was pale and kept her eyes fixed on the canon with observant insistence. Rosarito looked with amazement at her cousin. The latter, bending toward her, whispered under his breath:

"Don't mind me, little cousin; I am talking all this nonsense only to enrage the canon."

VII

The Disagreement Increases

Perhaps you think," said Doña Perfecta, with a tinge of conceit in her tones, "that Señor Don Inocencio is going to remain silent and not give you an answer to each and everyone of those points."

"Oh, no!" exclaimed the canon, arching his eyebrows. "I will not attempt to measure my poor abilities with a champion so valiant and at the same time so well armed. Señor Don José knows everything; that is to say, he has at his command the whole arsenal of the exact sciences. Of course I know that the doctrines he upholds are false; but I have neither the talent nor the eloquence to combat them. I would employ theological arguments, drawn from revelation, from faith, from the Divine Word; but alas! Señor Don José, who is an eminent savant, would laugh at theology, at faith, at revelation, at the holy prophets, at the gospel. A poor ignorant priest, an unhappy man who knows neither mathematics, nor German philosophy with its *ego* and its *non ego*, a poor dominie, who knows only the science of God and something of the Latin poets, cannot enter into combat with so valiant a champion."

Pepe Rey burst into a frank laugh.

"I see that Señor Don Inocencio," he said, "has taken seriously all the nonsense I have have been talking. Come, Señor Canon, regard the whole matter as a jest, and let it end there. I am quite sure that my opinions do not in reality differ greatly from yours. You are a pious and learned man; it is I who am ignorant. If I have allowed myself to speak in jest, pardon me, all of you—that is my way."

"Thanks!" responded the presbyter, visibly annoyed. "Is that the way you want to get out of it now? I am well aware, we are all well aware, that the views you have sustained are your own. It could not be otherwise. You are the man of the age. It cannot be denied that you have a wonderful, a truly wonderful intellect. While you were talking, at the same time that I inwardly deplored errors so great, I could not but admire, I will confess it frankly, the loftiness of expression, the prodigious fluency, the surprising method of your reasoning, the force of your arguments. What a head, Señora Doña Perfecta, what a head your young nephew has! When I was in Madrid and they took me to the Atheneum, I confess that I was amazed to see the wonderful talent which God has bestowed on the atheists and the Protestants."

"Señor Don Inocencio," said Doña Perfecta, looking alternately at her nephew and her friend, "I think that in judging this boy you are more than benevolent. Don't get angry, Pepe, or mind what I say, for I am neither a savante, nor a philosopher, nor a theologian; but it seems to me that Señor Don Inocencio has just given a proof of his great modesty and Christian charity in not crushing you as he could have done if he had wished."

"Oh, señora!" said the ecclesiastic.

"That is the way with him," continued Doña Perfecta, "always pretending to know nothing. And he knows more than the seven doctors put together. Ah, Señor Don Inocencio, how well the name you have suits you! But don't affect an unseasonable humility now. Why, my nephew has no pretensions. All he knows is what he has been taught. If he has been taught error, what more can he desire than that you should enlighten him and take him out of the limbo of his false doctrines?"

"Just so; I desire nothing more than that the Señor Penitentiary should take me out,"—murmured Pepe, comprehending that without intending it, he had got himself into a labyrinth.

"I am a poor priest, whose only learning is some knowledge of the ancients," responded Don Inocencio. "I recognize the immense value, from a worldly point of view, of Señor Don José's scientific knowledge, and before so brilliant an oracle I prostrate myself and am silent."

So saying, the canon folded his hands across his breast and bent his head. Pepe Rey was somewhat disturbed because of the turn which his aunt had chosen to give to an idle discussion jestingly followed up, and in which he had engaged only to enliven the conversation a little. He thought that the most prudent course to pursue would be to end at once so dangerous a debate, and for this purpose he addressed a question to Señor Don Cayetano when the latter, shaking off the drowsiness which had overcome him after the dessert, offered the guests the indispensable toothpicks stuck in a china peacock with outspread tail.

"Yesterday I discovered a hand grasping the handle of an amphora, on which there are a number of hieratic characters. I will show it to you," said Don Cayetano, delighted to introduce a favorite theme.

"I suppose that Señor de Rey is very expert in archaeological matters also," said the canon, who, still implacable, pursued his victim to his last retreat.

"Of course," said Doña Perfecta. "What is there that these clever children of our day do not understand? They have all the sciences at their fingers' ends. The universities and the academies teach them everything in a twinkling, giving them a patent of learning."

"Oh, that is unjust!" responded the canon, observing the pained expression of the engineer's countenance.

"My aunt is right," declared Pepe. "At the present day we learn a little of everything, and leave school with the rudiments of various studies."

"I was saying," continued the canon, "that you are no doubt a great archaeologist."

"I know absolutely nothing of that science," responded the young man. "Ruins are ruins, and I have never cared to cover myself with dust going among them."

Don Cayetano made an expressive grimace.

"That is not to say that I condemn archæology," said Doña Perfecta's nephew quickly, observing with pain that he could not utter a word without wounding someone. "I know that from that dust issues history. Those studies are delightful and very useful."

"You," said the Penitentiary, putting his toothpick into the last of his back teeth, "are no doubt more inclined to controversial studies. An excellent idea has just occurred to me, Señor Don José; you ought to be a lawyer."

"Law is a profession which I abhor," replied Pepe Rey. "I know many estimable lawyers, among them my father, who is the best of men; but, in spite of so favorable a specimen, I could never have brought myself to practise a profession which consists in defending with equal readiness the *pro* and the *contra* of a question. I know of no greater misjudgment, no greater prejudice, no greater blindness, than parents show in their eagerness to dedicate their sons to the law. The chief and the most terrible plague of Spain is the crowd of our young lawyers, for whose existence a fabulous number of lawsuits are necessary. Lawsuits multiply in proportion to the demand. And even thus, numbers are left without employment, and, as a jurisconsult cannot put his hand to the plough or seat himself at the loom, the result is that brilliant squadron of idlers full of pretensions, who clamor for places, embarrass the administration, agitate public opinion, and breed revolutions. In some way they must make a living. It would be a greater misfortune if there were lawsuits enough for all of them."

"Pepe, for Heaven's sake, take care what you say," said Doña Perfecta, in a tone of marked severity. "But excuse him, Señor Don Inocencio, for he is not aware that you have a nephew who, although he has only lately left the university, is a prodigy in the law."

"I speak in general terms," said Pepe, with firmness. "Being, as I am, the son of a distinguished lawyer, I cannot be ignorant of the fact that there are many men who practise that noble profession with honor to themselves."

"No; my nephew is only a boy yet," said the canon, with affected humility. "Far be it from me to assert that he is a prodigy of learning, like Señor de Rey. In time, who can tell? His talents are neither brilliant nor seductive. Of course, Jacinto's ideas are solid and his judgment is sound. What he knows he knows thoroughly. He is unacquainted with sophistries and hollow phrases."

Pepe Rey appeared every moment more and more disturbed. The idea that, without desiring it, his opinions should be in opposition to those of the friends of his aunt, vexed him, and he resolved to remain silent lest he and Don Inocencio should end by throwing the plates at each other's heads. Fortunately the cathedral bell, calling the canon to the important duties of the choir, extricated him from his painful position. The venerable ecclesiastic rose and took leave of everyone, treating Rey with as much amiability and kindness as if they had been old and dear friends. The canon, after offering his services to Pepe for all that he might require, promised to present his nephew to him in order that the young man might accompany him to see the town, speaking in the most affectionate terms and deigning, on leaving the room, to pat him on the shoulder. Pepe Rey, accepting with pleasure these formulas of concord, nevertheless felt indescribably relieved when the priest had left the dining-room and the house.

VIII

In all Haste

A little later the scene had changed. Don Cayetano, finding rest from his sublime labors in a gentle slumber that had overcome him after dinner, reclined comfortably in an arm-chair in the dining-room. Rosarito, seated at one of the windows that opened into the garden, glanced at her cousin, saying to him with the mute eloquence of her eyes:

"Cousin, sit down here beside me and tell me everything you have to say to me."

Her cousin, mathematician though he was, understood.

"My dear cousin," said Pepe, "how you must have been bored this afternoon by our disputes! Heaven knows that for my own pleasure I would not have played the pedant as I did; the canon was to blame for it. Do you know that that priest appears to me to be a singular character?"

"He is an excellent person!" responded Rosarito, showing the delight she felt at being able to give her cousin all the data and the information that he might require.

"Oh, yes! An excellent person. That is very evident!"

"When you know him a little better, you will see that."

"That he is beyond all price! But it is enough for him to be your friend and your mamma's to be my friend also," declared the young man. "And does he come here often?"

"Everyday. He spends a great deal of his time with us," responded Rosarito ingenuously. "How good and kind he is! And how fond he is of me!"

"Come! I begin to like this gentleman."

"He comes in the evening, besides, to play tresillo," continued the young girl; "for every night some friends meet here—the judge of the lower court, the attorney-general, the dean, the bishop's secretary, the alcalde, the collector of taxes, Don Inocencio's nephew—"

"Ah! Jacintito, the lawyer."

"Yes; he is a simple-hearted boy, as good as gold. His uncle adores him. Since he returned from the university with his doctor's tassel—for he is a doctor in two sciences, and he took honors besides—what do you think of that?—well, as I was saying, since his return, he has come here very often with his uncle. Mamma too is very fond of him. He is a very sensible boy. He goes home early with his uncle; he never goes at night to the Casino, nor plays nor squanders money, and he is employed in the office of Don Lorenzo Ruiz, who is the best lawyer in Orbajosa. They say Jacinto will be a great lawyer, too."

"His uncle did not exaggerate when he praised him, then," said Pepe. "I am very sorry that I talked all that nonsense I did about lawyers. I was very perverse, was I not, my dear cousin?"

"Not at all; for my part, I think you were quite right."

"But, really, was I not a little—"

"Not in the least, not in the least!"

"What a weight you have taken off my mind! The truth is that I found myself constantly, and without knowing why, in distressing opposition to that venerable priest. I am very sorry for it."

"What I think," said Rosarito, looking at him with eyes full of affection, "is that you will not find yourself at home among us."

"What do you mean by that?"

"I don't know whether I can make myself quite clear, cousin. I mean that it will not be easy for you to accustom yourself to the society and the ideas of the people of Orbajosa. I imagine so—it is a supposition."

"Oh, no! I think you are mistaken."

"You come from a different place, from another world, where the people are very clever, and very learned, and have refined manners, and a witty way of talking, and an air—perhaps I am not making myself clear. I mean that you are accustomed to live among people of refinement; you know a great deal. Here there is not what you need; here the people are not learned or very polished. Everything is plain, Pepe. I imagine you will be bored, terribly bored, and that in the end you will have to go away."

The expression of sadness which was natural in Rosarito's countenance here became so profound that Pepe Rey was deeply moved.

"You are mistaken, my dear cousin. I did not come here with the ideas you fancy, nor is there between my character and my opinions and the character and opinions of the people here the want of harmony you imagine. But let us suppose for a moment that there were."

"Let us suppose it."

"In that case I have the firm conviction that between you and me, between us two, dear Rosarito, perfect harmony would still exist. On this point I cannot be mistaken. My heart tells me that I am not mistaken."

Rosarito blushed deeply, but making an effort to conceal her embarrassment under smiles and fugitive glances, she said:

"Come, now, no pretences. But if you mean that I shall always approve of what you say, you are right."

"Rosario," exclaimed the young man, "the moment I saw you my soul was filled with gladness; I felt at the same time a regret that I had not come before to Orbajosa."

"Now, that I am not going to believe," she said, affecting gayety to conceal her emotion. "So soon? Don't begin to make protestations already. See, Pepe, I am only a country girl, I can talk only about common things; I don't know French; I don't dress with elegance; all I know is how to play the piano; I—"

"Oh, Rosario!" cried the young man, with ardor; "I believed you to be perfect before; now I am sure you are so."

Her mother at this moment entered the room. Rosarito, who did not know what to say in answer to her cousin's last words, was conscious, however, of the necessity of saying something, and, looking at her mother, she cried:

"Ah! I forgot to give the parrot his dinner."

"Don't mind that now. But why do you stay in here? Take your cousin for a walk in the garden."

Doña Perfecta smiled with maternal kindness at her nephew, as she pointed toward the leafy avenue which was visible through the glass door.

"Let us go there," said Pepe, rising.

Rosarito darted, like a bird released from its cage, toward the glass door.

"Pepe, who knows so much and who must understand all about trees," said Doña Perfecta, "will teach you how to graft. Let us see what he thinks of those young pear-trees that they are going to transplant."

"Come, come!" called Rosarito to her cousin impatiently from the garden.

Both disappeared among the foliage. Doña Perfecta watched them until they were out of sight and then busied herself with the parrot. As she changed its food she said to herself with a contemplative air:

"How indifferent he is! He has not even given a caress to the poor bird."

Then, thinking it possible that she had been overheard by her brother-in-law, she said aloud:

"Cayetano, what do you think of my nephew? Cayetano!"

A low grunt gave evidence that the antiquary was returning to the consciousness of this miserable world.

"Cayetano!"

"Just so, just so!" murmured the scientist in a sleepy voice. "That young gentleman will maintain, as everyone does, that the statues of Mundogrande belong to the first Phoenician immigration. But I will convince him—"

"But, Cayetano!"

"But, Perfecta! There! Now you will insist upon it again that I have been asleep."

"No, indeed; how could I insist upon anything so absurd! But you haven't told me what you think about that young man."

Don Cayetano placed the palm of his hand before his mouth to conceal a yawn; then he and Doña Perfecta entered upon a long conversation. Those who have transmitted to us the necessary data for a compilation of this history omit this dialogue, no doubt because it was entirely confidential. As for what the engineer and Rosarito said in the garden that afternoon, it is evident that it was not worthy of mention.

On the afternoon of the following day, however, events took place which, being of the gravest importance, ought not to be passed over in silence. Late in the afternoon the two cousins found themselves alone, after rambling through different parts of the garden in friendly companionship and having eyes and ears only for each other.

"Pepe," Rosario was saying, "all that you have been telling me is pure fancy, one of those stories that you clever men know so well how to put together. You think that because I am a country girl I believe everything I am told."

"If you understood me as well as I think I understand you, you would know that I never say anything I do not mean. But let us have done with foolish subtleties and lovers' sophistries, that lead only to misunderstandings. I will speak to you only in the language of truth. Are you by chance a young lady whose acquaintance I have made on the promenade or at a party, and with whom I propose to spend a pleasant hour or two? No, you are my cousin. You are something more. Rosario, let us at once put things on their proper footing. Let us drop circumlocutions. I have come here to marry you."

Rosario felt her face burning, and her heart was beating violently.

"See, my dear cousin," continued the young man. "I swear to you that if you had not pleased me I should be already far away from this place. Although politeness and delicacy would have obliged me to make an effort to conceal my disappointment, I should have found it hard to do so. That is my character."

"Cousin, you have only just arrived," said Rosarito laconically, trying to laugh.

"I have only just arrived, and I already know all that I wanted to know; I know that I love you; that you are the woman whom my heart has long been announcing to me, saying to me night and day, 'Now she is coming, now she is near; now you are burning.'"

These words served Rosario as an excuse for breaking into the laugh that had been dimpling her lips. Her soul swelled with happiness; she breathed an atmosphere of joy.

"You persist in depreciating yourself," continued Pepe, "but for me you possess every perfection. You have the admirable quality of radiating on all around you the divine light of your soul. The moment one sees you one feels instinctively the nobility of your mind and the purity of your heart. To see you is to see a celestial being who, through the forgetfulness of Heaven, remains upon the earth; you are an angel, and I adore you."

When he had said this it seemed as if he had fulfilled an important mission. Rosarito, overcome by the violence of her emotion, felt her scant strength suddenly fail her, and, half-fainting, she sank on a stone that in those pleasant solitudes served as a seat. Pepe bent over her. Her eyes were closed, her forehead rested on the palm of her hand. A few moments later the daughter of Doña Perfecta Polentinos gave her cousin, amid happy tears, a tender glance followed by these words:

"I loved you before I had ever seen you."

Placing her hands in those of the young man she rose to her feet, and their forms disappeared among the leafy branches of an oleander walk. Night was falling and soft shadows enveloped the lower end of the garden, while the last rays of the setting sun crowned the tree-tops with fleeting splendors. The noisy republic of the birds kept up a deafening clamor in the upper branches. It was the hour in which, after flitting about in the joyous regions of the sky, they were all going to rest, and they were disputing with one another the branches they had selected for sleeping-places. Their chatter at times had a sound of recrimination and controversy, at times of mockery and merriment. In their voluble twitter the little rascals said the most insulting things to each other, pecking at each other and flapping their wings, as orators wave their arms when they want to make their hearers believe the lies they are telling them. But words of love were to be heard there too, for the peace of the hour and the beauty of the spot invited to it. A sharp ear might have distinguished the following:

"I loved you before I had even seen you, and if you had not come I should have died of grief. Mamma used to give me your father's letters to read, and he praised you so much in them that I used to say, 'That is the man who ought to be my husband.' For a long time your father said nothing about our marrying, which seemed to me great negligence. Uncle Cayetano, whenever he spoke of you, would say, 'There are not many men like him in the world. The woman who gets him for a husband may think herself fortunate.' At last your father said what he could not avoid saying. Yes, he could not avoid saying it—I was expecting it everyday."

Shortly after these words the same voice added uneasily: "Someone is following us."

Emerging from among the oleanders, Pepe, turning round, saw two men approaching them, and touching the leaves of a young tree near by, he said aloud to his companion:

"It is not proper to prune young trees like this for the first time until they have taken firm root. Trees recently planted have not sufficient strength to bear the operation. You know that the roots can grow only by means of the leaves, so that if you take the leaves from a tree—"

"Ah, Señor Don José," cried the Penitentiary, with a frank laugh, approaching the two young people and bowing to them, "are you giving lessons in horticulture? *Insere nunc Melibœe piros; pone ordine vites*, as the great singer of the labors of the field said. 'Graft the pear-tree, dear Melibœus, trim the vines.' And how are we now, Señor Don José?"

The engineer and the canon shook hands. Then the latter turned round, and indicating by a gesture a young man who was behind him, said, smiling:

"I have the pleasure of presenting to you my dear Jacintillo—a great rogue, a feather-head, Señor Don José."

IX

The Disagreement Continues to Increase, and Threatens to Become Discord

C lose beside the black cassock was a fresh and rosy face, that seemed fresher and rosier from the contrast. Jacinto saluted our hero, not without some embarrassment.

He was one of those precocious youths whom the indulgent university sends prematurely forth into the arena of life, making them fancy that they are men because they have received their doctor's degree. Jacinto had a round, handsome face with rosy cheeks, like a girl's, and without any beard save the down which announced its coming. In person he was plump and below the medium height. His age was a little over twenty. He had been educated from childhood under the direction of his excellent and learned uncle, which is the same as saying that the twig had not become crooked in the growing. A severe moral training had kept him always straight, and in the fulfilment of his scholastic duties he had been almost above reproach. Having concluded his studies at the university with astonishing success, for there was scarcely a class in which he did not take the highest honors, he entered on the practice of his profession, promising, by his application and his aptitude for the law, to maintain fresh and green in the forum the laurels of the lecture-hall.

At times he was as mischievous as a boy, at times as sedate as a man. In very truth, if Jacinto had not had a little, and even a great deal of liking for pretty girls, his uncle would have thought him perfect. The worthy man preached to him unceasingly on this point, hastening to clip the wings of every audacious fancy. But not even this mundane inclination of the young man could cool the great affection which our worthy canon bore the charming offspring of his dear niece, Maria Remedios. Where the young lawyer was concerned, everything else must give way. Even the grave and methodical habits of the worthy ecclesiastic were altered when they interfered with the affairs of his precocious pupil. That order and regularity, apparently as fixed as the laws of a planetary system, were interrupted whenever Jacinto was ill or had to take a journey. Useless celibacy of the clergy! The Council of

Trent prohibits them from having children of their own, but God—and not the Devil, as the proverb says—gives them nephews and nieces in order that they may know the tender anxieties of paternity.

Examining impartially the qualities of this clever boy, it was impossible not to recognize that he was not wanting in merit. His character was in the main inclined to uprightness, and noble actions awakened a frank admiration in his soul. With respect to his intellectual endowments and his social knowledge, they were sufficient to enable him to become in time one of those notabilities of whom there are so many in Spain; he might be what we take delight in calling hyperbolically a distinguished patrician, or an eminent public man; species which, owing to their great abundance, are hardly appreciated at their just value. In the tender age in which the university degree serves as a sort of solder between boyhood and manhood, few young men—especially if they have been spoiled by their masters—are free from an offensive pedantry, which, if it gives them great importance beside their mamma's arm-chair, makes them very ridiculous when they are among grave and experienced men. Jacinto had this defect, which was excusable in him, not only because of his youth, but also because his worthy uncle stimulated his puerile vanity by injudicious praise.

When the introduction was over they resumed their walk. Jacinto was silent. The canon, returning to the interrupted theme of the *pyros* which were to be grafted and the *vites* which were to be trimmed, said:

"I am already aware that Señor Don José is a great agriculturist."

"Not at all; I know nothing whatever about the subject," responded the young man, observing with no little annoyance the canon's mania of supposing him to be learned in all the sciences.

"Oh, yes! a great agriculturist," continued the Penitentiary; "but on agricultural subjects, don't quote the latest treatises to me. For me the whole of that science, Señor de Rey, is condensed in what I call the Bible of the Field, in the 'Georgics' of the immortal Roman. It is all admirable, from that grand sentence, *Nec vero terræ ferre omnes omnia possunt*—that is to say, that not every soil is suited to every tree, Señor Don José—to the exhaustive treatise on bees, in which the poet describes the habits of those wise little animals, defining the drone in these words:

> "*Ille horridus alter*
> *Desidia, latamque trahens inglorius alvum.*'

'Of a horrible and slothful figure, dragging along the ignoble weight of the belly,' Señor Don José."

"You do well to translate it for me," said Pepe, "for I know very little Latin."

"Oh, why should the men of the present day spend their time in studying things that are out of date?" said the canon ironically. "Besides, only poor creatures like Virgil and Cicero and Livy wrote in Latin. I, however, am of a different way of thinking; as witness my nephew, to whom I have taught that sublime language. The rascal knows it better than I do. The worst of it is, that with his modern reading he is forgetting it; and some fine day, without ever having suspected it, he will find out that he is an ignoramus. For, Señor Don José, my nephew has taken to studying the newest books and the most extravagant theories, and it is Flammarion here and Flammarion there, and nothing will do him but that the stars are full of people. Come, I fancy that you two are going to be very good friends. Jacinto, beg this gentleman to teach you the higher mathematics, to instruct you concerning the German philosophers, and then you will be a man."

The worthy ecclesiastic laughed at his own wit, while Jacinto, delighted to see the conversation turn on a theme so greatly to his taste, after excusing himself to Pepe Rey, suddenly hurled this question at him:

"Tell me, Señor Don José, what do you think of Darwinism?"

Our hero smiled at this inopportune pedantry, and he felt almost tempted to encourage the young man to continue in this path of childish vanity; but judging it more prudent to avoid intimacy, either with the nephew or the uncle, he answered simply:

"I can think nothing at all about the doctrines of Darwin, for I know scarcely anything about him. My professional labors have not permitted me to devote much of my time to those studies."

"Well," said the canon, laughing, "it all reduces itself to this, that we are descended from monkeys. If he had said that only in the case of certain people I know, he would have been right."

"The theory of natural selection," said Jacinto emphatically, "has, they say, a great many partisans in Germany."

"I do not doubt it," said the ecclesiastic. "In Germany they would have no reason to be sorry if that theory were true, as far as Bismarck is concerned."

Doña Perfecta and Señor Don Cayetano at this moment made their appearance.

"What a beautiful evening!" said the former. "Well, nephew, are you getting terribly bored?"

"I am not bored in the least," responded the young man.

"Don't try to deny it. Cayetano and I were speaking of that as we came along. You are bored, and you are trying to hide it. It is not every young man of the present day who would have the self-denial to spend his youth, like Jacinto, in a town where there are neither theatres, nor opera bouffe, nor dancers, nor philosophers, nor athenæums, nor magazines, nor congresses, nor any other kind of diversions or entertainments."

"I am quite contented here," responded Pepe. "I was just now saying to Rosario that I find this city and this house so pleasant that I would like to live and die here."

Rosario turned very red and the others were silent. They all sat down in a summer-house, Jacinto hastening to take the seat on the left of the young girl.

"See here, nephew, I have a piece of advice to give you," said Doña Perfecta, smiling with that expression of kindness that seemed to emanate from her soul, like the aroma from the flower. "But don't imagine that I am either reproving you or giving you a lesson—you are not a child, and you will easily understand what I mean."

"Scold me, dear aunt, for no doubt I deserve it," replied Pepe, who was beginning to accustom himself to the kindnesses of his father's sister.

"No, it is only a piece of advice. These gentlemen, I am sure, will agree that I am in the right."

Rosario was listening with her whole soul.

"It is only this," continued Doña Perfecta, "that when you visit our beautiful cathedral again, you will endeavor to behave with a little more decorum while you are in it."

"Why, what have I done?"

"It does not surprise me that you are not yourself aware of your fault," said his aunt, with apparent good humor. "It is only natural; accustomed as you are to enter athenæums and clubs, and academies and congresses without any ceremony, you think that you can enter a temple in which the Divine Majesty is in the same manner."

"But excuse me, señora," said Pepe gravely, "I entered the cathedral with the greatest decorum."

"But I am not scolding you, man; I am not scolding you. If you take it in that way I shall have to remain silent. Excuse my nephew, gentlemen. A little carelessness, a little heedlessness on his part is not to be wondered at. How many years is it since you set foot in a sacred place before?"

"Señora, I assure you— But, in short, let my religious ideas be what they may, I am in the habit of observing the utmost decorum in church."

"What I assure you is— There, if you are going to be offended I won't go on. What I assure you is that a great many people noticed it this morning. The Señores de Gonzalez, Doña Robustiana, Serafinita—in short, when I tell you that you attracted the attention of the bishop— His lordship complained to me about it this afternoon when I was at my cousin's. He told me that he did not order you to be put out of the church only because you were my nephew."

Rosario looked anxiously at her cousin, trying to read in his countenance, before he uttered it, the answer he would make to these charges.

"No doubt they mistook me for someone else."

"No, no! it was you. But there, don't get angry! We are talking here among friends and in confidence. It was you. I saw you myself."

"You saw me!"

"Just so. Will you deny that you went to look at the pictures, passing among a group of worshippers who were hearing mass? I assure you that my attention was so distracted by your comings and goings that— well, you must not do it again. Then you went into the chapel of San Gregorio. At the elevation of the Host at the high altar you did not even turn around to make a gesture of reverence. Afterward you traversed the whole length of the church, you went up to the tomb of the Adelantado, you touched the altar with your hands, then you passed a second time among the group of worshippers, attracting the notice of everyone. All the girls looked at you, and you seemed pleased at disturbing so finely the devotions of those good people."

"Good Heavens! How many things I have done!" exclaimed Pepe, half angry, half amused. "I am a monster, it seems, without ever having suspected it."

"No, I am very well aware that you are a good boy," said Doña Perfecta, observing the canon's expression of unalterable gravity, which gave his face the appearance of a pasteboard mask. "But, my dear boy, between thinking things and showing them in that irreverent manner, there is a distance which a man of good sense and good breeding should never cross. I am well aware that your ideas are— Now, don't get angry! If you get angry, I will be silent. I say that it is one thing to have certain ideas about religion and another thing to express them. I will take good care not to reproach you because you believe that God did not create us in his image and likeness, but that we are descended from the monkeys; nor because you deny the existence of the soul, asserting that it is a drug, like the little papers of rhubarb and magnesia that are sold at the apothecary's—"

"Señora, for Heaven's sake!" exclaimed Pepe, with annoyance. "I see that I have a very bad reputation in Orbajosa."

The others still remained silent.

"As I said, I will not reproach you for entertaining those ideas. And, besides, I have not the right to do so. If I should undertake to argue with you, you, with your wonderful talents, would confute me a thousand times over. No, I will not attempt anything of that kind. What I say is that these poor and humble inhabitants of Orbajosa are pious and good Christians, although they know nothing about German philosophy, and that, therefore, you ought not publicly to manifest your contempt for their beliefs."

"My dear aunt," said the engineer gravely, "I have shown no contempt for anyone, nor do I entertain the ideas which you attribute to me. Perhaps I may have been a little wanting in reverence in the church. I am somewhat absent-minded. My thoughts and my attention were engaged with the architecture of the building and, frankly speaking, I did not observe—But this was no reason for the bishop to think of putting me out of the church, nor for you to suppose me capable of attributing to a paper from the apothecary's the functions of the soul. I may tolerate that as a jest, but only as a jest."

The agitation of Pepe Rey's mind was so great that, notwithstanding his natural prudence and moderation, he was unable to conceal it.

"There! I see that you are angry," said Doña Perfecta, casting down her eyes and clasping her hands. "I am very sorry. If I had known that you would have taken it in that way, I should not have spoken to you. Pepe, I ask your pardon."

Hearing these words and seeing his kind aunt's deprecating attitude, Pepe felt ashamed of the sternness of his last words, and he made an effort to recover his serenity. The venerable Penitentiary extricated him from his embarrassing position, saying with his accustomed benevolent smile:

"Señora Doña Perfecta, we must be tolerant with artists. Oh, I have known a great many of them! Those gentlemen, when they have before them a statue, a piece of rusty armor, a mouldy painting, or an old wall, forget everything else. Señor Don José is an artist, and he has visited our cathedral as the English visit it, who would willingly carry it away with them to their museums, to its last tile, if they could. That the worshippers were praying, that the priest was elevating the Sacred Host, that the moment of supreme piety and devotion had come—what of that? What does all that matter to an artist? It is true that I do not know what art is worth, apart from the sentiments which it expresses, but, in fine, at the present day, it is the custom to adore the form, not the idea. God preserve me from undertaking to discuss this question with Señor Don José, who knows so much, and who, reasoning with the admirable subtlety of the moderns, would instantly confound my mind, in which there is only faith."

"The determination which you all have to regard me as the most learned man on earth annoys me exceedingly," said Pepe, speaking in his former hard tone. "Hold me for a fool; for I would rather be regarded as a fool than as the possessor of that Satanic knowledge which is here attributed to me."

Rosarito laughed, and Jacinto thought that a highly opportune moment had now arrived to make a display of his own erudition.

"Pantheism or panentheism," he said, "is condemned by the Church, as well as by the teachings of Schopenhauer and of the modern Hartmann."

"Ladies and gentlemen," said the canon gravely, "men who pay so fervent a worship to art, though it be only to its form, deserve the greatest respect. It is better to be an artist, and delight in the contemplation of beauty, though this be only represented by nude nymphs, than to be indifferent and incredulous in everything. The mind that consecrates itself to the contemplation of beauty, evil will not take complete possession of. *Est Deus in nobis. Deus*, be it well understood. Let Señor Don José, then, continue to admire the marvels of our church; I, for one, will willingly forgive him his acts of irreverence, with all due respect for the opinions of the bishop."

"Thanks, Señor Don Inocencio," said Pepe, feeling a bitter and rebellious sentiment of hostility springing up within him toward the canon, and unable to conquer his desire to mortify him. "But let none of you imagine, either, that it was the beauties of art, of which you suppose the temple to be full, that engaged my attention. Those beauties, with the exception of the imposing architecture of a portion of the edifice and of the three tombs that are in the chapel of the apse, I do not see. What occupied my mind was the consideration of the deplorable decadence of the religious arts; and the innumerable monstrosities, of which the cathedral is full, caused me not astonishment, but disgust."

The amazement of all present was profound.

"I cannot endure," continued Pepe, "those glazed and painted images that resemble so much—God forgive me for the comparison—the dolls that little girls play with. And what am I to say of the theatrical robes that cover them? I saw a St. Joseph with a mantle whose appearance I will not describe, out of respect for the holy patriarch and for the church of which he is the patron. On the altar are crowded together images in the worst possible taste; and the innumerable crowns, branches, stars, moons, and other ornaments of metal or gilt paper have an air of an ironmongery that offends the religious sentiment and depresses the soul. Far from lifting itself up to religious contemplation, the soul sinks, and the idea of the ludicrous distracts it. The great works of art which give sensible form to ideas, to dogmas, to religious faith, to mystic exaltation, fulfil a noble mission. The caricatures, the aberrations of taste, the grotesque works with which a mistaken piety fills the churches, also fulfil their object; but this is a sad one enough: They encourage superstition, cool enthusiasm, oblige the eyes of the believer to turn away from the altar, and, with the eyes, the souls that have not a very profound and a very firm faith turn away also."

"The doctrine of the iconoclasts, too," said Jacinto, "has, it seems, spread widely in Germany."

"I am not an iconoclast, although I would prefer the destruction of all the images to the exhibition of buffooneries of which I speak," continued the young man. "Seeing it, one may justly advocate a return of religious worship to the august simplicity of olden times. But no; let us not renounce the admirable aid which all the arts, beginning with poetry and ending with music, lend to the relations between man and God. Let the arts live; let the utmost pomp be displayed in religious ceremonies. I am a partisan of pomp."

"An artist, an artist, and nothing more than an artist!" exclaimed the canon, shaking his head with a sorrowful air. "Fine pictures, fine statues, beautiful music; pleasure for the senses, and let the devil take the soul!"

"Apropos of music," said Pepe Rey, without observing the deplorable effect which his words produced on both mother and daughter, "imagine how disposed my mind would be to religious contemplation on entering the cathedral, when just at that moment, and precisely at the offertory at high mass, the organist played a passage from 'Traviata.'"

"Señor de Rey is right in that," said the little lawyer emphatically. "The organist played the other day the whole of the drinking song and the waltz from the same opera, and afterward a rondeau from the 'Grande Duchesse.'"

"But when I felt my heart sink," continued the engineer implacably, "was when I saw an image of the Virgin, which seems to be held in great veneration, judging from the crowd before it and the multitude of tapers which lighted it. They have dressed her in a puffed-out garment of velvet, embroidered with gold, of a shape so extraordinary that it surpasses the most extravagant of the fashions of the day. Her face is almost hidden under a voluminous frill, made of innumerable rows of lace, crimped with a crimping-iron, and her crown, half a yard in height, surrounded by golden rays, looks like a hideous catafalque erected over her head. Of the same material, and embroidered in the same manner, are the trousers of the Infant Jesus. I will not go on, for to describe the Mother and the Child might perhaps lead me to commit some irreverence. I will only say that it was impossible for me to keep from smiling, and for a short time I contemplated the profaned image, saying to myself: 'Mother and Lady mine, what a sight they have made of you!'"

As he ended Pepe looked at his hearers, and although, owing to the gathering darkness, he could not see their countenances distinctly, he fancied that in some of them he perceived signs of angry consternation.

"Well, Señor Don José!" exclaimed the canon quickly, smiling with a triumphant expression, "that image, which to your philosophy and pantheism appears so ridiculous, is Our Lady of Help, patroness and advocate of Orbajosa, whose inhabitants regard her with so much veneration that they would be quite capable of dragging anyone through the streets who should speak ill of her. The chronicles and history, Señor Don José, are full of the miracles which she has wrought, and even at the present day we receive constantly incontrovertible proofs of her protection. You must know also that your aunt, Dona Perfecta, is chief lady in waiting to the Most Holy Virgin of Help, and that the dress that to you appears so grotesque—well, the dress, I repeat, which, to

BENITO PÉREZ GALDÓS

your impious eyes, appears so grotesque—went out from this house, and that the trousers of the Infant are the work of the skilful needle and the ardent piety combined of your cousin Rosarito, who is now listening to us."

Pepe Rey was greatly disconcerted. At the same instant Doña Perfecta rose abruptly from her seat, and, without saying a word, walked toward the house, followed by the Penitentiary. The others rose also. Recovering from his stupefaction, the young man was about to beg his cousin's pardon for his irreverence, when he observed that Rosarito was weeping. Fixing on her cousin a look of friendly and gentle reproof, she said:

"What ideas you have!"

The voice of Doña Perfecta was heard crying in an altered accent:

"Rosario! Rosario!"

The latter ran toward the house.

X

The Existence of Discord is Evident

Pepe Rey was disturbed and perplexed, enraged with himself and everyone else; he tried in vain to imagine what could be the conflict that had arisen, in spite of himself, between his ideas and the ideas of his aunt's friends. Thoughtful and sad, foreseeing future discord, he remained for a short time sitting on the bench in the summer-house, his chin resting on his breast, his forehead gathered in a frown, his hands clasped. He thought himself alone.

Suddenly he heard a gay voice humming the refrain of a song from a zarzuela. He looked up and saw Don Jacinto sitting in the opposite corner of the summer-house.

"Ah, Señor de Rey!" said the youth abruptly, "one does not offend with impunity the religious sentiments of the great majority of a nation. If you doubt it, consider what happened in the first French revolution."

When Pepe heard the buzzing of this insect his irritation increased. Nevertheless there was no anger in his soul toward the youthful doctor of laws. The latter annoyed him, as a fly might annoy him, but nothing more. Rey felt the irritation which every importunate being inspires, and with the air of one who brushes away a buzzing drone, he answered:

"What has the French revolution to do with the robe of the Virgin?"

He got up and walked toward the house, but he had not taken half a dozen steps before he heard again beside him the buzzing of the mosquito, saying:

"Señor Don José, I wish to speak to you about an affair in which you are greatly interested and which may cause you some trouble."

"An affair?" said the young man, drawing back. "Let us hear what affair is that."

"You suspect what it is, perhaps," said Jacinto, approaching Pepe, and smiling with the air of a man of business who has some unusually important matter on hand; "I want to speak to you about the lawsuit."

"The lawsuit! My friend, I have no lawsuits. You, as a good lawyer, dream of lawsuits and see stamped paper everywhere."

"What! You have not heard of your lawsuit?" exclaimed the youth, with amazement.

"Of my lawsuit! But I have no lawsuits, nor have I ever had any."

"Well, if you have not heard of it, I am all the better pleased to have spoken to you about it, so that you may be on your guard. Yes, senor, you are going to have a suit at law."

"And with whom?"

"With Uncle Licurgo and other land-owners whose property borders on the estate called The Poplars."

Pepe Rey was astounded.

"Yes, señor," continued the little lawyer. "Today Uncle Licurgo and I had a long conference. As I am such a friend of the family, I wanted to let you know about it, so that, if you think well of it, you may hasten to arrange the matter."

"But what have I to arrange? What do those rascals claim from me?"

"It seems that a stream of water which rises in your property has changed its course and flows over some tile-works of the aforesaid Uncle Licurgo and the mill of another person, occasioning considerable damage. My client—for he is determined that I shall get him out of this difficulty—my client, as I said, demands that you shall restore the water to its former channel, so as to avoid fresh injuries, and that you shall indemnify him for the damage which his works have already sustained through the neglect of the superior proprietor."

"And I am the superior proprietor! If I engage in a lawsuit, that will be the first fruit that those famous Poplars, which were mine and which now, as I understand, belong to everybody, will have ever produced me, for Licurgo, as well as some of the other farmers of the district, have been filching from me, little by little, year after year, pieces of land, and it will be very difficult to re-establish the boundaries of my property."

"That is a different question."

"That is not a different question. The real suit," exclaimed the engineer, unable to control his anger, "will be the one that I will bring against that rabble who no doubt propose to themselves to tire me out and drive me to desperation—so that I may abandon everything and let them continue in possession of what they have stolen. We shall see if there are lawyers and judges who will uphold the infamous conduct of those village legists, who are forever at law, and who waste and consume the property of others. I am obliged to you, young gentleman, for having informed me of the villanous intentions of those boors, who are more perverse than Satan himself. When I tell you that that very tile-yard and that very mill on which Licurgo bases his claim are mine—"

"The title-deeds of the property ought to be examined, to see if possession may not constitute a title in this case."

"Possession! Those scoundrels are not going to have the pleasure of laughing at me in that way. I suppose that justice is honestly and faithfully administered in the city of Orbajosa."

"Oh, as to that!" exclaimed the little lawyer, with an approving look, "the judge is an excellent person! He comes here every evening. But it is strange that you should have received no notice of Señor Licurgo's claims. Have you not yet been summoned to appear before the tribunal of arbitration?"

"No."

"It will be tomorrow, then. Well, I am very sorry that Señor Licurgo's precipitation has deprived me of the pleasure and honor of defending you, but what is to be done? Licurgo was determined that I should take him out of his troubles. I will study the matter with the greatest care. This vile slavery is the great drawback of jurisprudence."

Pepe entered the dining-room in a deplorable state of mind. Doña Perfecta was talking with the Penitentiary, as he entered, and Rosarito was sitting alone, with her eyes fixed on the door. She was no doubt waiting for her cousin.

"Come here, you rascal," said his aunt, smiling with very little spontaneity. "You have insulted us, you great atheist! but we forgive you. I am well aware that my daughter and myself are two rustics who are incapable of soaring to the regions of mathematics where you dwell, but for all that it is possible that you may one day get down on your knees to us and beg us to teach you the Christian doctrine."

Pepe answered with vague phrases and formulas of politeness and repentance.

"For my part," said Don Inocencio, with an affected air of meekness and amiability, "if in the course of these idle disputes I have said anything that could offend Señor Don José, I beg his pardon for it. We are all friends here."

"Thanks. It is of no consequence."

"In spite of everything," said Doña Perfecta, smiling with more naturalness than before, "I shall always be the same for my dear nephew; in spite of his extravagant and anti-religious ideas. In what way do you suppose I am going to spend this evening? Well, in trying to make Uncle Licurgo give up those obstinate notions which would otherwise cause you annoyance. I sent for him, and he is waiting for me now in the hall. Make yourself easy, I will arrange the matter; for although I know that he is not altogether without right on his side—"

"Thanks, dear aunt," responded the young man, his whole being invaded by a wave of the generous emotion which was so easily aroused in his soul.

Pepe Rey looked in the direction of his cousin, intending to join her, but some wily questions of the canon retained him at Dona Perfecta's side. Rosario looked dejected, and was listening with an air of melancholy indifference to the words of the little lawyer, who, having installed himself at her side, kept up a continuous stream of fulsome flatteries, seasoned with ill-timed jests and fatuous remarks in the worst possible taste.

"The worst of it is," said Doña Perfecta to her nephew—surprising the glance which he cast in the direction of the ill-assorted pair—"the worst of it is, that you have offended poor Rosario. You must do all in your power to make your peace with her. The poor child is so good!"

"Oh, yes! so good," added the canon, "that I have no doubt that she will forgive her cousin."

"I think that Rosario has already forgiven me," affirmed Rey.

"And if not, angelic breasts do not harbor resentment long," said Don Inocencio mellifluously. "I have a great deal of influence with the child, and I will endeavor to dissipate in her generous soul whatever prejudice may exist there against you. As soon as I say a word or two to her—"

Pepe Rey felt a cloud darken his soul and he said with meaning:

"Perhaps it may not be necessary."

"I will not speak to her now," added the capitular, "because she is listening entranced to Jacinto's nonsense. Ah, those children! When they once begin there is no stopping them."

The judge of the lower court, the alcalde's lady, and the dean of the cathedral now made their appearance. They all saluted the engineer, manifesting in their words and manner, on seeing him, the satisfaction of gratified curiosity. The judge was one of those clever and intelligent young men who everyday spring into notice in official circles; aspiring, almost before they are out of the shell, to the highest political and administrative positions. He gave himself airs of great importance, and in speaking of himself and of his juvenile toga, he seemed indirectly to manifest great offence because he had not been all at once made president of the supreme court. In such inexpert hands, in a brain thus swollen with vanity, in this incarnation of conceit, had the state placed the most delicate and the most difficult functions of human justice. His manners were those of a perfect courtier, and revealed a scrupulous and minute attention to all that concerned his own person. He had the insufferable habit of taking off and putting on every moment his gold eye-glasses, and in his conversation he manifested with frequency the strong desire which he had to be transferred to Madrid, in order that he might give his invaluable services to the Department of Grace and Justice.

The alcalde's lady was a good-natured woman, whose only weakness was to fancy that she had a great many acquaintances at the court. She asked Pepe Rey various questions about the fashions, mentioning establishments in which she had had a mantle or a skirt made on her last journey to the capital, contemporaneous with the visit of Muley-Abbas, and she also mentioned the names of a dozen duchesses and marchionesses; speaking of them with as much familiarity as if they had been friends of her school-days. She said also that the Countess of M. (famous for her parties) was a friend of hers and that in '60 she had paid her a visit, when the countess had invited her to her box at the Teatro Real, where she saw Muley-Abbas in Moorish dress and accompanied by his retinue of Moors. The alcalde's wife talked incessantly and was not wanting in humor.

The dean was a very old man, corpulent and red-faced, plethoric and apoplectic looking, a man so obese that he seemed bursting out of his skin. He had belonged to one of the suppressed religious orders; he talked only of religious matters; and from the very first manifested the most profound contempt for Pepe Rey. The latter appeared every moment more unable to accommodate himself to a society so little to his taste. His disposition—not at all malleable, hard, and very little flexible—rejected the duplicities and the compromises of language to simulate concord when it did not exist. He remained, then, very grave during the whole of the tiresome evening, obliged as he was to endure the oratorical vehemence of the alcalde's wife, who, without being Fame, had the privilege of fatiguing with a hundred tongues the ears of men. If, in some brief respite which this lady gave her hearers, Pepe Rey made an attempt to approach his cousin, the Penitentiary attached himself to him instantly, like the mollusk to the rock; taking him apart with a mysterious air to propose to him an excursion with Señor Don Cayetano to Mundogrande, or a fishing party on the clear waters of the Nahara.

At last the evening came to an end, as everything does in this world. The dean retired, leaving the house, as it seemed, empty, and very soon there remained of the alcalde's wife only an echo, like the buzz which remains in the air after a storm has passed away. The judge also deprived the company of his presence, and at last Don Inocencio gave his nephew the signal for departure.

"Come, boy, come; for it is late," he said, smiling. "How you have tormented poor Rosarito, has he not, child? Home, you rogue, home, without delay."

"It is time to go to bed," said Doña Perfecta.

"Time to go to work," responded the little lawyer.

"I am always telling him that he ought to get through with his business in the day-time, but he will not mind me."

"There is so much, so very much business to be got through."

"No, say rather, that confounded work which you have undertaken. He does not wish to say it, Señor Don José, but the truth is that he is writing a book on 'The Influence of Woman in Christian Society,' and, in addition to that, 'A Glance at the Catholic Movement in'—somewhere or other. What do you know about glances or influences? But these youths of the present day have audacity enough for anything. Oh, what boys! Well, let us go home. Goodnight, Señora Doña Perfecta—goodnight, Señor Don José—Rosarito."

"I will wait for Señor Don Cayetano," said Jacinto, "to ask him to give me the Augusto Nicolas."

"Always carrying books. Why, sometimes you come into the house laden like a donkey. Very well, then, let us wait."

"Señor Don Jacinto does not write hastily," said Pepe Rey; "he prepares himself well for his work, so that his books may be treasures of learning."

"But that boy will injure his brain," objected Doña Perfecta. "For Heaven's sake be careful! I would set a limit to his reading."

"Since we are going to wait," said the little doctor, in a tone of insufferable conceit, "I will take with me also the third volume of Concilios. What do you think, uncle?"

"Take that, of course. It would never do to leave that behind you."

Fortunately Señor Don Cayetano (who generally spent his evenings at the house of Don Lorenzo Ruiz) soon arrived, and the books being received, uncle and nephew left the house.

Rey read in his cousin's sad countenance a keen desire to speak to him. He approached her while Dona Perfecta and Don Cayetano were discussing some domestic matter apart.

"You have offended mamma," said Rosarito.

Her features expressed something like terror.

"It is true," responded the young man; "I have offended your mamma—I have offended you."

"No, not me. I already imagined that the Infant Jesus ought not to wear trousers."

"But I hope that you will both forgive me. Your mamma was so kind to me a little while ago."

Doña Perfecta's voice suddenly vibrated through the dining-room, with so discordant a tone that her nephew started as if he had heard a cry of alarm. The voice said imperiously:

"Rosario, go to bed!"

Startled, her mind filled with anxious fears, the girl lingered in the room, going here and there as if she was looking for something. As she passed her cousin she whispered softly and cautiously these words:

"Mamma is angry."

"But—"

"She is angry—be on your guard, be on your guard."

Then she left the room. Her mother, for whom Uncle Licurgo was waiting, followed her, and for sometime the voices of Doña Perfecta and the countryman were heard mingled together in familiar conference. Pepe was left with Don Cayetano, who, taking a light, said:

"Goodnight, Pepe. But don't suppose that I am going to sleep, I am going to work. But why are you so thoughtful? What is the matter with you?—Just as I say, to work. I am making notes for a 'Memorial Discourse on the Genealogies of Orbajosa.' I have already found data and information of the utmost value. There can be no dispute about it. In every period of our history the Orbajosans have been distinguished for their delicate sense of honor, their chivalry, their valor, their intellectuality. The conquest of Mexico, the wars of the Emperor, the wars of Philip against the heretics, testify to this. But are you ill? What is the matter with you? As I say, eminent theologians, valiant warriors, conquerors, saints, bishops, statesmen—all sorts of illustrious men—have flourished in this humble land of the garlic. No, there is not in Christendom a more illustrious city than ours. Its virtues and its glories are in themselves enough and more than enough to fill all the pages of our country's history. Well, I see that it is sleepy you are—goodnight. As I say, I would not exchange the glory of being a son of this noble city for all the gold in the world. Augusta, the ancients called it; Augustissima,

I call it now; for now, as then, high-mindedness, generosity, valor, magnanimity, are the patrimony of all. Well, goodnight, dear Pepe. But I fancy you are not well. Has the supper disagreed with you?—Alonzo Gonzalez de Bustamante was right when he said in his "Floresta Amena' that the people of Orbajosa suffice in themselves to confer greatness and honor on a kingdom. Don't you think so?"

"Oh, yes, señor; undoubtedly," responded Pepe Rey, going abruptly toward his room.

XI

The Discord Grows

During the following days Pepe Rey made the acquaintance of several of the people of the place; he visited the Casino, and formed friendships with some of the individuals who spent their lives in the rooms of that corporation.

But the youth of Orbajosa did not spend all their time in the Casino, as evil-minded people might imagine. In the afternoons there were to be seen at the corner of the cathedral, and in the little plaza formed by the intersection of the Calle del Condestable and the Calle de la Triperia, several gentlemen who, gracefully enveloped in their cloaks, stood there like sentinels, watching the people as they passed by. If the weather was fine, those shining lights of the Urbs Augustan culture bent their steps, still enveloped in the indispensable cloak, toward the promenade called the Paseo de las Descalzas, which was called the Paseo de las Descalzas, which was formed by a double row of consumptive-looking elms and some withered bushes of broom. There the brilliant Pleiad watched the daughters of this fellow-townsman or that, who had also come there for a walk, and the afternoon passed tolerably. In the evening, the Casino filled up again; and while some of the members gave their lofty minds to the delights of monte, others read the newspaper, while the majority discussed in the coffee-room subjects of various kinds, such as politics, horses, bulls, or the gossip of the place. The result of every discussion was the renewed conviction of the supremacy of Orbajosa and its inhabitants over all the other towns and peoples on the face of the earth.

These distinguished men were the cream of the illustrious city; some rich landowners, others very poor, but all alike free from lofty aspirations. They had the imperturbable tranquillity of the beggar who desires nothing more so long as he has a crust of bread with which to cheat hunger, and the sun to warm him. What chiefly distinguished the Orbajosans of the Casino was a sentiment of bitter hostility toward all strangers, and whenever any stranger of note appeared in its august halls, they believed that he had come there to call in question the superiority of the land of the garlic, or to dispute with it, through envy, the incontestable advantages which nature had bestowed upon it.

BENITO PÉREZ GALDÓS

When Pepe Rey presented himself in the Casino, they received him with something of suspicion, and as facetious persons abounded in it, before the new member had been there a quarter of an hour, all sorts of jokes had been made about him. When in answer to the reiterated questions of the members he said that he had come to Orbajosa with a commission to explore the basin of the Nahara for coal, and to survey a road, they all agreed that Señor Don José was a conceited fellow who wished to give himself airs, discovering coalbeds and planning railroads. Someone added:

"He has come to a bad place for that, then. Those gentlemen imagine that here we are all fools, and that they can deceive us with fine words. He has come to marry Doña Perfecta's daughter, and all that he says about coalbeds is only for the sake of appearances."

"Well, this morning," said another, a merchant who had failed, "they told me at the Dominguez' that the gentleman has not a peseta, and that he has come here in order to be supported by his aunt and to see if he can catch Rosarito."

"It seems that he is no engineer at all," added an olive-planter, whose plantations were mortgaged for double their value. "But it is as you say: those starvelings from Madrid think they are justified in deceiving poor provincials, and as they believe that here we all wear tails—"

"It is plain to be seen that he is penniless—"

"Well, half-jest and whole earnest, he told us last night that we were lazy barbarians."

"That we spent our time sunning ourselves, like the Bedouins."

"That we lived with the imagination."

"That's it; that we lived with the imagination."

"And that this city was precisely like a city in Morocco."

"Well! one has no patience to listen to those things. Where else could he see (unless it might be in Paris) a street like the Calle del Condestable, that can show seven houses in a row, all of them magnificent, from Doña Perfecta's house to that of Nicolasita Hernandez? Does the fellow suppose that one has never seen anything, or has never been in Paris?"

"He also said, with a great deal of delicacy, that Orbajosa was a city of beggars; and he gave us to understand that in his opinion we live in the meanest way here without being ourselves aware of it."

"What insolence! If he ever says that to me, there will be a scene in the Casino," exclaimed the collector of taxes. "Why didn't they tell him how many arrobas of oil Orbajosa produced last year? Doesn't the fool know that in good years Orbajosa produces wheat enough to supply all Spain, and even all Europe, with bread? It is true that the crops have been bad for several years past, but that is not the rule. And the crop of garlic! I wager the gentleman doesn't know that the garlic of Orbajosa made the gentlemen of the jury in the Exposition of London stare!"

These and other conversations of a similar kind were to be heard in the rooms of the Casino in those days. Notwithstanding this boastful talk, so common in small towns, which, for the very reason that they are small, are generally arrogant, Rey was not without finding sincere friends among the members of the learned corporation, for they were not all gossips, nor were there wanting among them persons of good sense. But our hero had the misfortune—if misfortune it can be called—to be unusually frank in the manifestation of his feelings, and this awakened some antipathy toward him.

Days passed. In addition to the natural disgust which the social customs of the episcopal city produced in him, various causes, all of them disagreeable, began to develop in his mind a profound sadness, chief among these causes being the crowd of litigants that swarmed about him like voracious ants. Many others of the neighboring landowners besides Uncle Licurgo claimed damages from him, or asked him to render accounts for lands managed by his grandfather. A claim was also brought against him because of a certain contract of partnership entered into by his mother and which, as it appeared, had not been fulfilled; and he was required in the same way to acknowledge a mortgage on the estate of The Poplars executed in an irregular form by his uncle. Claims swarmed around him, multiplying with ant-like rapidity. He had come to the determination to renounce the ownership of his lands, but meanwhile his dignity required that he should not yield to the wily manœuvres of the artful rustics; and as the town-council brought a claim against him also on account of a pretended confusion of the boundary lines of his estate with those of an adjoining wood belonging to the town-lands, the unfortunate young man found himself at every step obliged to prove his rights, which were being continually called in question. His honor was engaged, and he had no alternative but to defend his rights to the death.

Doña Perfecta had promised in her magnanimity to help him to free himself from these disgraceful plots by means of an amicable arrangement; but the days passed, and the good offices of the exemplary lady had produced no result whatever. The claims multiplied with the dangerous swiftness of a violent disease. Pepe Rey passed hour after hour at court, making declarations and answering the same questions over and over again, and when he returned home tired and angry, there appeared before him the sharp features and grotesque face of the notary, who had brought him a thick bundle of stamped papers full of horrible formulas—that he might be studying the question.

It will be easily understood that Pepe Rey was not a man to endure such annoyances when he might escape from them by leaving the town. His mother's noble city appeared to his imagination like a horrible monster which had fastened its ferocious claws in him and was drinking his blood. To free himself from this monster nothing more was necessary, he believed, than flight. But a weighty interest—an interest in which his heart was concerned—kept him where he was; binding him to the rock of his martyrdom with very strong bonds. Nevertheless, he had come to feel so dissatisfied with his position; he had come to regard himself as so utterly a stranger, so to say, in that gloomy city of lawsuits, of old-fashioned customs and ideas, of envy and of slander, that he resolved to leave it without further delay, without, however, abandoning the project which had brought him to it. One morning, finding a favorable occasion, he opened his mind to Doña Perfecta on this point.

"Nephew," responded that lady, with her accustomed gentleness, "don't be rash. Why! you are like fire. Your father was just the same—what a man he was! You are like a flash—I have already told you that I will be very glad to call you my son. Even if you did not possess the good qualities and the talents which distinguish you (in spite of some little defects, for you have those, too); even if you were not as good as you are; it is enough that this union has been proposed by your father, to whom both my daughter and myself owe so much, for me to accept it. And Rosarito will not oppose it since I wish it. What is wanting, then? Nothing; there is nothing wanting but a little time. The marriage cannot be concluded with the haste you desire and which might, perhaps, give ground for interpretations discreditable to my dear daughter's reputation. But as you think of nothing but machines, you want everything done by steam. Wait, man, wait; what hurry are you in? This hatred that you have taken to our poor Orbajosa is nothing but a caprice. But of course you can only live among counts and marquises and orators and diplomats—all you want is to get married and separate me forever from my daughter," she added, wiping away a tear. "Since that is the case, inconsiderate boy, at least have the charity to delay for a little this marriage, for which you are so eager. What impatience! What ardent love! I did not suppose that a poor country girl like my daughter could inspire so violent a passion."

The arguments of his aunt did not convince Pepe Rey, but he did not wish to contradict her. A fresh cause of anxiety was soon added to those which already embittered his existence. He had now been in Orbajosa for two weeks, and during that time he had received no letter from his father. This could not be attributed to carelessness on the part of the officials of the post-office of Orbajosa, for the functionary who had charge of that service being the friend and *protégé* of Doña Perfecta, the latter everyday recommended him to take the greatest care that the letters addressed to her nephew did not go astray. The letter-carrier, named Cristoval Ramos, and nicknamed Caballuco—a personage whose acquaintance we have already made—also visited the house, and to him Dona Perfecta was accustomed to address warnings and reprimands as energetic as the following:

"A pretty mail service you have! How is it that my nephew has not received a single letter since he has been in Orbajosa? When the carrying of the mail is entrusted to such a giddy-pate, how can things be expected to go well? I will speak to the governor of the province so that he may be careful what kind of people he puts in the post-office."

Caballuco, shrugging his shoulders, looked at Rey with the most complete indifference.

One day he entered the house with a letter in his hand.

"Thank Heaven!" said Doña Perfecta to her nephew. "Here are letters from your father. Rejoice, man! A pretty fright we have had through my brother's laziness about writing. What does he say? He is well, no doubt," she added, seeing that Pepe Rey opened the letter with feverish impatience.

The engineer turned pale as he glanced over the first lines.

"Good Heavens! Pepe, what is the matter?" exclaimed Doña Perfecta, rising in alarm. "Is your father ill?"

"This letter is not from my father," responded Pepe, revealing in his countenance the greatest consternation.

"What is it, then?"

"An order from the Minister of Public Works, relieving me from the charge which was confided to me."

"What! Can it be possible!"

"A dismissal pure and simple, expressed in terms very little flattering to me."

"Was there ever anything so unjust!" exclaimed Doña Perfecta, when she had recovered from her amazement.

"What a humiliation!" exclaimed the young man. "It is the first time in my life that I have received an affront like this."

"But the Government is unpardonable! To put such a slight upon you! Do you wish me to write to Madrid? I have very good friends there, and I may be able to obtain satisfaction for you from the Government and reparation for this brutal affront."

"Thanks, señora, I desire no recommendations," said the young man, with ill-humor.

"But what a piece of injustice! what a high-handed proceeding! To discharge in this way a young man of your merit, an eminent scientist. Why, I cannot contain my anger!"

"I will find out," said Pepe, with energy, "who it is that occupies himself in injuring me."

"That minister—but what is to be expected from those infamous politicasters?"

"In this there is the hand of someone who is determined to drive me to desperation," declared the young man, visibly disturbed. "This is not the act of the minister; this and other contrarieties that I am experiencing are the result of a revengeful plot, of a secret and well-laid plan of some implacable enemy, and this enemy is here in Orbajosa, this plot has been hatched in Orbajosa, doubt it not, dear aunt."

"You are out of your mind," replied Doña Perfecta, with a look of compassion. "You have enemies in Orbajosa, you say? Someone wishes to revenge himself upon you? Come, Pepillo, you have lost your senses. The reading of those books in which they say that we have for ancestors monkeys or parrots has turned your brain."

She smiled sweetly as she uttered the last words, and taking a tone of familiar and affectionate admonition, she added:

"My dear boy, the people of Orbajosa may be rude and boorish rustics, without learning, or polish, or fine manners; but in loyalty and good faith we yield to no one—to no one, I say, no one."

"Don't suppose," said the young man, "that I accuse anyone in this house. But that my implacable and cruel enemy is in this city, I am persuaded."

"I wish you would show me that stage villain," responded Doña Perfecta, smiling again. "I suppose you will not accuse Uncle Licurgo, nor any of the others who have brought suits against you; for the poor people believe they are only defending their rights. And between ourselves, they are not altogether wanting in reason in this case. Besides, Uncle Licurgo likes you greatly. He has told me so himself. From the moment he saw you, you took his fancy, and the poor old man has conceived such an affection for you—"

"Oh, yes—a profound affection!" murmured Pepe.

"Don't be foolish," continued his aunt, putting her hand on his shoulder and looking at him closely. "Don't imagine absurdities; convince yourself that your enemy, if you have one, is in Madrid, in that centre of corruption, of envy and rivalry, not in this peaceful and tranquil corner, where all is good-will and concord. Someone, no doubt, who is envious of your merit—There is one thing I wish to say now— and that is, that if you desire to go there to learn the cause of this affront and ask an explanation of it from the Government, you must not neglect doing so on our account."

Pepe Rey fixed his eyes on his aunt's countenance, as if he wished to penetrate with his glance the inmost depths of her soul.

"I say that if you wish to go, do so," repeated Dona Perfecta, with admirable serenity, while her countenance expressed the most complete and unaffected sincerity.

"No, señora; I do not wish to go."

"So much the better; I think you are right. You are more tranquil here, notwithstanding the suspicions with which you are tormenting yourself. Poor Pepillo! We poor rustics of Orbajosa live happy in our ignorance. I am very sorry that you are not contented here. But is it my fault if you vex and worry yourself without cause? Do I not treat you like a son? Have I not received you as the hope of my house? Can I do more for you? If in spite of all this you do not like us, if you show so much indifference toward us, if you ridicule our piety, if you insult our friends, is it by chance because we do not treat you well?"

Doña Perfecta's eyes grew moist.

"My dear aunt," said Pepe, feeling his anger vanish, "I too have committed some faults since I have been a guest in this house."

"Don't be foolish. Don't talk about committing faults. Among persons of the same family everything is forgiven."

"But Rosarito—where is she?" asked the young man, rising. "Am I not to see her today, either?"

"She is better. Do you know that she did not wish to come down stairs?"

BENITO PÉREZ GALDÓS

"I will go up to her then."

"No, it would be of no use. That girl has some obstinate notions—today she is determined not to leave her room. She has locked herself in."

"What a strange idea!"

"She will get over it. Undoubtedly she will get over it. We will see tonight if we cannot put these melancholy thoughts out of her head. We will get up a party to amuse her. Why don't you go to Don Inocencio's and ask him to come here tonight and bring Jacintillo with him."

"Jacintillo!"

"Yes, when Rosarito has these fits of melancholy, the only one who can divert her is that young man."

"But I will go upstairs—"

"No, you must not."

"What etiquette there is in this house!"

"You are ridiculing us. Do as I ask you."

"But I wish to see her."

"But you cannot see her. How little you know the girl!"

"I thought I knew her well. I will stay here, then. But this solitude is horrible."

"There comes the notary."

"Maledictions upon him!"

"And I think the attorney-general has just come in too—he is an excellent person."

"He be hanged with his goodness!"

"But business affairs, when they are one's own, serve as a distraction. Someone is coming. I think it is the agricultural expert. You will have something to occupy you now for an hour or two."

"An hour or two of hell!"

"Ah, ha! if I am not mistaken Uncle Licurgo and Uncle Paso Largo have just entered. Perhaps they have come to propose a compromise to you."

"I would throw myself into the pond first!"

"How unnatural you are! For they are all very fond of you. Well, so that nothing may be wanting, there comes the constable too. He is coming to serve a summons on you."

"To crucify me."

All the individuals named were now entering the parlor one by one.

"Goodbye, Pepe; amuse yourself," said Doña Perfecta.

"Earth, open and swallow me!" exclaimed the young man desperately.

"Señor Don José."

"My dear Don José."

"Esteemed Don José."

"My dearest Don José."

"My respected friend, Don José."

Hearing these honeyed and insinuating preliminaries, Pepe Rey exhaled a deep sigh and gave himself up. He gave himself up, soul and body, to the executioners, who brandished horrible leaves of stamped paper while the victim, raising his eyes to heaven with a look of Christian meekness, murmured:

"Father, why hast thou forsaken me?"

XII

Here was Troy

L ove, friendship, a wholesome moral atmosphere, spiritual light, sympathy, an easy interchange of ideas and feelings, these were what Pepe Rey's nature imperatively demanded. Deprived of them, the darkness that shrouded his soul grew deeper, and his inward gloom imparted a tinge of bitterness and discontent to his manner. On the day following the scenes described in the last chapter, what vexed him more than anything else was the already prolonged and mysterious seclusion of his cousin, accounted for at first by a trifling indisposition and then by caprices and nervous feelings difficult of explanation.

Rey was surprised by conduct so contrary to the idea which he had formed of Rosarito. Four days had passed during which he had not seen her; and certainly it was not because he did not desire to be at her side; and his situation threatened soon to become humiliating and ridiculous, if, by boldly taking the initiative, he did not at once put an end to it.

"Shall I not see my cousin today, either?" he said to his aunt, with manifest ill-humor, when they had finished dining.

"No, not today, either. Heaven knows how sorry I am for it. I gave her a good talking to this morning. This afternoon we will see what can be done."

The suspicion that in this unreasonable seclusion his adorable cousin was rather the helpless victim than the free and willing agent, induced him to control himself and to wait. Had it not been for this suspicion he would have left Orbajosa that very day. He had no doubt whatever that Rosario loved him, but it was evident that some unknown influence was at work to separate them, and it seemed to him to be the part of an honorable man to discover whence that malign influence proceeded and to oppose it, as far as it was in his power to do so.

"I hope that Rosarito's obstinacy will not continue long," he said to Doña Perfecta, disguising his real sentiments.

On this day he received a letter from his father in which the latter complained of having received none from Orbajosa, a circumstance which increased the engineer's disquietude, perplexing him still further. Finally, after wandering about alone in the garden for a long time, he left the house and went to the Casino. He entered it with the desperate air of a man about to throw himself into the sea.

In the principal rooms he found various people talking and discussing different subjects. In one group they were solving with subtle logic difficult problems relating to bulls; in another, they were discussing the relative merits of different breeds of donkeys of Orbajosa and Villahorrenda. Bored to the last degree, Pepe Rey turned away from these discussions and directed his steps toward the reading-room, where he looked through various reviews without finding any distraction in the reading, and a little later, passing from room to room, he stopped, without knowing why, at the gaming-table. For nearly two hours he remained in the clutches of the horrible yellow demon, whose shining eyes of gold at once torture and charm. But not even the excitement of play had power to lighten the gloom of his soul, and the same tedium which had impelled him toward the green cloth sent him away from it. Shunning the noise, he found himself in an apartment used as an assembly-room, in which at the time there was not a living soul, and here he seated himself wearily at a window over-looking the street.

This was very narrow, with more corners and salient angles than houses, and was overshaded throughout its whole extent by the imposing mass of the cathedral that lifted its dark and time-corroded walls at one end of it. Pepe Rey looked up and down and in every direction; no sign of life—not a footstep, not a voice, not a glance, disturbed the stillness, peaceful as that of a tomb, that reigned everywhere. Suddenly strange sounds, like the whispering of feminine voices, fell on his ear, and then the rustling of curtains that were being drawn, a few words, and finally the humming of a song, the bark of a lap-dog, and other signs of social life, which seemed very strange in such a place. Observing attentively, Pepe Rey perceived that these noises proceeded from an enormous balcony with blinds which displayed its corpulent bulk in front of the window at which he was sitting. Before he had concluded his observations, a member of the Casino suddenly appeared beside him, and accosted him laughingly in this manner:

"Ah, Señor Don Pepe! what a rogue you are! so you have shut yourself in here to ogle the girls, eh?"

The speaker was Don Juan Tafetan, a very amiable man, and one of the few members of the Casino who had manifested for Pepe Rey cordial friendship and genuine admiration. With his red cheeks, his little dyed mustache, his restless laughing eyes, his insignificant figure, his hair carefully combed to hide his baldness, Don Juan Tafetan was far from being an Antinous in appearance, but he was very witty and very agreeable and he had a happy gift for telling a good story. He was much given to laughter, and when he laughed his face, from his forehead to his chin, became one mass of grotesque wrinkles. In spite of these qualities, and of the applause which might have stimulated his taste for spicy jokes, he was not a scandal-monger. Everyone liked him, and Pepe Rey spent with him many pleasant hours. Poor Tafetan, formerly an employé in the civil department of the government of the capital of the province, now lived modestly on his salary as a clerk in the bureau of charities; eking out his income by gallantly playing the clarionet in the processions, in the solemnities of the cathedral, and in the theatre, whenever some desperate company of players made their appearance in those parts with the perfidious design of giving representations in Orbajosa.

But the most curious thing about Don Juan Tafetan was his liking for pretty girls. He himself, in the days when he did not hide his baldness with half a dozen hairs plastered down with pomade, when he did not dye his mustache, when, in the freedom from care of youthful years, he walked with shoulders unstooped and head erect, had been a formidable *Tenorio*. To hear him recount his conquests was something to make one die laughing; for there are *Tenorios* and *Tenorios*, and he was one of the most original.

"What girls? I don't see any girls," responded Pepe Rey.

"Yes, play the anchorite!"

One of the blinds of the balcony was opened, giving a glimpse of a youthful face, lovely and smiling, that disappeared instantly, like a light extinguished by the wind.

"Yes, I see now."

"Don't you know them?"

"On my life I do not."

"They are the Troyas—the Troya girls. Then you don't know something good. Three lovely girls, the daughters of a colonel of staff, who died in the streets of Madrid in '54."

The blind opened again, and two faces appeared.

"They are laughing at us," said Tafetan, making a friendly sign to the girls.

"Do you know them?"

"Why, of course I know them. The poor things are in the greatest want. I don't know how they manage to live. When Don Francisco Troya died a subscription was raised for them, but that did not last very long."

"Poor girls! I imagine they are not models of virtue."

"And why not? I do not believe what they say in the town about them."

Once more the blinds opened.

"Good-afternoon, girls!" cried Don Juan Tafetan to the three girls, who appeared, artistically grouped, at the window. "This gentleman says that good things ought not to hide themselves, and that you should throw open the blinds."

But the blind was closed and a joyous concert of laughter diffused a strange gayety through the gloomy street. One might have fancied that a flock of birds was passing.

"Shall we go there?" said Tafetan suddenly.

His eyes sparkled and a roguish smile played on his discolored lips.

"But what sort of people are they, then?"

"Don't be afraid, Señor de Rey. The poor things are honest. Bah! Why, they live upon air, like the chameleons. Tell me, can anyone who doesn't eat, sin? The poor girls are virtuous enough. And even if they did sin, they fast enough to make up for it."

"Let us go, then."

A moment later Don Juan Tafetan and Pepe Rey were entering the parlor of the Troyas. The poverty he saw, that struggled desperately to disguise itself, afflicted the young man. The three girls were very lovely, especially the two younger ones, who were pale and dark, with large black eyes and slender figures. Well-dressed and well shod they would have seemed the daughters of a duchess, and worthy to ally themselves with princes.

When the visitors entered, the three girls were for a moment abashed: but very soon their naturally gay and frivolous dispositions became apparent. They lived in poverty, as birds live in confinement, singing behind iron bars as they would sing in the midst of the abundance of the forest. They spent the day sewing, which showed at least honorable principles; but no one in Orbajosa, of their own station in life, held any intercourse with them. They were, to a certain extent, proscribed, looked down upon, avoided, which also showed that there existed some cause for scandal. But, to be just, it must be said that the bad reputation of the Troyas consisted, more than in anything else, in the name they had of being gossips and mischief-makers, fond of playing practical jokes, and bold and free in their manners. They wrote anonymous letters to grave personages; they gave nicknames to every living being in Orbajosa, from the bishop down to the lowest vagabond; they threw pebbles at the passersby; they hissed behind the window bars, in order to amuse themselves with the perplexity and annoyance of the startled passerby; they found out everything that occurred in the neighborhood; to which end they made constant use of every window and aperture in the upper part of the house; they sang at night in the balcony; they masked themselves during the Carnival, in order to obtain entrance into the houses of the highest families; and they played many other mischievous pranks peculiar to small towns. But whatever its cause, the fact was that on the Troya triumvirate rested one of those stigmas that, once affixed on anyone by a susceptible community, accompanies that person implacably even beyond the tomb.

"This is the gentleman they say has come to discover the gold-mines?" said one of the girls.

"And to pull down the cathedral to build a shoe-factory with the stones?" added another.

"And to do away with the cultivation of garlic in Orbajosa to plant cotton or cinnamon trees in its stead?"

Pepe could not help laughing at these absurdities.

"All he has come for is to make a collection of pretty girls to take back with him to Madrid," said Tafetan.

"Ah! I'd be very glad to go!" cried one.

"I will take the three of you with me," said Pepe. "But I want to know one thing; why were you laughing at me when I was at the window of the Casino?"

These words were the signal for fresh bursts of laughter.

"These girls are silly things," said the eldest.

"It was because we said you deserved something better than Doña Perfecta's daughter."

"It was because this one said that you are only losing your time, for Rosarito cares only for people connected with the Church."

"How absurd you are! I said nothing of the kind! It was you who said that the gentleman was a Lutheran atheist, and that he enters the cathedral smoking and with his hat on."

"Well, I didn't invent it; that is what Suspiritos told me yesterday."

"And who is this Suspiritos who says such absurd things about me?"

"Suspiritos is—Suspiritos."

"Girls," said Tafetan, with smiling countenance, "there goes the orange-vender. Call him; I want to invite you to eat oranges."

One of the girls called the orange-vender.

The conversation started by the Troyas displeased Pepe Rey not a little, dispelling the slight feeling of contentment which he had experienced at finding himself in such gay and communicative company. He could not, however, refrain from smiling when he saw Don Juan Tafetan take down a guitar and begin to play upon it with all the grace and skill of his youthful years.

"I have been told that you sing beautifully," said Rey to the girls.

"Let Don Juan Tafetan sing."

"I don't sing."

"Nor I," said the second of the girls, offering the engineer some pieces of the skin of the orange she had just peeled.

"Maria Juana, don't leave your sewing," said the eldest of the Troyas. "It is late, and the cassock must be finished tonight."

"There is to be no work today. To the devil with the needles!" exclaimed Tafetan.

And he began to sing a song.

"The people are stopping in the street," said the second of the girls, going out on the balcony. "Don Juan Tafetan's shouts can be heard in the Plaza—Juana, Juana!"

"Well?"

"Suspiritos is walking down the street."

"Throw a piece of orange-peel at her."

Pepe Rey looked out also; he saw a lady walking down the street at whom the youngest of the Troyas, taking a skilful aim, threw a large piece of orange-peel, which struck her straight on the back of the head. Then they hastily closed the blinds, and the three girls tried to stifle their laughter so that it might not be heard in the street.

"There is to be no work today," cried one, overturning the sewing-basket with the tip of her shoe.

"That is the same as saying, tomorrow there is to be no eating," said the eldest, gathering up the sewing implements.

Pepe Rey instinctively put his hand into his pocket. He would gladly have given them an alms. The spectacle of these poor orphans, condemned by the world because of their frivolity, saddened him beyond measure. If the only sin of the Troyas, if the only pleasure which they had to compensate them for solitude, poverty, and neglect, was to throw orange-peels at the passersby, they might well be excused for doing it. The austere customs of the town in which they lived had perhaps preserved them from vice, but the unfortunate girls lacked decorum and good-breeding, the common and most visible signs of modesty, and it might easily be supposed that they had thrown out of the window something more than orange-peels. Pepe Rey felt profound pity for them. He noted their shabby dresses, made over, mended, trimmed, and retrimmed, to make them look like new; he noted their broken shoes—and once more he put his hand in his pocket.

"Vice may reign here," he said to himself, "but the faces, the furniture, all show that this is the wreck of a respectable family. If these poor girls were as bad as it is said they are, they would not live in such poverty and they would not work. In Orbajosa there are rich men."

The three girls went back and forward between him and the window, keeping up a gay and sprightly conversation, which indicated, it must be said, a species of innocence in the midst of all their frivolity and unconventionality.

"Señor Don José, what an excellent lady Doña Perfecta is!"

"She is the only person in Orbajosa who has no nickname, the only person in Orbajosa who is not spoken ill of."

"Everyone respects her."

"Everyone adores her."

To these utterances the young man responded by praises of his aunt, but he had no longer any inclination to take money from his pocket and say, "Maria Juana, take this for a pair of boots." "Pepa, take this to buy a dress for yourself." "Florentina, take this to provide yourself with a week's provisions," as he had been on the point of doing. At a moment when the three girls had run out to the balcony to see who was passing, Don Juan Tafetan approached Rey and whispered to him:

"How pretty they are! Are they not? Poor things! It seems impossible that they should be so gay when it may be positively affirmed that they have not dined today."

"Don Juan, Don Juan!" cried Pepilla. "Here comes a friend of yours, Nicolasito Hernandez, in other words, Cirio Pascual, with his three-story hat. He is praying to himself, no doubt, for the souls of those whom he has sent to the grave with his extortion."

"I wager that neither of you will dare to call him by his nickname."

"It is a bet."

"Juana, shut the blinds, wait until he passes, and when he is turning the corner, I will call out, 'Cirio, Cirio Pascual!'"

Don Juan Tafetan ran out to the balcony.

"Come here, Don José, so that you may know this type," he called.

Pepe Rey, availing himself of the moment in which the three girls and Don Juan were making merry in the balcony, calling Nicolasito Hernandez the nickname which so greatly enraged him, stepped cautiously to one of the sewing baskets in the room and placed in it a half ounce which he had left after his losses at play.

Then he hurried out to the balcony just as the two youngest cried in the midst of wild bursts of laughter, "Cirio, Cirio Pascual!"

XIII

A Casus Belli

After this prank the Troyas commenced a conversation with their visitors about the people and the affairs of the town. The engineer, fearing that his exploit might be discovered while he was present, wished to go, which displeased the Troyas greatly. One of them who had left the room now returned, saying:

"Suspiritos is now in the yard; she is hanging out the clothes."

"Don José will wish to see her," said another of the girls.

"She is a fine-looking woman. And now she arranges her hair in the Madrid fashion. Come, all of you."

They took their visitors to the dining-room—an apartment very little used—which opened on a terrace, where there were a few flowers in pots and many broken and disused articles of furniture. The terrace overlooked the yard of an adjoining house, with a piazza full of green vines and plants in pots carefully cultivated. Everything about it showed it to be the abode of neat and industrious people of modest means.

The Troyas, approaching the edge of the roof, looked attentively at the neighboring house, and then, imposing silence by a gesture on their cavaliers, retreated to a part of the terrace from which they could not see into the yard, and where there was no danger of their being seen from it.

"She is coming out of the kitchen now with a pan of peas," said Maria Juana, stretching out her neck to look.

"There goes!" cried another, throwing a pebble into the yard.

The noise of the projectile striking against the glass of the piazza was heard, and then an angry voice crying:

"Now they have broken another pane of glass!"

The girls, hidden, close beside the two men, in a corner of the terrace, were suffocating with laughter.

"Señora Suspiritos is very angry," said Rey. "Why do they call her by that name?"

"Because, when she is talking, she sighs after every word, and although she has everything she wants, she is always complaining."

There was a moment's silence in the house below. Pepita Troya looked cautiously down.

"There she comes again," she whispered, once more imposing silence by a gesture. "Maria, give me a pebble. Give it here—bang! there it goes!"

"You didn't hit her. It struck the ground."

"Let me see if I can. Let us wait until she comes out of the pantry again."

"Now, now she is coming out. Take care, Florentina."

"One, two, three! There it goes!"

A cry of pain was heard from below, a malediction, a masculine exclamation, for it was a man who uttered it. Pepe Rey could distinguish clearly these words:

"The devil! They have put a hole in my head, the—Jacinto, Jacinto! But what an abominable neighborhood this is!"

"Good Heavens! what have I done!" exclaimed Florentina, filled with consternation. "I have struck Señor Don Inocencio on the head."

"The Penitentiary?" said Pepe Rey.

"Yes."

"Does he live in that house?"

"Why, where else should he live?"

"And the lady of the sighs—"

"Is his niece, his housekeeper, or whatever else she may be. We amuse ourselves with her because she is very tiresome, but we are not accustomed to play tricks on his reverence, the Penitentiary."

While this dialogue was being rapidly carried on, Pepe Rey saw, in front of the terrace and very near him, a window belonging to the bombarded house open; he saw a smiling face appear at it—a familiar face—a face the sight of which stunned him, terrified him, made him turn pale and tremble. It was that of Jacinto, who, interrupted in his grave studies, appeared at it with his pen behind his ear. His modest, fresh, and smiling countenance, appearing in this way, had an auroral aspect.

"Good-afternoon, Señor Don José," he said gayly.

"Jacinto, Jacinto, I say!"

"I am coming. I was saluting a friend."

"Come away, come away!" cried Florentina, in alarm. "The Penitentiary is going up to Don Nominative's room and he will give us a blessing."

"Yes, come away; let us close the door of the dining-room."

They rushed pell-mell from the terrace.

"You might have guessed that Jacinto would see you from his temple of learning," said Tafetan to the Troyas.

"Don Nominative is our friend," responded one of the girls. "From his temple of science he says a great many sweet things to us on the sly, and he blows us kisses besides."

"Jacinto?" asked the engineer. "What the deuce is that name you gave him?"

"Don Nominative."

The three girls burst out laughing.

"We call him that because he is very learned."

"No, because when we were little he was little too. But, yes, now I remember. We used to play on the terrace, and we could hear him studying his lessons aloud."

"Yes, and the whole blessed day he used to spend singing."

"Declining, girl! That is what it was. He would go like this: 'Nominative, rosa, Genitive, Dative, Accusative.'"

"I suppose that I have my nickname too," said Pepe Rey.

"Let Maria Juana tell you what it is," said Florentina, hiding herself.

"I? Tell it to him you, Pepa."

"You haven't any name yet, Don José."

"But I shall have one. I promise you that I will come to hear what it is and to receive confirmation," said the young man, making a movement to go.

"What, are you going?"

"Yes. You have lost time enough already. To work, girls! Throwing stones at the neighbors and the passersby is not the most suitable occupation for girls as pretty and as clever as you are. Well, goodbye."

And without waiting for further remonstrances, or answering the civilities of the girls, he left the house hastily, leaving Don Juan Tafetan behind him.

The scene which he had just witnessed, the indignity suffered by the canon, the unexpected appearance of the little doctor of laws, added still further to the perplexities, the anxieties, and the disagreeable presentiments that already disturbed the soul of the unlucky engineer. He regretted with his whole soul having entered the house of the Troyas, and, resolving to employ his time better while his hypochondriasm lasted, he made a tour of inspection through the town.

He visited the market, the Calle de la Triperia, where the principal stores were; he observed the various aspects presented by the industry and commerce of the great city of Orbajosa, and, finding only new motives of weariness, he bent his steps in the direction of the Paseo de las Descalzas; but he saw there only a few stray dogs, for, owing to the disagreeable wind which prevailed, the usual promenaders had remained at home. He went to the apothecary's, where various species of ruminant friends of progress, who chewed again and again the cud of the same endless theme, were accustomed to meet, but there he was still more bored. Finally, as he was passing the cathedral, he heard the strains of the organ and the beautiful chanting of the choir. He entered, knelt before the high altar, remembering the warnings which his aunt had given him about behaving with decorum in church; then visited a chapel, and was about to enter another when an acolyte, warden, or beadle approached him, and with the rudest manner and in the most discourteous tone said to him:

"His lordship says that you are to get out of the church."

The engineer felt the blood rush to his face. He obeyed without a word. Turned out everywhere, either by superior authority or by his own tedium, he had no resource but to return to his aunt's house, where he found waiting for him:

First, Uncle Licurgo, to announce a second lawsuit to him; second, Señor Don Cayetano, to read him another passage from his discourse on the "Genealogies of Orbajosa"; third, Caballuco, on some business which he had not disclosed; fourth, Doña Perfecta and her affectionate smile, for what will appear in the following chapter.

XIV

The Discord Continues to Increase

A fresh attempt to see his cousin that evening failed, and Pepe Rey shut himself up in his room to write several letters, his mind preoccupied with one thought.

"Tonight or tomorrow," he said to himself, "this will end one way or another."

When he was called to supper Doña Perfecta, who was already in the dining-room, went up to him and said, without preface:

"Dear Pepe, don't distress yourself, I will pacify Señor Don Inocencio. I know everything already. Maria Remedios, who has just left the house, has told me all about it."

Doña Perfecta's countenance radiated such satisfaction as an artist, proud of his work, might feel.

"About what?"

"Set your mind at rest. I will make an excuse for you. You took a few glasses too much in the Casino, that was it, was it not? There you have the result of bad company. Don Juan Tafetan, the Troyas! This is horrible, frightful. Did you consider well?"

"I considered everything," responded Pepe, resolved not to enter into discussions with his aunt.

"I shall take good care not to write to your father what you have done."

"You may write whatever you please to him."

"You will exculpate yourself by denying the truth of this story, then?"

"I deny nothing."

"You confess then that you were in the house of those—"

"I was."

"And that you gave them a half ounce; for, according to what Maria Remedios has told me, Florentina went down to the shop of the Extramaduran this afternoon to get a half ounce changed. They could not have earned it with their sewing. You were in their house today; consequently—"

"Consequently I gave it to her. You are perfectly right."

"You do not deny it?"

"Why should I deny it? I suppose I can do whatever I please with my money?"

"But you will surely deny that you threw stones at the Penitentiary."

"I do not throw stones."

"I mean that those girls, in your presence—"

"That is another matter."

"And they insulted poor Maria Remedios, too."

"I do not deny that, either."

"And how do you excuse your conduct! Pepe in Heaven's name, have you nothing to say? That you are sorry, that you deny—"

"Nothing, absolutely nothing, señora!"

"You don't even give me any satisfaction."

"I have done nothing to offend you."

"Come, the only thing there is left for you to do now is—there, take that stick and beat me!"

"I don't beat people."

"What a want of respect! What, don't you intend to eat any supper?"

"I intend to take supper."

For more than a quarter of an hour no one spoke. Don Cayetano, Doña Perfecta, and Pepe Rey ate in silence. This was interrupted when Don Inocencio entered the dining-room.

"How sorry I was for it, my dear Don José! Believe me, I was truly sorry for it," he said, pressing the young man's hand and regarding him with a look of compassion.

The engineer was so perplexed for a moment that he did not know what to answer.

"I refer to the occurrence of this afternoon."

"Ah, yes!"

"To your expulsion from the sacred precincts of the cathedral."

"The bishop should consider well," said Pepe Rey, "before he turns a Christian out of the church."

"That is very true. I don't know who can have put it into his lordship's head that you are a man of very bad habits; I don't know who has told him that you make a boast of your atheism everywhere; that you ridicule sacred things and persons, and even that you are planning to pull down the cathedral to build a large tar factory with the stones. I tried my best to dissuade him, but his lordship is a little obstinate."

"Thanks for so much kindness."

"And it is not because the Penitentiary has any reason to show you these considerations. A little more, and they would have left him stretched on the ground this afternoon."

"Bah!" said the ecclesiastic, laughing. "But have you heard of that little prank already? I wager Maria Remedios came with the story. And I forbade her to do it—I forbade her positively. The thing in itself is of no consequence, am I not right, Señor de Rey?"

"Since you think so—"

"That is what I think. Young people's pranks! Youth, let the moderns say what they will, is inclined to vice and to vicious actions. Señor de Rey, who is a person of great endowments, could not be altogether perfect—why should it be wondered at that those pretty girls should have captivated him, and, after getting his money out of him, should have made him the accomplice of their shameless and criminal insults to their neighbors? My dear friend, for the painful part that I had in this afternoon's sport," he added, raising his hand to the wounded spot, "I am not offended, nor will I distress you by even referring to so disagreeable an incident. I am truly sorry to hear that Maria Remedios came here to tell all about it. My niece is so fond of gossiping! I wager she told too about the half ounce, and your romping with the girls on the terrace, and your chasing one another about, and the pinches and the capers of Don Juan Tafetan. Bah! those things ought not to be told."

Pepe Rey did not know which annoyed him most—his aunt's severity or the hypocritical condescension of the canon.

"Why should they not be told?" said Doña Perfecta. "He does not seem ashamed of his conduct himself. I assure you all that I keep this from my dear daughter only because, in her nervous condition, a fit of anger might be dangerous to her."

"Come, it is not so serious as all that, señora," said the Penitentiary. "I think the matter should not be again referred to, and when the one who was stoned says that, the rest may surely be satisfied. And the blow was no joke, Señor Don José. I thought they had split my head open and that my brains were oozing out."

"I am truly sorry for the occurrence!" stammered Pepe Rey. "It gives me real pain, although I had no part in it—"

"Your visit to those Señoras Troyas will be talked about all over the town," said the canon. "We are not in Madrid, in that centre of corruption, of scandal—"

"There you can visit the vilest places without anyone knowing it," said Doña Perfecta.

"Here we are very observant of one another," continued Don Inocencio. "We take notice of everything our neighbors do, and with such a system of vigilance public morals are maintained at a proper height. Believe me, my friend, believe me,—and I do not say this to mortify you,—you are the first gentleman of your position who, in the light of day—the first, yes, señor—*Trojæ qui primus ab oris*."

And bursting into a laugh, he clapped the engineer on the back in token of amity and good-will.

"How grateful I ought to be," said the young man, concealing his anger under the sarcastic words which he thought the most suitable to answer the covert irony of his interlocutors, "to meet with so much generosity and tolerance, when my criminal conduct would deserve—"

"What! Is a person of one's own blood, one who bears one's name," said Doña Perfecta, "to be treated like a stranger? You are my nephew, you are the son of the best and the most virtuous of men, of my dear brother Juan, and that is sufficient. Yesterday afternoon the secretary of the bishop came here to tell me that his lordship is greatly displeased because I have you in my house."

"And that too?" murmured the canon.

"And that too. I said that in spite of the respect which I owe the bishop, and the affection and reverence which I bear him, my nephew is my nephew, and I cannot turn him out of my house."

"This is another singularity which I find in this place," said Pepe Rey, pale with anger. "Here, apparently, the bishop governs other people's houses."

"He is a saint. He is so fond of me that he imagines—he imagines that you are going to contaminate us with your atheism, your disregard for public opinion, your strange ideas. I have told him repeatedly that, at bottom, you are an excellent young man."

"Some concession must always be made to superior talent," observed Don Inocencio.

"And this morning, when I was at the Cirujedas'—oh, you cannot imagine in what a state they had my head! Was it true that you had come to pull down the cathedral; that you were commissioned by the English Protestants to go preaching heresy throughout Spain; that you spent the whole night gambling in the Casino; that you were drunk in the streets? 'But, señoras,' I said to them, 'would you have me send my nephew to the hotel?' Besides, they are wrong about the

BENITO PÉREZ GALDÓS

drunkenness, and as for gambling—I have never yet heard that you gambled."

Pepe Rey found himself in that state of mind in which the calmest man is seized by a sudden rage, by a blind and brutal impulse to strangle someone, to strike someone in the face, to break someone's head, to crush someone's bones. But Doña Perfecta was a woman and was, besides, his aunt; and Don Inocencio was an old man and an ecclesiastic. In addition to this, physical violence is in bad taste and unbecoming a person of education and a Christian. There remained the resource of giving vent to his suppressed wrath in dignified and polite language; but this last resource seemed to him premature, and only to be employed at the moment of his final departure from the house and from Orbajosa. Controlling his fury, then, he waited.

Jacinto entered as they were finishing supper.

"Good-evening, Señor Don José," he said, pressing the young man's hand. "You and your friends kept me from working this afternoon. I was not able to write a line. And I had so much to do!"

"I am very sorry for it, Jacinto. But according to what they tell me, you accompany them sometimes in their frolics."

"I!" exclaimed the boy, turning scarlet. "Why, you know very well that Tafetan never speaks a word of truth. But is it true, Señor de Rey, that you are going away?"

"Is that the report in the town?"

"Yes. I heard it in the Casino and at Don Lorenzo Ruiz's."

Rey contemplated in silence for a few moments the fresh face of Don Nominative. Then he said:

"Well, it is not true; my aunt is very well satisfied with me; she despises the calumnies with which the Orbajosans are favoring me—and she will not turn me out of her house, even though the bishop himself should try to make her do so."

"As for turning you out of the house—never. What would your father say?"

"Notwithstanding all your kindness, dearest aunt, notwithstanding the cordial friendship of the reverend canon, it is possible that I may myself decide to go away."

"To go away!"

"To go away—you!"

A strange light shone in Doña Perfecta's eyes. The canon, experienced though he was in dissimulation, could not conceal his joy.

"Yes, and perhaps this very night."

"Why, man, how impetuous you are; Why don't you at least wait until morning? Here—Juan, let someone go for Uncle Licurgo to get the nag ready. I suppose you will take some luncheon with you. Nicolasa, that piece of veal that is on the sideboard! Librada, the señorito's linen."

"No, I cannot believe that you would take so rash a resolution," said Don Cayetano, thinking himself obliged to take some part in the question.

"But you will come back, will you not?" asked the canon.

"At what time does the morning train pass?" asked Doña Perfecta, in whose eyes was clearly discernible the feverish impatience of her exaltation.

"I am going away tonight."

"But there is no moon."

In the soul of Doña Perfecta, in the soul of the Penitentiary, in the little doctor's youthful soul echoed like a celestial harmony the word, "Tonight!"

"Of course, dear Pepe, you will come back. I wrote today to your father, your excellent father," exclaimed Doña Perfecta, with all the physiognomic signs that make their appearance when a tear is about to be shed.

"I will trouble you with a few commissions," said the savant.

"A good opportunity to order the volume that is wanting in my copy of the Abbé Gaume's work," said the youthful lawyer.

"You take such sudden notions, Pepe; you are so full of caprices," murmured Doña Perfecta, smiling, with her eyes fixed on the door of the dining-room. "But I forgot to tell you that Caballuco is waiting to speak to you."

XV

DISCORD CONTINUES TO GROW UNTIL WAR IS DECLARED

Everyone looked toward the door, at which appeared the imposing figure of the Centaur, serious-looking and frowning; embarrassed by his anxiety to salute the company politely; savagely handsome, but disfigured by the violence which he did himself in smiling civilly and treading softly and holding his herculean arms in a correct posture.

"Come in, Señor Ramos," said Pepe Rey.

"No, no!" objected Doña Perfecta. "What he has to say to you is an absurdity."

"Let him say it."

"I ought not to allow such ridiculous questions to be discussed in my house."

"What is Señor Ramos' business with me?"

Caballuco uttered a few words.

"Enough, enough!" exclaimed Doña Perfecta. "Don't trouble my nephew anymore. Pepe, don't mind this simpleton. Do you wish me to tell you the cause of the great Caballuco's anger?" she said, turning to the others.

"Anger? I think I can imagine," said the Penitentiary, leaning back in his chair and laughing with boisterous hilarity.

"I wanted to say to Señor Don José—" growled the formidable horseman.

"Hold your tongue, man, for Heaven's sake! and don't tire us anymore with that nonsense."

"Señor Caballuco," said the canon, "it is not to be wondered at that gentlemen from the capital should cut out the rough riders of this savage country."

"In two words, Pepe, the question is this: Caballuco is—"

She could not go on for laughing.

"Is—I don't know just what," said Don Inocencia, "of one of the Troya girls, of Mariquita Juana, if I am not mistaken."

"And he is jealous! After his horse, the first thing in creation for him is Mariquilla Troya."

"A pretty insinuation that!" exclaimed Doña Perfecta. "Poor Cristobal! Did you suppose that a person like my nephew—let us hear, what were you going to say to him? Speak."

"Señor Don José and I will talk together presently," responded the bravo of the town brusquely.

And without another word he left the room.

Shortly afterward Pepe Rey left the dining-room to retire to his own room. In the hall he found himself face to face with his Trojan antagnist, and he could not repress a smile at sight of the fierce and gloomy countenance of the offended lover.

"A word with you," said the latter, planting himself insolently in front of the engineer. "Do you know who I am?"

As he spoke he laid his heavy hand on the young man's shoulder with such insolent familiarity that the latter, incensed, flung him off with violence, saying:

"It is not necessary to crush one to say that."

The bravo, somewhat disconcerted, recovered himself in a moment, and looking at Rey with provoking boldness, repeated his refrain:

"Do you know who I am?"

"Yes; I know now that you are a brute."

He pushed the bully roughly aside and went into his room. As traced on the excited brain of our unfortunate friend at this moment, his plan of action might be summed up briefly and definitely as follows: To break Caballuco's head without loss of time; then to take leave of his aunt in severe but polite words which should reach her soul; to bid a cold adieu to the canon and give an embrace to the inoffensive Don Cayetano; to administer a thrashing to Uncle Licurgo, by way of winding up the entertainment, and leave Orbajosa that very night, shaking the dust from his shoes at the city gates.

But in the midst of all these mortifications and persecutions the unfortunate young man had not ceased to think of another unhappy being, whom he believed to be in a situation even more painful and distressing than his own. One of the maidservants followed the engineer into his room.

"Did you give her my message?" he asked.

"Yes, señor, and she gave me this."

Rey took from the girl's hand a fragment of a newspaper, on the margin of which he read these words:

"They say you are going away. I shall die if you do."

When he returned to the dining-room Uncle Licurgo looked in at the door and asked:

"At what hour do you want the horse?"

"At no hour," answered Rey quickly.

"Then you are not going tonight?" said Doña Perfecta. "Well, it is better to wait until tomorrow."

"I am not going tomorrow, either."

"When are you going, then?"

"We will see presently," said the young man coldly, looking at his aunt with imperturbable calmness. "For the present I do not intend to go away."

His eyes flashed forth a fierce challenge.

Doña Perfecta turned first red, then pale. She looked at the canon, who had taken off his gold spectacles to wipe them, and then fixed her eyes successively on each of the other persons in the room, including Caballuco, who, entering shortly before, had seated himself on the edge of a chair. Doña Perfecta looked at them as a general looks at his trusty body-guard. Then she studied the thoughtful and serene countenance of her nephew—of that enemy, who, by a strategic movement, suddenly reappeared before her when she believed him to be in shameful flight.

Alas! Bloodshed, ruin, and desolation! A great battle was about to be fought.

XVI

NIGHT

Orbajosa slept. The melancholy street-lamps were shedding their last gleams at street-corners and in by-ways, like tired eyes struggling in vain against sleep. By their dim light, wrapped in their cloaks, glided past like shadows vagabonds, watchmen, and gamblers. Only the hoarse shout of the drunkard or the song of the serenader broke the peaceful silence of the historic city. Suddenly the "Ave Maria Purisima" of some drunken watchman would be heard, like a moan uttered in its sleep by the town.

In Doña Perfecta's house also silence reigned, unbroken but for a conversation which was taking place between Don Cayetano and Pepe Rey, in the library of the former. The savant was seated comfortably in the arm-chair beside his study table, which was covered with papers of various kinds containing notes, annotations, and references, all arranged in the most perfect order. Rey's eyes were fixed on the heap of papers, but his thoughts were doubtless far away from this accumulated learning.

"Perfecta," said the antiquary, "although she is an excellent woman, has the defect of allowing herself to be shocked by any little act of folly. In these provincial towns, my dear friend, the slightest slip is dearly paid for. I see nothing particular in your having gone to the Troyas' house. I fancy that Don Inocencio, under his cloak of piety, is something of a mischief-maker. What has he to do with the matter?"

"We have reached a point, Señor Don Cayetano, in which it is necessary to take a decisive resolution. I must see Rosario and speak with her."

"See her, then!"

"But they will not let me," answered the engineer, striking the table with his clenched hand. "Rosario is kept a prisoner."

"A prisoner!" repeated the savant incredulously. "The truth is that I do not like her looks or her air, and still less the vacant expression in her beautiful eyes. She is melancholy, she talks little, she weeps—friend Don José, I greatly fear that the girl may be attacked by the terrible malady to which so many of the members of my family have fallen victims."

"A terrible malady! What is it?"

"Madness—or rather mania. Not a single member of my family has been free from it. I alone have escaped it."

"You! But leaving aside the question of madness," said Rey, with impatience, "I wish to see Rosario."

"Nothing more natural. But the isolation in which her mother keeps her is a hygienic measure, dear Pepe, and the only one that has been successfully employed with the various members of my family. Consider that the person whose presence and voice would make the strongest impression on Rosarillo's delicate nervous system is the chosen of her heart."

"In spite of all that," insisted Pepe, "I wish to see her."

"Perhaps Perfecta will not oppose your doing so," said the savant, giving his attention to his notes and papers. "I don't want to take any responsibility in the matter."

The engineer, seeing that he could obtain nothing from the good Polentinos, rose to retire.

"You are going to work," he said, "and I will not trouble you any longer."

"No, there is time enough. See the amount of precious information that I collected today. Listen: 'In 1537 a native of Orbajosa, called Bartolomé del Hoyo, went to Civita-Vecchia in one of the galleys of the Marquis of Castel Rodrigo.' Another: 'In the same year two brothers named Juan and Rodrigo Gonzalez del Arco embarked in one of the six ships which sailed from Maestricht on the 20th of February, and which encountered in the latitude of Calais an English vessel and the Flemish fleet commanded by Van Owen.' That was truly an important exploit of our navy. I have discovered that it was an Orbajosan, one Mateo Diaz Coronel, an ensign in the guards, who, in 1709, wrote and published in Valencia the 'Metrical Encomium, Funeral Chant, Lyrical Eulogy, Numerical Description, Glorious Sufferings, and Sorrowful Glories of the Queen of the Angels.' I possess a most precious copy of this work, which is worth the mines of Peru. Another Orbajosan was the author of that famous 'Treatise on the Various Styles of Horsemanship' which I showed you yesterday; and, in short, there is not a step I take in the labyrinth of unpublished history that I do not stumble against some illustrious compatriot. It is my purpose to draw all these names out of the unjust obscurity and oblivion in which they have so long lain. How pure a joy, dear Pepe, to restore all their lustre to the glories, epic and literary, of one's native place! And how could a man better employ the scant intellect with which Heaven has endowed him, the fortune which he has inherited, and the brief period of time on earth allowed to even the longest life. Thanks to me it will be seen that Orbajosa is the illustrious cradle of Spanish genius. But what do I say? Is not its illustrious ancestry evident in the nobleness and high-mindedness of the present Urbs Augustan generation? We know few places where all the virtues, unchoked by the malefic weeds of vice, grow more luxuriantly. Here all is peace, mutual respect, Christian humility. Charity is practised here as it was in Biblical times; here envy is unknown; here the criminal passions are unknown, and if you hear thieves and murderers spoken of, you may be sure that they are not the children of this noble soil; or, that if they are, they belong to the number of unhappy creatures perverted by the teachings of demagogues. Here you will see the national character in all its purity—upright, noble, incorruptible, pure, simple, patriarchal, hospitable, generous. Therefore it is that I live so happy in this solitude far from the turmoil of cities where, alas! falsehood and vice reign. Therefore it is that the many friends whom I have in Madrid have not been able to tempt me from this place; therefore it is that I spend my life in the sweet companionship of my faithful townspeople and my books, breathing the wholesome atmosphere of integrity, which is gradually becoming circumscribed in our Spain to the humble and Christian towns that have preserved it with the emanations of their virtues. And believe me, my dear Pepe, this peaceful isolation has greatly contributed to preserve me from the terrible malady connatural in my family. In my youth I suffered, like my brothers and my father, from a lamentable propensity to the most absurd manias; but here you have me so miraculously cured that all I know of the malady is what I see of it in others. And it is for that reason that I am so uneasy about my little niece."

"I am rejoiced that the air of Orbajosa has proved so beneficial to you," said Rey, unable to resist the jesting mood that, by a strange contradiction, came over him in the midst of his sadness. "With me it has agreed so badly that I think I shall soon become mad if I remain in it. Well, goodnight, and success to your labors."

"Goodnight."

Pepe went to his room, but feeling neither a desire for sleep nor the need of physical repose,—on the contrary, a violent excitation of mind which impelled him to move, to act,—he walked up and down the room,

BENITO PÉREZ GALDÓS

torturing himself with useless cavilling. After a time he opened the window which overlooked the garden and, leaning his elbows on the parapet, he gazed out on the limitless darkness of the night. Nothing could be seen, but he who is absorbed in his own thoughts sees with the mental vision, and Pepe Rey, his eyes fixed on the darkness, saw the varied panorama of his misfortunes unroll itself upon it before him. The obscurity did not permit him to see the flowers of the earth, nor those of the heavens, which are the stars. The very absence of light produced the effect of an illusory movement in the masses of foliage, which seemed to stretch away, to recede slowly, and come curling back like the waves of a shadowy sea. A vast flux and reflux, a strife between forces vaguely comprehended, agitated the silent sky. The mathematician, contemplating this strange projection of his soul upon the night, said to himself:

"The battle will be terrible. Let us see who will come out of it victorious."

The nocturnal insects whispered in his ear mysterious words. Here a shrill chirp; there a click, like the click made with the tongue; further on, plaintive murmurs; in the distance a tinkle like that of the bell on the neck of the wandering ox. Suddenly Rey heard a strange sound, a rapid note, that could be produced only by the human tongue and lips. This sibilant breathing passed through the young man's brain like a flash of lightning. He felt that swift "s-s-s" dart snake-like through him, repeated again and then again, with augmented intensity. He looked all around, then he looked toward the upper part of the house, and he fancied that in one of the windows he could distinguish an object like a white bird flapping its wings. Through Pepe Rey's excited mind flashed instantly the idea of the phœnix, of the dove, of the regal heron, and yet the bird he saw was nothing more than a handkerchief.

The engineer sprang from the balcony into the garden. Observing attentively, he saw the hand and the face of his cousin. He thought he could perceive the gesture commonly employed of imposing silence by laying the finger on the lips. Then the dear shade pointed downward and disappeared. Pepe Rey returned quickly to his room, entered the hall noiselessly, and walked slowly forward. He felt his heart beat with violence. He waited for a few moments, and at last he heard distinctly light taps on the steps of the stairs. One, two, three—the sounds were produced by a pair of little shoes.

He walked in the direction whence they proceeded, and stretched out his hands in the obscurity to assist the person who was descending the stairs. In his soul there reigned an exalted and profound tenderness, but—why seek to deny it—mingling with this tender feeling, there suddenly arose within him, like an infernal inspiration, another sentiment, a fierce desire for revenge. The steps continued to descend, coming nearer and nearer. Pepe Rey went forward, and a pair of hands, groping in the darkness, came in contact with his own. The two pairs of hands were united in a close clasp.

XVII

Light in the Darkness

The hall was long and broad. At one end of it was the door of the room occupied by the engineer, in the centre that of the dining-room, and at the other end were the staircase and a large closed door reached by a step. This door opened into a chapel in which the Polentinos performed their domestic devotions. Occasionally the holy sacrifice of the mass was celebrated in it.

Rosario led her cousin to the door of the chapel and then sank down on the doorstep.

"Here?" murmured Pepe Rey.

From the movements of Rosarito's right hand he comprehended that she was blessing herself.

"Rosario, dear cousin, thanks for allowing me to see you!" he exclaimed, embracing her ardently.

He felt the girl's cold fingers on his lips, imposing silence. He kissed them rapturously.

"You are frozen. Rosario, why do you tremble so?"

Her teeth were chattering, and her whole frame trembled convulsively. Rey felt the burning heat of his cousin's face against his own, and he cried in alarm.

"Your forehead is burning! You are feverish."

"Very."

"Are you really ill?"

"Yes."

"And you have left your room—"

"To see you."

The engineer wrapped his arms around her to protect her from the cold, but it was not enough.

"Wait," he said quickly, rising. "I am going to my room to bring my travelling rug."

"Put out the light, Pepe."

Rey had left the lamp burning in his room, through the door of which issued a faint streak of light, illuminating the hall. He returned in an instant. The darkness was now profound. Groping his way along the wall he reached the spot where his cousin was sitting, and wrapped the rug carefully around her.

"You are comfortable now, my child."

"Yes, so comfortable! With you!"

"With me—and forever!" exclaimed the young man, with exaltation.

But he observed that she was releasing herself from his arms and was rising.

"What are you doing?"

A metallic sound was heard. Rosario had put the key into the invisible lock and was cautiously opening the door on the threshold of which they had been sitting. The faint odor of dampness, peculiar to rooms that have been long shut up, issued from the place, which was as dark as a tomb. Pepe Rey felt himself being guided by the hand, and his cousin's voice said faintly:

"Enter!"

They took a few steps forward. He imagined himself being led to an unknown Elysium by the angel of night. Rosario groped her way. At last her sweet voice sounded again, murmuring:

"Sit down."

They were beside a wooden bench. Both sat down. Pepe Rey embraced Rosario again. As he did so, his head struck against a hard body.

"What is this?" he asked.

"The feet."

"Rosario—what are you saying?"

"The feet of the Divine Jesus, of the image of Christ crucified, that we adore in my house."

Pepe Rey felt a cold chill strike through him.

"Kiss them," said the young girl imperiously.

The mathematician kissed the cold feet of the holy image.

"Pepe," then cried the young girl, pressing her cousin's hand ardently between her own, "do you believe in God?"

"Rosario! What are you saying? What absurdities are you imagining?" responded her cousin, perplexed.

"Answer me."

Pepe Rey felt drops of moisture on his hands.

"Why are you crying?" he said, greatly disturbed. "Rosario, you are killing me with your absurd doubts. Do I believe in God? Do you doubt it?"

"I do not doubt it; but they all say that you are an atheist."

"You would suffer in my estimation, you would lose your aureole of purity—your charm—if you gave credit to such nonsense."

"When I heard them accuse you of being an atheist, although I could bring no proof to the contrary, I protested from the depths of my soul against such a calumny. You cannot be an atheist. I have within me as strong and deep a conviction of your faith as of my own."

"How wisely you speak! Why, then, do you ask me if I believe in God?"

"Because I wanted to hear it from your own lips, and rejoice in hearing you say it. It is so long since I have heard the sound of your voice! What greater happiness than to hear it again, saying: 'I believe in God?'"

"Rosario, even the wicked believe in him. If there be atheists, which I doubt, they are the calumniators, the intriguers with whom the world is infested. For my part, intrigues and calumnies matter little to me; and if you rise superior to them and close your heart against the discord which a perfidious hand would sow in it, nothing shall interfere with our happiness."

"But what is going on around us? Pepe, dear Pepe, do you believe in the devil?"

The engineer was silent. The darkness of the chapel prevented Rosario from seeing the smile with which her cousin received this strange question.

"We must believe in him," he said at last.

"What is going on? Mamma forbids me to see you; but, except in regard to the atheism, she does not say anything against you. She tells me to wait, that you will decide; that you are going away, that you are coming back— Speak to me with frankness—have you formed a bad opinion of my mother?"

"Not at all," replied Rey, urged by a feeling of delicacy.

"Do you not believe, as I do, that she loves us both, that she desires only our good, and that we shall in the end obtain her consent to our wishes?"

"If you believe it, I do too. Your mamma adores us both. But, dear Rosario, it must be confessed that the devil has entered this house."

"Don't jest!" she said affectionately. "Ah! mamma is very good. She has not once said to me that you were unworthy to be my husband. All she insists upon is the atheism. They say, besides, that I have manias, and that I have the mania now of loving you with all my soul. In our family it is a rule not to oppose directly the manias that are hereditary in it, because to oppose them aggravates them."

"Well, I believe that there are skilful physicians at your side who have determined to cure you, and who will, in the end, my adored girl, succeed in doing so."

"No, no; a thousand times no!" exclaimed Rosario, leaning her forehead on her lover's breast. "I am willing to be mad if I am with you. For you I am suffering, for you I am ill; for you I despise life and I risk death. I know it now—tomorrow I shall be worse, I shall be dangerously ill, I shall die. What does it matter to me?"

"You are not ill," he responded, with energy; "there is nothing the matter with you but an agitation of mind which naturally brings with it some slight nervous disturbances; there is nothing the matter with you but the suffering occasioned by the horrible coercion which they are using with you. Your simple and generous soul does not comprehend it. You yield; you forgive those who injure you; you torment yourself, attributing your suffering to baleful, supernatural influences; you suffer in silence; you give your innocent neck to the executioner, you allow yourself to be slain, and the very knife which is plunged into your breast seems to you the thorn of a flower that has pierced you in passing. Rosario, cast those ideas from your mind; consider our real situation, which is serious; seek its cause where it really is, and do not give way to your fears; do not yield to the tortures which are inflicted upon you, making yourself mentally and physically ill. The courage which you lack would restore you to health, because you are not really ill, my dear girl, you are—do you wish me to say it?—you are frightened, terrified. You are under what the ancients, not knowing how to express it, called an evil spell. Courage, Rosario, trust in me! Rise and follow me. That is all I will say."

"Ah, Pepe—cousin! I believe that you are right," exclaimed Rosario, drowned in tears. "Your words resound within my heart, arousing in it new energy, new life. Here in this darkness, where we cannot see each other's faces, an ineffable light emanates from you and inundates my soul. What power have you to transform me in this way? The moment I saw you I became another being. In the days when I did not see you I returned to my former insignificance, my natural cowardice. Without you, my Pepe, I live in Limbo. I will do as you tell me, I will arise and follow you. We will go together wherever you wish. Do you know that

I feel well? Do you know that I have no fever; that I have recovered my strength; that I want to run about and cry out; that my whole being is renewed and enlarged, and multiplied a hundred-fold in order to adore you? Pepe, you are right. I am not sick, I am only afraid; or rather, bewitched."

"That is it, bewitched."

"Bewitched! Terrible eyes look at me, and I remain mute and trembling. I am afraid, but of what? You alone have the strange power of calling me back to life. Hearing you, I live again. I believe if I were to die and you were to pass by my grave, that deep under the ground I should feel your footsteps. Oh, if I could see you now! But you are here beside me, and I cannot doubt that it is you. So many days without seeing you! I was mad. Each day of solitude appeared to me a century. They said to me, tomorrow and tomorrow, and always tomorrow. I looked out of the window at night, and the light of the lamp in your room served to console me. At times your shadow on the window was for me a divine apparition. I stretched out my arms to you, I shed tears and cried out inwardly, without daring to do so with my voice. When I received the message you sent me with the maid, when I received your letter telling me that you were going away, I grew very sad, I thought my soul was leaving my body and that I was dying slowly. I fell, like the bird wounded as it flies, that falls and, falling, dies. Tonight, when I saw that you were awake so late, I could not resist the longing I had to speak to you; and I came down stairs. I believe that all the courage of my life has been used up in this single act, and that now I can never be anything again but a coward. But you will give me courage; you will give me strength; you will help me, will you not? Pepe, my dear cousin, tell me that you will; tell me that I am strong, and I will be strong; tell me that I am not ill, and I will not be ill. I am not ill now. I feel so well that I could laugh at my ridiculous maladies."

As she said this she felt herself clasped rapturously in her cousin's arms. An "Oh!" was heard, but it came, not from her lips, but from his, for, in bending his head, he had struck it violently against the feet of the crucifix. In the darkness it is that the stars are seen.

In the exalted state of his mind, by a species of hallucination natural in the darkness, it seemed to Pepe Rey not that his head had struck against the sacred foot, but that this had moved, warning him in the briefest and most eloquent manner. Raising his head he said, half seriously, half gayly:

"Lord, do not strike me; I will do nothing wrong."

At the same moment Rosario took the young man's hand and pressed it against her heart. A voice was heard, a pure, grave, angelic voice, full of feeling, saying:

"Lord whom I adore, Lord God of the world, and guardian of my house and of my family; Lord whom Pepe also adores; holy and blessed Christ who died on the cross for our sins; before thee, before thy wounded body, before thy forehead crowned with thorns, I say that this man is my husband, and that, after thee, he is the being whom my heart loves most; I say that I declare him to be my husband, and that I will die before I belong to another. My heart and my soul are his. Let not the world oppose our happiness, and grant me the favor of this union, which I swear to be true and good before the world, as it is in my conscience."

"Rosario, you are mine!" exclaimed Pepe Rey, with exaltation. "Neither your mother nor anyone else shall prevent it."

Rosario sank powerless into her cousin's arms. She trembled in his manly embrace, as the dove trembles in the talons of the eagle.

Through the engineer's mind the thought flashed that the devil existed; but the devil then was he. Rosario made a slight movement of fear; she felt the thrill of surprise, so to say, that gives warning that danger is near.

"Swear to me that you will not yield to them," said Pepe Rey, with confusion, observing the movement.

"I swear it to you by my father's ashes that are—"

"Where?"

"Under our feet."

The mathematician felt the stone rise under his feet—but no, it was not rising; he only fancied, mathematician though he was, that he felt it rise.

"I swear it to you," repeated Rosario, "by my father's ashes, and by the God who is looking at us— May our bodies, united as they are, repose under those stones when God wills to take us out of this world."

"Yes," repeated the Pepe Rey, with profound emotion, feeling his soul filled with an inexplicable trouble.

Both remained silent for a short time. Rosario had risen.

"Already?" he said.

She sat down again.

"You are trembling again," said Pepe. "Rosario, you are ill; your forehead is burning."

"I think I am dying," murmured the young girl faintly. "I don't know what is the matter with me."

She fell senseless into her cousin's arms. Caressing her, he noticed that her face was covered with a cold perspiration.

"She is really ill," he said to himself. "It was a piece of great imprudence to have come down stairs."

He lifted her up in his arms, endeavoring to restore her to consciousness, but neither the trembling that had seized her nor her insensibility passed away; and he resolved to carry her out of the chapel, in the hope that the fresh air would revive her. And so it was. When she recovered consciousness Rosario manifested great disquietude at finding herself at such an hour out of her own room. The clock of the cathedral struck four.

"How late it is!" exclaimed the young girl. "Release me, cousin. I think I can walk. I am really very ill."

"I will go upstairs with you."

"Oh, no; on no account! I would rather drag myself to my room on my hands and feet. Don't you hear a noise?"

Both were silent. The anxiety with which they listened made the silence intense.

"Don't you hear anything, Pepe?"

"Absolutely nothing."

"Pay attention. There, there it is again. It is a noise that sounds as if it might be either very, very distant, or very near. It might either be my mother's breathing or the creaking of the vane on the tower of the cathedral. Ah! I have a very fine ear."

"Too fine! Well, dear cousin, I will carry you upstairs in my arms."

"Very well; carry me to the head of the stairs. Afterward I can go alone. As soon as I rest a little I shall be as well as ever. But don't you hear?"

They stopped on the first step.

"It is a metallic sound."

"Your mother's breathing?"

"No, it is not that. The noise comes from a great distance. Perhaps it is the crowing of a cock?"

"Perhaps so."

"It sounds like the words, 'I am going there, I am going there!'"

"Now, now I hear," murmured Pepe Rey.

"It is a cry."

"It is a cornet."

"A cornet!"

"Yes. Let us hurry. Orbajosa is going to wake up. Now I hear it clearly. It is not a trumpet but a clarionet. The soldiers are coming."

"Soldiers!"

"I don't know why I imagine that this military invasion is going to be advantageous to me. I feel glad. Up, quickly, Rosario!"

"I feel glad, too. Up, up!"

In an instant he had carried her upstairs, and the lovers took a whispered leave of each other.

"I will stand at the window overlooking the garden, so that you may know I have reached my room safely. Goodbye."

"Goodbye, Rosario. Take care not to stumble against the furniture."

"I can find my way here perfectly, cousin. We shall soon see each other again. Stand at your window if you wish to receive my telegraphic despatch."

Pepe Rey did as he was bade; but he waited a long time, and Rosario did not appear at the window. The engineer fancied he heard agitated voices on the floor above him.

XVIII

The Soldiers

The inhabitants of Orbajosa heard in the twilight vagueness of their morning slumbers the same sonorous clarionet, and they opened their eyes, saying:

"The soldiers!"

Some murmured to themselves between sleeping and waking:

"At last they have sent us that rabble."

Others got out of bed hastily, growling:

"Let us go take a look at those confounded soldiers."

Some soliloquized in this way:

"It will be necessary to hurry up matters. They say drafts and contributions; we will say blows and more blows."

In another house were heard these words uttered joyfully:

"Perhaps my son is coming! Perhaps my brother is coming!"

Everywhere people were springing out of bed, dressing hastily, opening the windows to see the regiment that caused all this excitement entering the city in the early dawn. The city was gloom, silence, age; the army gayety, boisterousness, youth. As the army entered the city it seemed as if the mummy received by some magic art the gift of life and sprang with noisy gayety from its damp sarcophagus to dance around it. What movement, what shouting, what laughter, what merriment! There is nothing so interesting as a regiment. It is our country in its youthful and vigorous aspect. All the ineptitude, the turbulence, the superstition at times, and at times the impiety of the country as represented in the individual, disappears under the iron rule of discipline, which of so many insignificant figures makes an imposing whole. The soldier, or so to say, the corpuscle, separating at the command "Break ranks!" from the mass in which he has led a regular and at times a sublime life, occasionally preserves some of the qualities peculiar to the army. But this is not the general rule. The separation is most often accompanied by a sudden deterioration, with the result that if an army is the glory and honor of a nation, an assemblage of soldiers may be an insupportable calamity; and the towns that shed tears of joy and enthusiasm when they see a victorious battalion enter their precincts, groan with terror and tremble with apprehension when they see the same soldiers separate and off duty.

This last was what happened in Orbajosa, for in those days there were no glorious deeds to celebrate, nor was there any motive for weaving wreaths or tracing triumphal inscriptions, or even for making mention of the exploits of our brave soldiers, for which reason all was fear and suspicion in the episcopal city, which, although poor, did not lack treasures in chickens, fruits, money, and maidenhood, all of which ran great risk from the moment when the beforementioned sons of Mars entered it. In addition to this, the native town of the Polentinos, as a city remote from the movement and stir brought with them by traffic, the newspapers, railroads, and other agents which it is unnecessary now to specify, did not wish to be disturbed in its tranquil existence.

Besides which, it manifested on every favorable occasion a strong aversion to submitting to the central authority which, badly or well, governs us; and calling to mind its former privileges and ruminating upon them anew, as the camel chews the cud of the grass which it ate yesterday, it would occasionally display a certain rebellious independence, and vicious tendencies much to be deplored, which at times gave no little anxiety to the governor of the province.

It must also be taken into account that Orbajosa had rebellious antecedents, or rather ancestry. Doubtless it still retained some of those energetic fibres which, in remote ages, according to the enthusiastic opinion of Don Cayetano, impelled it to unexampled epic deeds; and, even in its decadence, occasionally felt an eager desire to do great things, although they might be only barbarities and follies. As it had given to the world so many illustrious sons, it desired, no doubt, that its actual scions, the Caballucos, Merengues, and Pelosmalos, should renew the glorious *Gesta* of their predecessors.

Whenever there was disaffection in Spain, Orbajosa gave proof that it was not in vain that it existed on the face of the earth, although it is true that it was never the theatre of a real war. The spirit of the town, its situation, its history, all reduced it to the secondary part of raising guerillas. It bestowed upon the country this national product in 1827, at the time of the Apostolics, during the Seven Years' War, in 1848, and at other epochs of less resonance in the national history. The guerillas and their chiefs were always popular, a fatal circumstance due to the War of Independence, one of those good things which have been the origin of an infinite number of detestable things. *Corruptio optimi pessima*. And with the popularity of the guerillas and their chiefs coincided, in ever-increasing proportion, the unpopularity of everyone who entered Orbajosa in the character of a delegate or instrument of the central power. The soldiers were held in such disrepute there that, whenever the old people told of any crime, any robbery, assassination, or the like atrocity, they added: "This happened when the soldiers were here."

And now that these important observations have been made, it will be well to add that the battalions sent there during the days in which the events of our story took place did not go to parade through the streets, but for another purpose which will be clearly and minutely set forth later on. As a detail of no little interest, it may be noted that the events here related took place at a period neither very remote nor very recent. It may also be said that Orbajosa (called by the Romans Urbs Augusta, although some learned moderns, enquiring into the etymology of the termination *ajosa*,* are of opinion that it comes by it from being the richest garlic-growing country in the world) is neither very near Madrid nor very far from it; nor can we say whether its glorious foundations are laid toward the north or toward the south, toward the east or toward the west; but that it may be supposed to be in any part of Spain where the pungent odor of its garlic is to be perceived.

The billets of residence being distributed by the authorities, each soldier went to seek his borrowed home. They were received by their hosts with a very ill grace and assigned the most atrociously uninhabitable parts of the houses. The girls of the city were not indeed among those who were most dissatisfied, but a strict watch was kept over them, and it was considered not decent to show pleasure at the visit of such rabble. The few soldiers who were natives of the district only were treated like kings. The others were regarded as invaders.

At eight in the morning a lieutenant-colonel of cavalry entered the house of Doña Perfecta Polentinos with his billet. He was received by the servants, by order of its mistress, who, being at the time in a deplorable state of mind, did not wish to go down stairs to meet the soldier, and by them he was shown to the only room in the house which, it seemed, was disposable, the room occupied by Pepe Rey.

---

* Rich in garlic.

"Let them settle themselves as best they can," said Doña Perfecta, with an expression of gall and vinegar. "And if they have not room enough, let them go into the street."

Was it her intention to annoy in this way her detested nephew, or was there really no other unoccupied room in the house? This we do not know, nor do the chronicles from which this true history is taken say a word on this important point. What we know positively is that, far from displeasing the two guests to be thus boxed up together, it gave them great pleasure, as they happened to be old friends. They were greatly surprised and delighted when they met, and they were never tired of asking each other questions and uttering exclamations, dwelling on the strange chance that had brought them together in such a place and on such an occasion.

"Pinzon—you here! Why, what is this? I had no suspicion that you were in this neighborhood."

"I heard that you were in this part of the country, Pepe; but I had no idea, either, that I should meet you in this horrible, this barbarous Orbajosa."

"But what a fortunate chance! For this chance is most fortunate—providential. Pinzon, between us both we are going to do a great thing in this wretched town."

"And we shall have time enough to consult about it," answered the other, seating himself on the bed in which the engineer was lying, "for it appears that we are both to occupy this room. What the devil sort of a house is this?"

"Why, man, it is my aunt's. Speak with more respect about it. Have you not met my aunt? But I am going to get up."

"I am very glad of it, for then I can lie down and rest; and badly I need it. What a road, friend Pepe, what a road, and what a town!"

"Tell me, have you come to set fire to Orbajosa?"

"Fire!"

"I ask you because, in that case, I might help you."

"What a town! But what a town!" exclaimed the soldier, removing his shako, and laying aside sword and shoulder-belt, travelling case and cloak. "This is the second time they have sent us here. I swear to you that the third time I will ask my discharge."

"Don't talk ill of these good people! But you have come in the nick of time. It seems as if Providence has sent you to my aid, Pinzon. I have a terrible project on hand, an adventure,—a plot, if you wish to call it so, my friend,—and it would have been difficult for me to carry it through without you. A moment ago I was in despair, wondering how I should manage, and saying to myself anxiously, 'If I only had a friend here, a good friend!'"

"A project, a plot, an adventure! One of two things, Señor Mathematician: it is either the discovery of aërial navigation, or else some love affair."

"It is serious, very serious. Go to bed, sleep a while, and afterward we will talk about it."

"I will go to bed, but I will not sleep. You may say all you wish to me. All that I ask is that you will say as little as possible about Orbajosa."

"It is precisely about Orbajosa that I wish to speak to you. But have you also an antipathy to this cradle of illustrious men?"

"These garlic-venders—we call them the garlic-venders—may be as illustrious as you choose, but to me they are as irritating as the product of the country. This is a town ruled by people who teach distrust, superstition, and hatred of the whole human race. When we have leisure I will relate to you an occurrence—an adventure, half-comic, half-tragic—that happened to me here last year. When I tell it to you, you will laugh and I shall be fuming. But, in fine, what is past is past."

"In what is happening to me there is nothing comic."

"But I have various reasons for hating this wretched place. You must know that my father was assassinated here in '48 by a party of barbarous guerillas. He was a brigadier, and he had left the service. The Government sent for him, and he was passing through Villahorrenda on his way to Madrid, when he was captured by half a dozen ruffians. Here there are several dynasties of guerilla chiefs—the Aceros, the Caballucos, the Pelosmalos—a periodical eruption, as someone has said who knew very well what he was talking about."

"I suppose that two infantry regiments and some cavalry have not come here solely for the pleasure of visiting these delightful regions."

"Certainly not! We have come to survey the country. There are many deposits of arms here. The Government does not venture, as it desires, to remove from office the greater number of the municipal councils without first distributing a few companies of soldiers through these towns. As there is so much disturbance in this part of the country, as two of the neighboring provinces are already infested, and as this municipal district of Orbajosa has, besides, so brilliant a record in all the civil wars, there are fears that the bravos of the place may take to the roads and rob all they can lay hands on."

"A good precaution! But I am firmly convinced that not until these people die and are born over again, not until the very stones have changed their form, will there be peace in Orbajosa."

"That is my opinion too," said the officer, lighting a cigarette. "Don't you see that the guerilla chiefs are the pets of this place? Those who desolated the district in 1848 and at other epochs, or, if not they, their sons, are employed in the market inspector's office, at the town gates, in the town-hall, in the post-office; among them are constables, sacristans, bailiffs. Some have become powerful party leaders and they are the ones who manage the elections, have influence in Madrid, bestow places—in short, this is terrible."

"And tell me, is there no hope of the guerilla chiefs performing some exploit in these days? If that should happen, you could destroy the town, and I would help you."

"If it depended upon me— They will play their usual pranks no doubt," said Pinzon, "for the insurrection in the two neighboring provinces is spreading like wildfire. And between ourselves, friend Rey, I think this is going to last for a long time. Some people smile and say that it would be impossible that there should be another insurrection like the last one. They don't know the country; they don't know Orbajosa and its inhabitants. I believe that the war that is now beginning will have serious consequences, and that we shall have another cruel and bloody struggle, that will last Heaven knows how long. What is your opinion?"

"Well, in Madrid I laughed at anyone who spoke of the possibility of a civil war as long and as terrible as the Seven Years' War; but since I have been here—"

"One must come to the heart of this enchanting country, see the people at home, and hear them talk, to know what the real state of affairs is."

"Just so. Without knowing precisely on what I base my opinion, the fact is that here I see things in a different light, and I now believe that it is possible that there may be a long and bloody war."

"Exactly so."

"But at present my thoughts are occupied less by the public war than by a private war in which I am engaged and which I declared a short time ago."

"You said this was your aunt's house. What is her name?"

BENITO PÉREZ GALDÓS

"Doña Perfecta Rey de Polentinos."

"Ah! I know her by reputation. She is an excellent person, and the only one of whom I have not heard the garlic-venders speak ill. When I was here before I heard her goodness, her charity, her innumerable virtues, everywhere extolled."

"Yes, my aunt is very kind, very amiable," said Rey.

Then he fell into a thoughtful silence.

"But now I remember!" exclaimed Pinzon suddenly. "How one thing fits in with another! Yes, I heard in Madrid that you were going to be married to a cousin of yours. All is clear now. Is it that beautiful and heavenly Rosarito?"

"Pinzon, we must have a long talk together."

"I imagine that there are difficulties."

"There is something more; there is violent opposition. I have need of a determined friend—a friend who is prompt to act, fruitful in resource, of great experience in emergencies, astute and courageous."

"Why, this is even more serious than a challenge."

"A great deal more serious. It would be easy to fight with another man. With women, with unseen enemies who work in the dark, it is impossible."

"Come, I am all ears."

Lieutenant-colonel Pinzon lay stretched at full length upon the bed. Pepe Rey drew a chair up to the bedside and, leaning his elbow on the bed and his head on his hand, began his conference, consultation, exposition of plan, or whatever else it might be called, and continued talking for a long time. Pinzon listened to him with profound attention and without interrupting him, except to ask an occasional question for the purpose of obtaining further details or additional light upon some obscure point. When Pepe Rey ended, Pinzon looked grave. He stretched himself, yawning with the satisfaction of one who has not slept for three nights, and then said:

"Your plan is dangerous and difficult."

"But not impossible."

"Oh, no! for nothing is impossible. Reflect well about it."

"I have reflected."

"And you are resolved to carry it through? Consider that these things are not now in fashion. They generally turn out badly and throw discredit on those who undertake them."

"I am resolved."

"For my part, then, although the business is dangerous and serious—very serious—I am ready to aid you in all things and for all things."

"Can I rely upon you?"

"To the death."

XIX

A Terrible Battle—Strategy

The opening of hostilities could not long be delayed. When the hour of dinner arrived, after coming to an agreement with Pinzon regarding the plan to be pursued, the first condition of which was that the friends should pretend not to know each other, Pepe Rey went to the dining-room. There he found his aunt, who had just returned from the cathedral where she had spent the morning, as was her habit. She was alone, and appeared to be greatly preoccupied. The engineer observed that on that pale and marble-like countenance, not without a certain beauty, there rested a mysterious shadow. When she looked up it recovered its sinister calmness, but she looked up seldom, and after a rapid examination of her nephew's countenance, that of the amiable lady would again take on its studied gloom.

They awaited dinner in silence. They did not wait for Don Cayetano, for he had gone to Mundogrande. When they sat down to table Doña Perfecta said:

"And that fine soldier whom the Government has sent us, is he not coming to dinner?"

"He seems to be more sleepy than hungry," answered the engineer, without looking at his aunt.

"Do you know him?"

"I have never seen him in all my life before."

"We are nicely off with the guests whom the Government sends us. We have beds and provisions in order to keep them ready for those vagabonds of Madrid, whenever they may choose to dispose of them."

"There are fears of an insurrection," said Pepe Rey, with sudden heat, "and the Government is determined to crush the Orbajosans—to crush them, to grind them to powder."

"Stop, man, stop, for Heaven's sake; don't crush us!" cried Doña Perfecta sarcastically. "Poor we! Be merciful, man, and allow us unhappy creatures to live. And would you, then, be one of those who would aid the army in the grand work of crushing us?"

"I am not a soldier. I will do nothing but applaud when I see the germs of civil war, of insubordination, of discord, of disorder, of robbery, and of barbarism that exist here, to the shame of our times and of our country, forever extirpated."

"All will be as God wills."

"Orbajosa, my dear aunt, has little else than garlic and bandits; for those who in the name of some political or religious idea set out in search of adventures every four or five years are nothing but bandits."

"Thanks, thanks, my dear nephew!" said Doña Perfecta, turning pale. "So Orbajosa has nothing more than that? Yet there must be something else here—something that you do not possess, since you have come to look for it among us."

Rey felt the cut. His soul was on fire. He found it very difficult to show his aunt the consideration to which her sex, her rank, and her relation to himself entitled her. He was on the verge of a violent outbreak, and a force that he could not resist was impelling him against his interlocutor.

"I came to Orbajosa," he said, "because you sent for me; you arranged with my father—"

"Yes, yes; it is true," she answered, interrupting him quickly and making an effort to recover her habitual serenity. "I do not deny it. I am the one who is really to blame. I am to blame for your ill-humor, for the slights you put upon us, for everything disagreeable that has been happening in my house since you entered it."

"I am glad that you are conscious of it."

"In exchange, you are a saint. Must I also go down on my knees to your grace and ask your pardon?"

"Señora," said Pepe Rey gravely, laying down his knife and fork, "I entreat you not to mock me in so pitiless a manner. I cannot meet you on equal ground. All I have said is that I came to Orbajosa at your invitation."

"And it is true. Your father and I arranged that you should marry Rosario. You came in order to become acquainted with her. I accepted you at once as a son. You pretended to love Rosario—"

"Pardon me," objected Pepe; "I loved and I love Rosario; you pretended to accept me as a son; receiving me with deceitful cordiality, you employed from the very beginning all the arts of cunning to thwart me and to prevent the fulfilment of the proposals made to my father; you determined from the first day to drive me to desperation, to tire me out; and with smiles and affectionate words on your lips you have been killing me, roasting me at a slow fire; you have let loose upon me

BENITO PÉREZ GALDÓS

in the dark and from behind an ambush a swarm of lawsuits; you have deprived me of the official commission which I brought to Orbajosa; you have brought me into disrepute in the town; you have had me turned out of the cathedral; you have kept me constantly separated from the chosen of my heart; you have tortured your daughter with an inquisitorial imprisonment which will cause her death, unless God interposes to prevent it."

Doña Perfecta turned scarlet. But the flush of offended pride passed away quickly, leaving her face of a greenish pallor. Her lips trembled. Throwing down the knife and fork with which she had been eating, she rose swiftly to her feet. Her nephew rose also.

"My God! Holy Virgin of Succor!" she cried, raising both her hands to her head and pressing it between them with the gesture indicative of desperation, "is it possible that I deserve such atrocious insults? Pepe, my son, is it you who speak to me in this way? If I have done what you say, I am indeed very wicked."

She sank on the sofa and covered her face with her hands. Pepe, approaching her slowly, saw that his aunt was sobbing bitterly and shedding abundant tears. In spite of his conviction he could not altogether conquer the feeling of compassion which took possession of him; and while he condemned himself for his cowardice he felt something of remorse for the severity and the frankness with which he had spoken.

"My dear aunt," he said, putting his hand on her shoulder, "if you answer me with tears and sighs, you will move me but you will not convince me. Proofs, not emotions, are what I require. Speak to me, tell me that I am mistaken in thinking what I think; then prove it to me, and I will acknowledge my error."

"Leave me, you are not my brother's son! If you were, you would not insult me as you have insulted me. So, then, I am an intriguer, an actress, a hypocritical harpy, a domestic plotter?"

As she spoke, Doña Perfecta uncovered her face and looked at her nephew with a martyr-like expression. Pepe was perplexed. The tears as well as the gentle voice of his father's sister could not be insignificant phenomena for the mathematician's soul. Words crowded to his lips to ask her pardon. A man of great firmness generally, any appeal to his emotions, anything which touched his heart, converted him at once into a child. Weaknesses of a mathematician! It is said that Newton was the same.

"I will give you the proofs you ask," said Doña Perfecta, motioning him to a seat beside her. "I will give you satisfaction. You shall see whether I am kind, whether I am indulgent, whether I am humble. Do you think that I am going to contradict you; to deny absolutely the acts of which you have accused me? Well, then, no; I do not deny them."

The engineer was astounded.

"I do not deny them," continued Doña Perfecta. "What I deny is the evil intention which you attribute to them. By what right do you undertake to judge of what you know only from appearances and by conjecture? Have you the supreme intelligence which is necessary to judge justly the actions of others and pronounce sentence upon them? Are you God, to know the intentions?"

Pepe was every moment more amazed.

"Is it not allowable at times to employ indirect means to attain a good and honorable end? By what right do you judge actions of mine that you do not clearly understand? I, my dear nephew, manifesting a sincerity which you do not deserve, confess to you that I have indeed employed subterfuges to attain a good end, to attain what was at the same time beneficial to you and to my daughter. You do not comprehend? You look bewildered. Ah! your great mathematician's and German philosopher's intellect is not capable of comprehending these artifices of a prudent mother."

"I am more and more astounded every moment," said the engineer.

"Be as astounded as you choose, but confess your barbarity," said the lady, with increasing spirit; "acknowledge your hastiness and your brutal conduct toward me in accusing me as you have done. You are a young man without any experience or any other knowledge than that which is derived from books, which teach nothing about the world or the human heart. All you know is how to make roads and docks. Ah, my young gentleman! one does not enter into the human heart through the tunnel of a railroad, or descend into its depths through the shaft of a mine. You cannot read in the conscience of another with the microscope of a naturalist, nor decide the question of another's culpability measuring ideas with a theodolite."

"For God's sake, dear aunt!"

"Why do you pronounce the name of God when you do not believe in him?" said Doña Perfecta, in solemn accents. "If you believed in him, if you were a good Christian, you would not dare to form evil judgments about my conduct. I am a devout woman, do you understand? I have a

BENITO PÉREZ GALDÓS

tranquil conscience, do you understand? I know what I am doing and why I do it, do you understand?"

"I understand, I understand, I understand!"

"God, in whom you do not believe, sees what you do not see and what you cannot see—the intention. I will say no more; I do not wish to enter into minute explanations, for I do not need to do so. Nor would you understand me if I should tell you that I desired to attain my object without scandal, without offending your father, without offending you, without giving cause for people to talk by an explicit refusal—I will say nothing of all this to you, for you would not understand it, either, Pepe. You are a mathematician. You see what is before your eyes, and nothing more; brute matter and nothing more. You see the effect, and not the cause. He who does not believe in God does not see causes. God is the supreme intention of the world. He who does not know this must necessarily judge things as you judge them—foolishly. In the tempest, for instance, he sees only destruction; in the conflagration, ruin; in the drought, famine; in the earthquake, desolation; and yet, arrogant young man, in all those apparent calamities we are to seek the good intention—yes, señor, the intention, always good, of Him who can do nothing evil."

This confused, subtle, and mystic logic did not convince Pepe Rey; but he did not wish to follow his aunt in the tortuous path of such a method of reasoning, and he said simply:

"Well, I respect intentions."

"Now that you seem to recognize your error," continued the pious lady, with ever-increasing confidence, "I will make another confession to you, and that is that I see now that I did wrong in adopting the course I did, although my object was excellent. In view of your impetuous disposition, in view of your incapacity to comprehend me, I should have faced the situation boldly and said to you, 'Nephew, I do not wish that you should be my daughter's husband.'"

"That is the language you should have used to me from the beginning," said the engineer, drawing a deep breath, as if his mind had been relieved from an enormous weight. "I am greatly obliged to you for those words. After having been stabbed in the dark, this blow on the face in the light of day is a great satisfaction to me."

"Well, I will repeat the blow, nephew," declared Doña Perfecta, with as much energy as displeasure. "You know it now—I do not wish you to marry Rosario!"

Pepe was silent. There was a long pause, during which the two regarded each other attentively, as if the face of each was for the other the most perfect work of art.

"Don't you understand what I have said to you?" she repeated. "That everything is at an end, that there is to be no marriage."

"Permit me, dear aunt," said the young man, with composure, "not to be terrified by the intimation. In the state at which things have arrived your refusal has little importance for me."

"What are you saying?" cried Doña Perfecta violently.

"What you hear. I will marry Rosario!"

Doña Perfecta rose to her feet, indignant, majestic, terrible. Her attitude was that of anathema incarnated in a woman. Rey remained seated, serene, courageous, with the passive courage of a profound conviction and an immovable resolve. The whole weight of his aunt's wrath, threatening to overwhelm him, did not make him move an eyelash. This was his character.

"You are mad. Marry my daughter, you! Marry her against my will!"

Doña Perfecta's trembling lips articulated these words in a truly tragic tone.

"Against your will! She is of a different way of thinking."

"Against my will!" repeated Doña Perfecta. "Yes, and I repeat it again and again. I do not wish it, I do not wish it!"

"She and I wish it."

"Fool! Is nothing else in the world to be considered but her and you? Are there not parents; is there not society; is there not a conscience; is there not a God?"

"Because there is society, because there is a conscience, because there is a God," affirmed Rey gravely, rising to his feet, and pointing with outstretched arm to the heavens, "I say and I repeat that I will marry her."

"Wretch! arrogant man! And if you would dare to trample everything under your feet, do you think there are not laws to prevent your violence?"

"Because there are laws, I say and I repeat that I will marry her."

"You respect nothing!"

"Nothing that is unworthy of respect."

"And my authority, my will, I—am I nothing?"

"For me your daughter is everything—the rest is nothing."

Pepe Rey's composure was, so to say, the arrogant display of invincible and conscious strength. The blows he gave were hard and

BENITO PÉREZ GALDÓS

crushing in their force, without anything to mitigate their severity. His words, if the comparison may be allowed, were like a pitiless discharge of artillery.

Doña Perfecta sank again on the sofa; but she shed no tears, and a convulsive tremor agitated her frame.

"So that for this infamous atheist," she exclaimed, with frank rage, "there are no social conventionalities, there is nothing but caprice. This is base avarice. My daughter is rich!"

"If you think to wound me with that treacherous weapon, evading the question and giving a distorted meaning to my sentiments in order to offend my dignity, you are mistaken, dear aunt. Call me mercenary, if you choose. God knows what I am."

"You have no dignity!"

"That is an opinion, like any other. The world may hold you to be infallible. I do not. I am far from believing that from your judgments there is no appeal to God."

"But is what you say true? But do you persist in your purpose, after my refusal? You respect nothing, you are a monster, a bandit."

"I am a man."

"A wretch! Let us end this at once. I refuse to give my daughter to you; I refuse her to you!"

"I will take her then! I shall take only what is mine."

"Leave my presence!" exclaimed Doña Perfecta, rising suddenly to her feet. "Coxcomb, do you suppose that my daughter thinks of you?"

"She loves me, as I love her."

"It is a lie! It is a lie!"

"She herself has told me so. Excuse me if, on this point, I put more faith in her words than in her mother's."

"How could she have told you so, when you have not seen her for several days?"

"I saw her last night, and she swore to me before the crucifix in the chapel that she would be my wife."

"Oh, scandal; oh, libertinism! But what is this? My God, what a disgrace!" exclaimed Doña Perfecta, pressing her head again between her hands and walking up and down the room. "Rosario left her room last night?"

"She left it to see me. It was time."

"What vile conduct is yours! You have acted like a thief; you have acted like a vulgar seducer!"

"I have acted in accordance with the teachings of your school. My intention was good."

"And she came down stairs! Ah, I suspected it! This morning at daybreak I surprised her, dressed, in her room. She told me she had gone out, I don't know for what. You were the real criminal, then. This is a disgrace! Pepe, I expected anything from you rather than an outrage like this. Everything is at an end! Go away! You are dead to me. I forgive you, provided you go away. I will not say a word about this to your father. What horrible selfishness! No, there is no love in you. You do not love my daughter!"

"God knows that I love her, and that is sufficient for me."

"Be silent, blasphemer! and don't take the name of God upon your lips!" exclaimed Doña Perfecta. "In the name of God, whom I can invoke, for I believe in him, I tell you that my daughter will never be your wife. My daughter will be saved, Pepe; my daughter shall not be condemned to a living hell, for a union with you would be a hell!"

"Rosario will be my wife," repeated the mathematician, with pathetic calmness.

The pious lady was still more exasperated by her nephew's calm energy. In a broken voice she said:

"Don't suppose that your threats terrify me. I know what I am saying. What! are a home and a family to be outraged like this? Are human and divine authority to be trampled under foot in this way?"

"I will trample everything under foot," said the engineer, beginning to lose his composure and speaking with some agitation.

"You will trample everything under foot! Ah! it is easy to see that you are a barbarian, a savage, a man who lives by violence."

"No, dear aunt; I am mild, upright, honorable, and an enemy to violence; but between you and me—between you who are the law and I who am to honor it—is a poor tormented creature, one of God's angels, subjected to iniquitous tortures. The spectacle of this injustice, this unheard-of violence, is what has converted my rectitude into barbarity; my reason into brute force; my honor into violence, like an assassin's or a thief's; this spectacle, señora, is what impels me to disregard your law, what impels me to trample it under foot, braving everything. This which appears to you lawlessness is obedience to an unescapable law. I do what society does when a brutal power, as illogical as irritating, opposes its progress. It tramples it under foot and destroys it in an outburst of frenzy. Such am I at this moment—I do not recognize myself. I was reasonable, and now I am a brute; I was respectful, and now I am insolent; I was civilized, and now I am a savage. You have brought me to this horrible extremity; infuriating me and driving me from the path of rectitude which I was tranquilly pursuing. Who is to blame—I or you?"

"You, you!"

"Neither you nor I can decide the question. I think we are both to blame: you for your violence and injustice, I for my injustice and violence. We have both become equally barbarous, and we struggle with and wound each other without compassion. God has permitted that it should be so; my blood will be upon your conscience, yours will be upon mine. Enough now, señora. I do not wish to trouble you with useless words. We will now proceed to acts."

"To acts, very well!" said Doña Perfecta, roaring rather than speaking. "Don't suppose that in Orbajosa there is no civil guard!"

"Goodbye, señora. I will now leave this house. I think we shall meet again."

"Go, go! go now!" she cried, pointing with an energetic gesture to the door.

Pepe Rey left the room. Doña Perfecta, after pronouncing a few incoherent words, which were the clearest expression of her anger, sank into a chair, with indications of fatigue, or of a coming attack of nerves. The maids came running in.

"Go for Señor Don Inocencio!" she cried. "Instantly—hurry! Ask him to come here!"

Then she tore her handkerchief with her teeth.

XX

Rumors—Fears

On the day following that of this lamentable quarrel, various rumors regarding Pepe Rey and his conduct spread through Orbajosa, going from house to house, from club to club, from the Casino to the apothecary's, and from the Paseo de las Descalzes to the Puerta de Baidejos. They were repeated by everybody, and so many were the comments made that, if Don Cayetano had collected and compiled them, he might have formed with them a rich "Thesaurus" of Orbajosan benevolence. In the midst of the diversity of the reports circulated, there was agreement in regard to certain important particulars, one of which was the following:

That the engineer, enraged at Doña Perfecta's refusal to marry Rosario to an atheist, had raised his hand to his aunt.

The young man was living in the widow De Cusco's hotel, an establishment mounted, as they say now, not at the height, but at the depth of the superlative backwardness of the town. Lieutenant-colonel Pinzon visited him with frequency, in order that they might discuss together the plot which they had on hand, and for the successful conduct of which the soldier showed the happiest dispositions. New artifices and stratagems occurred to him at every instant, and he hastened to put them into effect with excellent humor, although he would often say to his friend:

"The rôle I am playing, dear Pepe, is not a very dignified one; but to give an annoyance to the Orbajosans I would walk on my hands and feet."

We do not know what cunning stratagems the artful soldier, skilled in the wiles of the world, employed; but certain it is that before he had been in the house three days he had succeeded in making himself greatly liked by everybody in it. His manners were very pleasing to Doña Perfecta, who could not hear unmoved his flattering praises of the elegance of the house, and of the nobility, piety, and august magnificence of its mistress. With Don Inocencio he was hand and glove. Neither her mother nor the Penitentiary placed any obstacle in the way of his speaking with Rosario (who had been restored to liberty on the departure of her ferocious cousin); and, with his delicate compliments, his skilful flattery, and great address, he had acquired in the house of Polentinos considerable ascendency, and he had even succeeded in establishing himself in it on a footing of familiarity. But the object of all his arts was a servant maid named Librada, whom he had seduced (chastely speaking) that she might carry messages and notes to Rosario, of whom he pretended to be enamored. The girl allowed herself to be bribed with persuasive words and a good deal of money, because she was ignorant of the source of the notes and of the real meaning of the intrigue, for had she known that it was all a diabolical plot of Don José, although she liked the latter greatly, she would not have acted with treachery toward her mistress for all the money in the world.

One day Doña Perfecta, Don Inocencio, Jacinto, and Pinzon were conversing together in the garden. They were talking about the soldiers and the purpose for which they had been sent to Orbajosa, in which the Penitentiary found motive for condemning the tyrannical conduct of the Government; and, without knowing how it came about, Pepe Rey's name was mentioned.

"He is still at the hotel," said the little lawyer. "I saw him yesterday, and he gave me remembrances for you, Doña Perfecta."

"Was there ever seen such insolence! Ah, Señor Pinzon! do not be surprised at my using this language, speaking of my own nephew—that young man, you remember, who had the room which you occupy."

"Yes, I know. I am not acquainted with him, but I know him by sight and by reputation. He is an intimate friend of our brigadier."

"An intimate friend of the brigadier?"

"Yes, señor; of the commander of the brigade that has just arrived in this district, and which is quartered in the neighboring villages."

"And where is he?" asked the lady.

"In Orbajosa."

"I think he is stopping at Polavieja's," observed Jacinto.

"Your nephew and Brigadier Batalla are intimate friends," continued Pinzon; "they are always to be seen together in the streets."

"Well, my friend, that gives me a bad idea of your chief," said Doña Perfecta.

"He is—he is very good-natured," said Pinzon, in the tone of one who, through motives of respect, did not venture to use a harsher word.

"With your permission, Señor Pinzon, and making an honorable exception in your favor, it must be said that in the Spanish army there are some curious types—"

"Our brigadier was an excellent soldier before he gave himself up to spiritualism."

"To spiritualism!"

"That sect that calls up ghosts and goblins by means of the legs of a table!" said the canon, laughing.

"From curiosity, only from curiosity," said Jacintillo, with emphasis, "I ordered Allan Kardec's book from Madrid. It is well to know something about everything."

"But is it possible that such follies—Heavens! Tell me, Pinzon, does my nephew too belong to that sect of table-tippers?"

"I think it was he who indoctrinated our valiant Brigadier Batalla."

"Good Heavens!"

"Yes; and whenever he chooses," said Don Inocencio, unable to contain his laughter, "he can speak to Socrates, St. Paul, Cervantes, or Descartes, as I speak now to Librada to ask her for a match. Poor Señor de Rey! I was not mistaken in saying that there was something wrong with his head."

"Outside that," continued Pinzon, "our brigadier is a good soldier. If he errs at all, it is on the side of severity. He takes the orders of the Government so literally that, if he were to meet with much opposition here, he would be capable of not leaving one stone upon another in Orbajosa. Yes, I advise you all to be on your guard."

"But is that monster going to cut all our heads off, then? Ah, Señor Don Inocencio! these visits of the army remind me of what I have read in the lives of the martyrs about the visits of the Roman proconsuls to a Christian town."

"The comparison is not wanting in exactness," said the Penitentiary, looking at the soldier over his spectacles.

"It is not very agreeable, but if it is the truth, why should it not be said?" observed Pinzon benevolently. "Now you all are at our mercy."

"The authorities of the place," objected Jacinto, "still exercise their functions as usual."

"I think you are mistaken," responded the soldier, whose countenance Doña Perfecta and the Penitentiary were studying with profound interest. "The alcalde of Orbajosa was removed from office an hour ago."

"By the governor of the province?"

"The governor of the province has been replaced by a delegate from the Government, who was to arrive this morning. The municipal councils will all be removed from office today. The minister has so ordered becaused he suspected, I don't know on what grounds, that they were not supporting the central authority."

"This is a pretty state of things!" murmured the canon, frowning and pushing out his lower lip.

Doña Perfecta looked thoughtful.

"Some of the judges of the primary court, among them the judge of Orbajosa, have been deprived of office."

"The judge! Periquito—Periquito is no longer judge!" exclaimed Doña Perfecta, in a voice and with the manner of a person who has just been stung by a snake.

"The person who was judge in Orbajosa is judge no longer," said Pinzon. "Tomorrow the new judge will arrive."

"A stranger!"

"A stranger."

"A rascal, perhaps. The other was so honorable!" said Doña Perfecta, with alarm. "I never asked anything from him that he did not grant it to me at once. Do you know who will be the new alcalde?"

"They say a corregidor is coming."

"There, say at once that the Deluge is coming, and let us be done with it," said the canon, rising.

"So that we are at the brigadier's mercy!"

"For a few days only. Don't be angry with me. In spite of my uniform I am an enemy of militarism; but we are ordered to strike—and we strike. There could not be a viler trade than ours."

"That it is, that it is!" said Doña Perfecta, with difficulty concealing her fury. "Now that you have confessed it— So, then, neither alcalde nor judge—"

"Nor governor of the province."

"Let them take the bishop from us also and send us a choir boy in his stead."

"That is all that is wanting—if the people here will allow them to do it," murmured Don Inocencio, lowering his eyes. "They won't stop at trifles."

"And it is all because they are afraid of an insurrection in Orbajosa," exclaimed Doña Perfecta, clasping her hands and waving them up and down. "Frankly, Pinzon, I don't know why it is that even the very stones don't rise up in rebellion. I wish you no harm; but it would be a just judgment on you if the water you drink turned into mud. You say that my nephew is the intimate friend of the brigadier?"

"So intimate that they are together all day long; they were school-fellows. Batalla loves him like a brother, and would do anything to please him. In your place, señora, I would be uneasy."

"Oh, my God! I fear there will be an attack on the house!"

"Señora," declared the canon, with energy, "before I would consent that there should be an attack on this honorable house—before I would consent that the slightest harm should be done to this noble family—I, my nephew, all the people of Orbajosa—"

Don Inocencio did not finish. His anger was so great that the words refused to come. He took a few steps forward with a martial air, then returned to his seat.

"I think that your fears are not idle," said Pinzon. "If it should be necessary, I—"

"And I—" said Jacinto.

Doña Perfecto had fixed her eyes on the glass door of the dining-room, through which could be seen a graceful figure. As she looked at it, it seemed as if the cloud of apprehension which rested on her countenance grew darker.

"Rosario! come in here, Rosario!" she said, going to meet the young girl. "I fancy you look better today, and that you are more cheerful. Don't you think that Rosario looks better? She seems a different being."

They all agreed that the liveliest happiness was depicted on her countenance.

XXI

"Desperta Ferro"

A bout this time the following items of news appeared in the Madrid newspapers:

"There is no truth whatever in the report that there has been an insurrection in the neighborhood of Orbajosa. Our correspondent in that place informs us that the country is so little disposed for adventures that the further presence of the Batalla brigade in that locality is considered unnecessary."

"It is said that the Batalla brigade will leave Orbajosa, as troops are not required there, to go to Villajuan de Nahara, where guerillas have made their appearance."

"The news has been confirmed that the Aceros, with a number of mounted followers, are ranging the district of Villajuan, adjacent to the judicial district of Orbajosa. The governor of the province of X. has telegraphed to the Government that Francisco Acero entered Las Roquetas, where he demanded provisions and money. Domingo Acero (Faltriquera), was ranging the Jubileo mountains, actively pursued by the Civil Guards, who killed one of his men and captured another. Bartolomé Acero is the man who burned the registry office of Lugarnoble and carried away with him as hostages the alcalde and two of the principal landowners."

"Complete tranquillity reigns in Orbajosa, according to a letter which we have before us, and no one there thinks of anything but cultivating the garlic-fields, which promise to yield a magnificent crop. The neighboring districts, however, are infested with guerillas, but the Batalla brigade will make short work of these."

Orbajosa was, in fact, tranquil. The Aceros, that warlike dynasty, worthy, in the opinion of some, of figuring in the "Romancero," had taken possession of the neighboring province; but the insurrection was not spreading within the limits of the episcopal city. It might be supposed that modern culture had at last triumphed in its struggle with the turbulent habits of the great city of disorder, and that the latter was tasting the delights of a lasting peace. So true is this that Cabulluco himself, one of the most important figures of the historic rebellion of Orbajosa, said frankly to everyone that he did not wish to quarrel with the Government nor involve himself in a business which might cost him dear.

Whatever may be said to the contrary, the impetuous nature of Ramos had quieted down with years, and the fiery temper which he had received with life from the ancestral Caballucos, the most valiant race of warriors that had ever desolated the earth, had grown cooler. It is also related that in those days the new governor of the province held a conference with this important personage, and received from his lips the most solemn assurances that he would contribute as far as in him lay to the tranquillity of the country, and would avoid doing anything that might give rise to disturbances. Reliable witnesses declare that he was to be seen in friendly companionship with the soldiers, hobnobbing with this sergeant or the other in the tavern, and it was even said that an important position in the town-hall of the capital of the province was to be given him. How difficult it is for the historian who tries to be impartial to arrive at the exact truth in regard to the sentiments and opinions of the illustrious personages who have filled the world with their fame! He does not know what to hold by, and the absence of authentic records often gives rise to lamentable mistakes. Considering events of such transcendent importance as that of the 18th Brumaire, the sack of Rome by Bourbon, or the destruction of Jerusalem—where is the psychologist or the historian who would be able to determine what were the thoughts which preceded or followed them in the minds of Bonaparte, of Charles V, and of Titus? Ours is an immense responsibility. To discharge it in part we will report words, phrases, and even discourses of the Orbajosan emperor himself; and in this way everyone will be able to form the opinion which may seem to him most correct.

It is beyond a doubt that Cristobal Ramos left his house just after dark, crossed the Calle del Condestable, and, seeing three countrymen mounted on powerful mules coming toward him, asked them where they were going, to which they answered that they were going to Señora Doña Perfecta's house to take her some of the first fruits of their gardens and a part of the rent that had fallen due. They were Señor Paso Largo, a young man named Frasquito Gonzalez, and a third, a man of medium stature and robust make, who was called Vejarruco, although his real name was José Esteban Romero. Caballuco turned back, tempted by the agreeable society of these persons, who were old and intimate friends of his, and accompanied them to Doña Perfecta's house. This took place, according to the most reliable accounts, at nightfall, and two days after the day on which Doña Perfecta and Pinzon held the conversation which those who have read the preceding chapter will have seen recorded there. The great Ramos stopped for a moment to give Librada certain messages of trifling importance, which a neighbor had confided to his good memory, and when he entered the dining-room he found the three beforementioned countrymen and Señor Licurgo, who by a singular coincidence was also there, conversing about domestic matters and the crops. The Señora was in a detestable humor; she found fault with everything, and scolded them harshly for the drought of the heavens and the barrenness of the earth, pheomena for which they, poor men! were in no wise to blame. The Penitentiary was also present. When Caballuco entered, the good canon saluted him affectionately and motioned him to a seat beside himself.

"Here is the individual," said the mistress of the house disdainfully. "It seems impossible that a man of such little account should be so much talked about. Tell me, Caballuco, is it true that one of the soldiers slapped you on the face this morning?"

"Me! me!" said the Centaur, rising indignantly, as if he had received the grossest insult.

"That is what they say," said Doña Perfecta. "Is it not true? I believed it; for anyone who thinks so little of himself—they might spit in your face and you would think yourself honored with the saliva of the soldiers."

"Señora!" vociferated Ramos with energy, "saving the respect which I owe you, who are my mother, my mistress, my queen—saving the respect, I say, which I owe to the person who has given me all that I possess—saving the respect—"

"Well? One would think you were going to say something."

"I say then, that saving the respect, that about the slap is a slander," he ended, expressing himself with extraordinary difficulty. "My affairs are in everyone's mouth—whether I come in or whether I go out, where I am going and where I have come from—and why? All because they want to make me a tool to raise the country. Pedro is contented in his own house, ladies and gentlemen. The troops have come? Bad! but what are we going to do about it? The alcalde and the secretary and the judge have been removed from office? Very bad! I wish the very stones of Orbajosa might rise up against them; but I have given my word to the governor, and up to the present—"

He scratched his head, gathered his gloomy brows in a frown, and with ever-increasing difficulty of speech continued:

"I may be brutal, disagreeable, ignorant, quarrelsome, obstinate, and everything else you choose, but in honor I yield to no one."

"What a pity of the Cid Campeador!" said Doña Perfecta contemptuously. "Don't you agree with me, Señor Penitentiary, that there is not a single man left in Orbajosa who has any shame in him?"

"That is a serious view to take of the case," responded the capitular, without looking at his friend, or removing from his chin the hand on which he rested his thoughtful face; "but I think this neighborhood has accepted with excessive submission the heavy yoke of militarism."

Licurgo and the three countrymen laughed boisterously.

"When the soldiers and the new authorities," said Doña Perfecta, "have taken from us our last real, when the town has been disgraced, we will send all the valiant men of Orbajosa in a glass case to Madrid to be put in the museum there or exhibited in the streets."

"Long life to the mistress!" cried the man called Vejarruco demonstratively. "What she says is like gold. It won't be said on my account that there are no brave men here, for if I am not with the Aceros it is only because I have a wife and three children, and if anything was to happen—if it wasn't for that—"

"But haven't you given your word to the governor, too?" said Doña Perfecta.

"To the governor?" cried the man named Frasquito Gonzalez. "There is not in the whole country a scoundrel who better deserves a bullet. Governor and Government, they are all of a piece. Last Sunday the priest said so many rousing things in his sermon about the heresies and the profanities of the people of Madrid—oh! it was worth while hearing him! Finally, he shouted out in the pulpit that religion had no longer any defenders."

"Here is the great Cristobal Ramos!" said Doña Perfecta, clapping the Centaur on the back. "He mounts his horse and rides about in the Plaza and up and down the high-road to attract the attention of the soldiers; when they see him they are terrified at the fierce appearance of the hero, and they all run away, half-dead with fright."

Doña Perfecta ended with an exaggerated laugh, which the profound silence of her hearers made still more irritating. Caballuco was pale.

"Señor Paso Largo," continued the lady, becoming serious, "when you go home tonight, send me your son Bartolomé to stay here. I need to have brave people in the house; and even with that it may very well happen that, some fine morning, my daughter and myself will be found murdered in our beds."

"Señora!" exclaimed everyone.

"Señora!" cried Caballuco, rising to his feet, "is that a jest, or what is it?"

"Señor Vejarruco, Señor Paso Largo," continued Doña Perfecta, without looking at the bravo of the place, "I am not safe in my own house. No one in Orbajosa is, and least of all, I. I live with my heart in my mouth. I cannot close my eyes in the whole night."

"But who, who would dare—"

"Come," exclaimed Licurgo with fire, "I, old and sick as I am, would be capable of fighting the whole Spanish army if a hair of the mistress' head should be touched!"

"Señor Caballuco," said Frasquito Gonzalez, "will be enough and more than enough."

"Oh, no," responded Dona Perfecta, with cruel sarcasm, "don't you see that Ramos has given his word to the governor?"

Caballuco sat down again, and, crossing one leg ever the other, clasped his hands on them.

"A coward will be enough for me," continued the mistress of the house implacably, "provided he has not given his word to anyone. Perhaps I may come to see my house assaulted, my darling daughter torn from my arms, myself trampled under foot and insulted in the vilest manner—"

She was unable to continue. Her voice died away in her throat, and she burst into tears.

"Señora, for Heaven's sake calm yourself! Come, there is no cause yet!" said Don Inocencio hastily, and manifesting the greatest distress in his voice and his countenance. "Besides, we must have a little resignation and bear patiently the calamities which God sends us."

"But who, señora, who would dare to commit such outrages?" asked one of the four countrymen. "Orbajosa would rise as one man to defend the mistress."

"But who, who would do it?" they all repeated.

"There, don't trouble yourselves asking useless questions," said the Penitentiary officiously. "You may go."

"No, no, let them stay," said Doña Perfecta quickly, drying her tears. "The company of my loyal servants is a great consolation to me."

"May my race be accursed!" said Uncle Licurgo, striking his knee with his clenched hand, "if all this mess is not the work of the mistress' own nephew."

"Of Don Juan Rey's son?"

"From the moment I first set eyes on him at the station at Villahorrenda, and he spoke to me with his honeyed voice and his mincing manners," declared Licurgo, "I thought him a great—I will not say what, through respect for the mistress. But I knew him—I put my mark upon him from that moment, and I make no mistakes. A thread shows what the ball is, as the saying goes; a sample tells what the cloth is, and a claw what the lion is."

"Let no one speak ill of that unhappy young man in my presence," said Señora de Polentinos severely. "No matter how great his faults may be, charity forbids our speaking of them and giving them publicity."

"But charity," said Don Inocencio, with some energy, "does not forbid us protecting ourselves against the wicked, and that is what the question is. Since character and courage have sunk so low in unhappy Orbajosa; since our town appears disposed to hold up its face to be spat upon by half a dozen soldiers and a corporal, let us find protection in union among ourselves."

"I will protect myself in whatever way I can," said Doña Perfecta resignedly, clasping her hands. "God's will be done!"

"Such a stir about nothing! By the Lord! In this house they are all afraid of their shadows," exclaimed Caballuco, half seriously, half jestingly. "One would think this Don Pepito was a legion of devils. Don't be frightened, señora. My little nephew Juan, who is thirteen, will guard the house, and we shall see, nephew for nephew, which is the best man."

"We all know already what your boasting and bragging signify," replied Doña Perfecta. "Poor Ramos! You want to pretend to be very brave when we have already had proof that you are not worth anything."

Ramos turned slightly pale, while he fixed on Doña Perfecta a strange look in which terror and respect were blended.

"Yes, man; don't look at me in that way. You know already that I am not afraid of bugaboos. Do you want me to speak plainly to you now? Well, you are a coward."

Ramos, moving about restlessly in his chair, like one who is troubled with the itch, seemed greatly disturbed. His nostrils expelled and drew in the air, like those of a horse. Within that massive frame a storm of rage and fury, roaring and destroying, struggled to escape. After stammering a few words and muttering others under his breath, he rose to his feet and bellowed:

"I will cut off the head of Señor Rey!"

"What folly! You are as brutal as you are cowardly," said Doña Perfecta, turning pale. "Why do you talk about killing? I want no one killed, much less my nephew—a person whom I love, in spite of his wickedness."

"A homicide! What an atrocity!" exclaimed Doñ Inocencio, scandalized. "The man is mad!"

"To kill! The very idea of killing a man horrifies me, Caballuco," said Doña Perfecta, closing her mild eyes. "Poor man! Ever since you have been wanting to show your bravery, you have been howling like a ravening wolf. Go away, Ramos; you terrify me."

"Doesn't the mistress say she is afraid? Doesn't she say that they will attack the house; that they will carry off the young lady?"

"Yes, I fear so."

"And one man is going to do that," said Ramos contemptuously, sitting down again. "Don Pepe Poquita Cosa, with his mathematics, is going to do that. I did wrong in saying I would slit his throat. A doll of that kind one takes by the ear and ducks in the river."

"Yes, laugh now, you fool! It is not my nephew alone who is going to commit the outrages you have mentioned and which I fear; if it were he alone I should not fear him. I would tell Librada to stand at the door with a broom—and that would be sufficient. It is not he alone, no!"

"Who then?"

"Pretend you don't understand! Don't you know that my nephew and the brigadier who commands that accursed troop have been confabulating?"

"Confabulating!" repeated Caballuco, as if puzzled by the word.

"That they are bosom friends," said Licurgo. "Confabulate means to be like bosom friends. I had my suspicions already of what the mistress says."

"It all amounts to this—that the brigadier and the officers are hand and glove with Don José, and what he wants those brave soldiers want; and those brave soldiers will commit all kinds of outrages and atrocities, because that is their trade."

"And we have no alcalde to protect us."

"Nor judge."

"Nor governor. That is to say that we are at the mercy of that infamous rabble."

"Yesterday," said Vejarruco, "some soldiers enticed away Uncle Julian's youngest daughter, and the poor thing was afraid to go back home; they found her standing barefooted beside the old fountain, crying and picking up the pieces of her broken jar."

"Poor Don Gregorio Palomeque, the notary of Naharilla Alta!" said Frasquito. "Those rascals robbed him of all the money he had in his house. And all the brigadier said, when he was told about it, was it was a lie."

"Tyrants! greater tyrants were never born," said the other. "When I say that it is through punctilio that I am not with the Aceros!"

"And what news is there of Francisco Acero?" asked Doña Perfecta gently. "I should be sorry if any mischance were to happen to him. Tell me, Don Inocencio, was not Francisco Acero born in Orbajosa?"

"No; he and his brother are from Villajuan."

"I am sorry for it, for Orbajosa's sake," said Doña Perfecta. "This poor city has fallen into misfortune. Do you know if Francisco Acero gave his word to the governor not to trouble the poor soldiers in their abductions, in their impious deeds, in their sacrilegious acts, in their villanies?"

Caballuco sprang from his chair. He felt himself now not stung, but cut to the quick by a cruel stroke, like that of a sabre. With his face burning and his eyes flashing fire he cried:

"I gave my word to the governor because the governor told me that they had come for a good purpose."

"Barbarian, don't shout! Speak like other people, and we will listen to you."

"I promised that neither I nor any of my friends would raise guerillas in the neighborhood of Orbajosa. To those who wanted to take up arms because they were itching to fight I said: 'Go to the Aceros, for here we won't stir.' But I have a good many honest men, yes, señora; and true men, yes, señora; and valiant men, yes, señora; scattered about in the hamlets and villages and in the suburbs and the mountains, each in his own house, eh? And so soon as I say a quarter of a word to them, eh? they will be taking down their guns, eh? and setting out on horseback or on foot, for whatever place I tell them. And don't keep harping on words, for if I gave my word it was because I don't wish to fight; and if I want guerillas there will be guerillas; and if I don't there won't, for I am who I am, the same man that I always was, as everyone knows very well. And I say again don't keep harping on words, eh? and don't let people say one thing to me when they mean another, eh? and if people want me to fight, let them say so plainly, eh? for that is what God has given us tongues for, to say this thing or that. The mistress knows very well who I am, as I know that I owe to her the shirt on my back, and the bread I eat today, and the first pea I sucked after I was weaned, and the coffin in which my father was buried when he died, and the medicines and the doctor that cured me when I was sick; and the mistress knows very well that if she says to me, 'Caballuco, break your head,' I will go there to the corner and dash it against the wall; the mistress knows very well that if she tells me now that it is day, although I see that it is night, I will believe that I am mistaken, and that it is broad day; the mistress knows very well that she and her interests are for me before my own life, and that if a mosquito stings her in my presence, I pardon it, because it is a mosquito; the mistress knows very well that she is dearer to me than all there is besides under the sun. To a man of heart like me one says, 'Caballuco, you stupid fellow, do this or do that.' And let there be an end to sarcasms, and beating about the bush, and preaching one thing and meaning another, and a stab here, and a pinch there."

"There, man, calm yourself," said Doña Perfecta kindly. "You have worked yourself into a heat like those republican orators who came here to preach free religion, free love, and I don't know how many other free things. Let them bring you a glass of water."

Caballuco, twisting his handkerchief into a ball, wiped with it his broad forehead and his neck, which were bathed in perspiration. A glass of water was brought to him and the worthy canon, with a humility that was in perfect keeping with his sacerdotal character, took it from the servant's hand to give it to him himself, and held the plate while he drank. Caballuco gulped down the water noisily.

"Now bring another glass for me, Señora Librada," said Don Inocencio. "I have a little fire inside me too."

XXII

"Desperta!"

With regard to the guerillas," said Doña Perfecta, when they had finished drinking, "all I will say is—do as your conscience dictates to you."

"I know nothing about dictations," cried Ramos. "I will do whatever the mistress pleases!"

"I can give you no advice on so important a matter," answered Doña Perfecta with the cautiousness and moderation which so well became her. "This is a very serious business, and I can give you no advice about it."

"But your opinion—"

"My opinion is that you should open your eyes and see, that you should open your ears and hear. Consult your own heart—I will grant that you have a great heart. Consult that judge, that wise counsellor, and do as it bids you."

Caballuco reflected; he meditated as much as a sword can meditate.

"We counted ourselves yesterday in Naharilla Alta," said Vejarruco, "and we were thirteen—ready for any little undertaking. But as we were afraid the mistress might be vexed, we did nothing. It is time now for the shearing."

"Don't mind about the shearing," said Doña Perfecta. "There will be time enough for it. It won't be left undone for that."

"My two boys quarrelled with each other yesterday," said Licurgo, "because one of them wanted to join Francisco Acero and the other didn't. 'Easy, boys, easy,' I said to them; 'all in good time. Wait; we know how to fight here as well as they do anywhere else.'"

"Last night," said Uncle Paso Largo, "Roque Pelosmalos told me that the moment Señor Ramos said half a word they would all be ready, with their arms in their hands. What a pity that the two Burguillos brothers went to work in the fields in Lugarnoble!"

"Go for them you," said the mistress quickly. "Señor Lucas, do you provide Uncle Paso Largo with a horse."

"And if the mistress tells me to do so, and Señor Ramos agrees," said Frasquito Gonzalez, "I will go to Villahorrenda to see if Robustiano, the forester, and his brother Pedro will also—"

BENITO PÉREZ GALDÓS

"I think that is a good idea. Robustiano will not venture to come to Orbajosa, because he owes me a trifle. You can tell him that I forgive him the six dollars and a half. These poor people who sacrifice themselves so generously for a noble idea are satisfied with so little. Is it not so, Señor Don Inocencio?"

"Our good Ramos here tells me," answered the canon, "that his friends are displeased with him for his lukewarmness; but that, as soon as they see that he has decided, they will all put the cartridge-box in their belts."

"What, have you decided to take to the roads?" said the mistress. "I have not advised you to do any such thing, and if you do it, it is of your own free-will. Neither has Señor Don Inocencio said a word to you to that effect. But if that is your decision, you have no doubt strong reasons for coming to it. Tell me, Cristobal, will you have some supper? Will you take something—speak frankly."

"As far as my advising Señor Ramos to take the field is concerned," said Don Inocencio, looking over his spectacles, "Doña Perfecta is quite right. I, as an ecclesiastic, could advise nothing of the kind. I know that some priests do so, and even themselves take up arms; but that seems to me improper, very improper, and I for one will not follow their example. I carry my scrupulosity so far as not to say a word to Señor Ramos about the delicate question of his taking up arms. I know that Orbajosa desires it; I know that all the inhabitants of this noble city would bless him for it; I know that deeds are going to be done here worthy of being recorded in history; but notwithstanding, let me be allowed to maintain a discreet silence."

"Very well said," said Doña Perfecta. "I don't approve of ecclesiastics taking any part in such matters. That is the way an enlightened priest ought to act. Of course we know that on serious and solemn occasions, as when our country and our faith are in danger, for instance, it is within the province of an ecclesiastic to incite men to the conflict and even to take a part in it. Since God himself has taken part in celebrated battles, under the form of angels and saints, his ministers may very well do so also. During the wars against the infidels how many bishops headed the Castilian troops!"

"A great many, and some of them were illustrious warriors. But these times are not like those, señora. It is true that, if we examine the matter closely, the faith is in greater danger now than it was then. For what do the troops that occupy our city and the surrounding villages represent? What do they represent? Are they anything else but the vile instruments of which the atheists and Protestants who infest Madrid make use for their perfidious conquests and the extermination of the faith? In that centre of corruption, of scandal, of irreligion and unbelief, a few malignant men, bought by foreign gold, occupy themselves in destroying in our Spain the deeds of faith. Why, what do you suppose? They allow us to say mass and you to hear it through a remnant of consideration, for shame's sake—but, the day least expected—For my part, I am tranquil. I am not a man to disturb myself about any worldly and temporal interest. Doña Perfecta is well aware of that; all who know me are aware of it. My mind is at rest, and the triumph of the wicked does not terrify me. I know well that terrible days are in store for us; that all of us who wear the sacerdotal garb have our lives hanging by a hair, for Spain, doubt it not, will witness scenes like those of the French Revolution, in which thousands of pious ecclesiastics perished in a single day. But I am not troubled. When the hour to kill strikes, I will present my neck. I have lived long enough. Of what use am I? None, none!"

"May I be devoured by dogs," exclaimed Vejarruco, shaking his fist, which had all the hardness and the strength of a hammer, "if we do not soon make an end of that thievish rabble!"

"They say that next week they will begin to pull down the cathedral," observed Frasquito.

"I suppose they will pull it down with pickaxes and hammers," said the canon, smiling. "There are artificers who, without those implements, can build more rapidly than they can pull down. You all know that, according to holy tradition, our beautiful chapel of the Sagrario was pulled down by the Moors in a month, and immediately afterward rebuilt by the angels in a single night. Let them pull it down; let them pull it down!"

"In Madrid, as the curate of Naharilla told us the other night," said Vejarruco, "there are so few churches left standing that some of the priests say mass in the middle of the street, and as they are beaten and insulted and spat upon, there are many who don't wish to say it."

"Fortunately here, my children," observed Don Inocencio, "we have not yet had scenes of that nature. Why? Because they know what kind of people you are; because they have heard of your ardent piety and your valor. I don't envy the first ones who lay hands on our priests and our religion. Of course it is not necessary to say that, if they are not stopped

BENITO PÉREZ GALDÓS

in time, they will commit atrocities. Poor Spain, so holy and so meek and so good! Who would have believed she would ever arrive at such extremities! But I maintain that impiety will not triumph, no. There are courageous people still; there are people still like those of old. Am I not right, Señor Ramos?"

"Yes, señor, that there are," answered the latter.

"I have a blind faith in the triumph of the law of God. Someone must stand up in defence of it. If not one, it will be another. The palm of victory, and with it eternal glory, someone must bear. The wicked will perish, if not today, tomorrow. That which goes against the law of God will fall irremediably. Let it be in this manner or in that, fall it must. Neither its sophistries, nor its evasions, nor its artifices will save it. The hand of God is raised against it and will infallibly strike it. Let us pity them and desire their repentance. As for you, my children, do not expect that I shall say a word to you about the step which you are no doubt going to take. I know that you are good; I know that your generous determination and the noble end which you have in view will wash away from you all stain of the sin of shedding blood. I know that God will bless you; that your victory, the same as your death, will exalt you in the eyes of men and in the eyes of God. I know that you deserve palms and glory and all sorts of honors; but in spite of this, my children, my lips will not incite you to the combat. They have never done it, and they will not do it now. Act according to the impulse of your own noble hearts. If they bid you to remain in your houses, remain in them; if they bid you to leave them—why, then, leave them. I will resign myself to be a martyr and to bow my neck to the executioner, if that vile army remains here. But if a noble and ardent and pious impulse of the sons of Orbajosa contributes to the great work of the extirpation of our country's ills, I shall hold myself the happiest of men, solely in being your fellow-townsman; and all my life of study, of penitence, of resignation, will seem to me less meritorious, less deserving of heaven, than a single one of your heroic days."

"Impossible to say more or to say it better!" exclaimed Doña Perfecta, in a burst of enthusiasm.

Caballuco had leaned forward in his chair and was resting his elbows on his knees; when the canon ended he took his hand and kissed it with fervor.

"A better man was never born," said Uncle Licurgo, wiping, or pretending to wipe away a tear.

"Long life to the Señor Penitentiary!" cried Frasquito Gonzalez, rising to his feet and throwing his cap up to the ceiling.

"Silence!" said Doña Perfecta. "Sit down, Frasquito! You are one of those with whom it is always much cry and little wool."

"Blessed be God who gave you that eloquent tongue!" exclaimed Cristobal, inflamed with admiration. "What a pair I have before me! While these two live what need is there of anyone else? All the people in Spain ought to be like them. But how could that be, when there is nothing in it but roguery! In Madrid, which is the capital where the laws and the mandarins come from, everything is robbery and cheating. Poor religion, what a state they have brought it to! There is nothing to be seen but crimes. Señor Don Inocencio, Señora Doña Perfecta, by my father's soul, by the soul of my grandfather, by the salvation of my own soul, I swear that I wish to die!"

"To die!"

"That I wish those rascally dogs may kill me, and I say that I wish they may kill me, because I cannot cut them in quarters. I am very little."

"Ramos, you are great," said Doña Perfecta solemnly.

"Great? Great? Very great, as far as my courage is concerned; but have I fortresses, have I cavalry, have I artillery?"

"That is a thing, Ramos," said Doña Perfecta, smiling, "about which I would not concern myself. Has not the enemy what you lack?"

"Yes."

"Take it from him, then."

"We will take it from him, yes, señora. When I say that we will take it from him—"

"My dear Ramos," exclaimed Don Inocencio, "yours is an enviable position. To distinguish yourself, to raise yourself above the base multitude, to put yourself on an equality with the greatest heroes of the earth, to be able to say that the hand of God guides your hand—oh, what grandeur and honor! My friend, this is not flattery. What dignity, what nobleness, what magnanimity! No; men of such a temper cannot die. The Lord goes with them, and the bullet and the steel of the enemy are arrested in their course; they do not dare—how should they dare—to touch them, coming from the musket and the hand of heretics? Dear Caballuco, seeing you, seeing your bravery and your nobility, there come to my mind involuntarily the verses of that ballad on the conquest of the Empire of Trebizond:

> *"'Came the valiant Roland*
> *Armed at every point,*
> *On his war-horse mounted,*
> *The gallant Briador;*
> *His good sword Durlindana*
> *Girded to his side,*
> *Couched for the attack his lance,*
> *On his arm his buckler stout,*
> *Through his helmet's visor*
> *Flashing fire he came;*
> *Quivering like a slender reed*
> *Shaken by the wind his lance,*
> *And all the host united*
> *Defying haughtily.'"*

"Very good," exclaimed Licurgo, clapping his hands. "And I say like Don Renialdos:

> *"'Let none the wrath of Don Renialdos*
> *Dare brave and hope to escape unscathed;*
> *For he who seeks with him a quarrel,*
> *Shall pay so dearly for his rashness*
> *That he, and all his cause who champion,*
> *Shall at my hand or meet destruction*
> *Or chastisement severe shall suffer.'"*

"Ramos, you will take some supper, you will eat something; won't you?" said the mistress of the house.

"Nothing, nothing"; answered the Centaur. "Or if you give me anything, let it be a plate of gunpowder."

And bursting into a boisterous laugh, he walked up and down the room several times, attentively observed by everyone; then, stopping beside the group, he looked fixedly at Doña Perfecta and thundered forth these words:

"I say that there is nothing more to be said. Long live Orbajosa! death to Madrid!"

And he brought his hand down on the table with such violence that the floor shook.

"What a valiant spirit!" said Don Inocencio.

"What a fist you have!"

Everyone was looking at the table, which had been split in two by the blow.

Then they looked at the never-enough-to-be admired Renialdos or Caballuco. Undoubtedly there was in his handsome countenance, in his green eyes animated by a strange, feline glow, in his black hair, in his herculean frame, a certain expression and air of grandeur—a trace, or rather a memory, of the grand races that dominated the world. But his general aspect was one of pitiable degeneration, and it was difficult to discover the noble and heroic filiation in the brutality of the present. He resembled Don Cayetano's great men as the mule resembles the horse.

XXIII

Mystery

The conference lasted for sometime longer, but we omit what followed as not being necessary to a clear understanding of our story. At last they separated, Señor Don Inocencio remaining to the last, as usual. Before the canon and Doña Perfecta had had time to exchange a word, an elderly woman, Doña Perfecta's confidential servant and her right hand, entered the dining-room, and her mistress, seeing that she looked disturbed and anxious, was at once filled with disquietude, suspecting that something wrong was going on in the house.

"I can't find the señorita anywhere," said the servant, in answer to her mistress' questions.

"Good Heavens—Rosario! Where is my daughter?"

"Virgin of Succor protect us!" cried the Penitentiary, taking up his hat and preparing to hurry out with Doña Perfecta.

"Search for her well. But was she not with you in her room?"

"Yes, señora," answered the old woman, trembling, "but the devil tempted me, and I fell asleep."

"A curse upon your sleep! What is this? Rosario, Rosario! Librada!"

They went upstairs and came down again, they went up a second time and came down again; carrying a light and looking carefully in all the rooms. At last the voice of the Penitentiary was heard saying joyfully from the stairs:

"Here she is, here she is! She has been found."

A moment later mother and daughter were standing face to face in the hall.

"Where were you?" asked Doña Perfecta, in a severe voice, scrutinizing her daughter's face closely.

"In the garden," answered the girl, more dead than alive.

"In the garden at this hour? Rosario!"

"I was warm, I went to the window, my handkerchief dropped out, and I came down stairs for it!"

"Why didn't you ask Librada to get it for you? Librada! Where is that girl? Has she fallen asleep too?"

Librada at last made her appearance. Her pale face revealed the consternation and the apprehension of the delinquent.

"What is this? Where were you?" asked her mistress, with terrible anger.

"Why, señora, I came down stairs to get the clothes out of the front room—and I fell asleep."

"Everyone here seems to have fallen asleep tonight. Some of you, I faney, will not sleep in my house tomorrow night. Rosario, you may go."

Comprehending that it was necessary to act with promptness and energy, Doña Perfecta and the canon began their investigations without delay. Questions, threats, entreaties, promises, were skilfully employed to discover the truth regarding what had happened. Not even the shadow of guilt was found to attach to the old servant; but Librada confessed frankly between tears and sighs all her delinquencies, which we will sum up as follows:

Shortly after his arrival in the house Señor Pinzon had begun to cast loving glances at Señorita Rosario. He had given money to Librada, according to what the latter said, to carry messages and love-letters to her. The young lady had not seemed angry, but, on the contrary, pleased, and several days had passed in this manner. Finally, the servant declared that Rosario and Señor Pinzon had agreed to meet and talk with each other on this night at the window of the room of the latter, which opened on the garden. They had confided their design to the maid, who promised to favor it, in consideration of a sum which was at once given her. It had been agreed that Señor Pinzon was to leave the house at his usual hour and return to it secretly at nine o'clock, go to his room, and leave it and the house again, clandestinely also, a little later, to return, without concealment, at his usual late hour. In this way no suspicion would fall upon him. Librada had waited for Pinzon, who had entered the house closely enveloped in his cloak, without speaking a word. He had gone to his room at the same moment in which the young lady descended to the garden. During the interview, at which she was not present, Librada had remained on guard in the hall to warn Pinzon, if any danger should threaten; and at the end of an hour the latter had left the house enveloped in his cloak, as before, and without speaking a word. When the confession was ended Don Inocencio said to the wretched girl:

"Are you sure that the person who came into and went out of the house was Señor Pinzon?"

The culprit answered nothing, but her features expressed the utmost perplexity.

Her mistress turned green with anger.

"Did you see his face?"

"But who else could it be but he?" answered the maid. "I am certain that it was he. He went straight to his room—he knew the way to it perfectly well."

"It is strange," said the canon. "Living in the house there was no need for him to use such mystery. He might have pretended illness and remained in the house. Does it not seem so to you, señora?"

"Librada," exclaimed the latter, in a paroxysm of anger, "I vow that you shall go to prison."

And clasping her hands, she dug the nails of the one into the other with such force as almost to draw blood.

"Señor Don Inocencio," she exclaimed, "let us die—there is no remedy but to die."

Then she burst into a fit of inconsolable weeping.

"Courage, señora," said the priest, in a moved voice. "Courage—now it is necessary to be very brave. This requires calmness and a great deal of courage."

"Mine is immense," said Señora de Polentinos, in the midst of her sobs.

"Mine is very small," said the canon; "but we shall see, we shall see."

XXIV

The Confession

Meanwhile Rosario—with her heart torn and bleeding, unable to shed tears, unable to be at peace or rest, transpierced by grief as by a sharp sword, with her thoughts passing swiftly from the world to God and from God to the world, bewildered and half-crazed, her hands clasped, her bare feet resting on the floor—was kneeling, late in the evening, in her own room, beside her bed, on the edge of which she rested her burning forehead, in darkness, in solitude, and in silence. She was careful not to make the slightest noise, in order not to attract the attention of her mother, who was asleep, or seemed to be asleep, in the adjoining room. She lifted up her distracted thoughts to Heaven in this form:

"Lord, my God, why is it that before I did not know how to lie, and now I know? Why did I not know before how to deceive, and now I deceive? Am I a vile woman? Is this that I feel, is this that is happening to me, a fall from which there can be no arising? Have I ceased to be virtuous and good? I do not recognize myself. Is it I or is it someone else who is in this place? How many terrible things in a few days! How many different sensations! My heart is consumed with all it has felt! Lord, my God, dost thou hear my voice, or am I condemned to pray eternally without being heard? I am good, nothing will convince me that I am not good. To love, to love boundlessly, is that wickedness? But no—it is no illusion, no error—I am worse than the worst woman on earth. A great serpent is within me, and has fastened his poisonous fangs in my heart. What is this that I feel? My God, why dost thou not kill me? Why dost thou not plunge me forever into the depths of hell? It is frightful, but I confess it, I confess it to God, who hears me, and I will confess it to the priest—I hate my mother. Why is this? I cannot explain it to myself. He has not said a word to me against my mother. I do not know how this is come to pass. How wicked I am! The demons have taken possession of me. Lord, come to my help, for with my own strength alone I cannot vanquish myself. A terrible impulse urges me to leave this house. I wish to escape, to fly from it. If he does not take me, I will drag myself after him through the streets. What divine joy is this

BENITO PÉREZ GALDÓS

that mingles in my breast with so cruel a grief? Lord God, my Father, illumine me. I desire only to love. I was not born for this hatred that is consuming me. I was not born to deceive, to lie, to cheat. Tomorrow I will go out into the streets and cry aloud to all the passersby: 'I love! I hate!' My heart will relieve itself in this way. What happiness it would be to be able to reconcile everything, to love and respect everyone! May the Most Holy Virgin protect me. Again that terrible idea! I don't wish to think it, and I think it. Ah! I cannot deceive myself in regard to this. I can neither destroy it nor diminish it—but I can confess it; and I confess it, saying to thee: 'Lord, I hate my mother!'"

At last she fell into a doze. In her uneasy sleep her imagination reproduced in her mind all she had done that night, distorting it, without altering it in substance. She heard again the clock of the cathedral striking nine; she saw with joy the old servant fall into a peaceful sleep; and she left the room very slowly, in order to make no noise; she descended the stairs softly, step by step and on tiptoe, in order to avoid making the slightest sound. She went into the garden, going around through the servants' quarters and the kitchen; in the garden she paused for a moment to look up at the sky, which was dark and studded with stars. The wind was hushed. Not a breath disturbed the profound stillness of the night. It seemed to maintain a fixed and silent attention—the attention of eyes that look without winking and ears that listen attentively, awaiting a great event. The night was watching.

She then approached the glass door of the dining-room and looked cautiously through it, from a little distance, fearing that those within might perceive her. By the light of the dining-room lamp she saw her mother sitting with her back toward her. The Penitentiary was on her right, and his profile seemed to undergo a strange transformation; his nose grew larger and larger, seeming like the beak of some fabulous bird; and his whole face became a black silhouette with angles here and there, sharp, derisive, irritating. In front of him sat Caballuco, who resembled a dragon rather than a man. Rosario could see his green eyes, like two lanterns of convex glass. This glow, and the imposing figure of the animal, inspired her with fear. Uncle Licurgo and the other three men appeared to her imagination like grotesque little figures. She had seen somewhere, doubtless in some of the clay figures at the fairs, that foolish smile, those coarse faces, that stupid look. The dragon moved his arms which, instead of gesticulating, turned round, like the arms of a windmill, and the green globes, like the lights of a pharmacy, moved from side to side. His glance was blinding. The conversation appeared to be interesting. The Penitentiary was flapping his wings. He was a presumptuous bird, who tried to fly and could not. His beak lengthened itself, twisting round and round. His feathers stood out, as if with rage; and then, collecting himself and becoming pacified, he hid his bald head under his wings. Then the little clay figures began to move, wishing to be persons, and Frasquito Gonzalez was trying to pass for a man.

Rosario felt an inexplicable terror, witnessing this friendly conference. She went away from the door and advanced, step by step, looking around her to see if she was observed. Although she saw no one, she fancied that a million eyes were fastened upon her. But suddenly her fears and her shame were dispelled. At the window of the room occupied by Señor Pinzon appeared a man, dressed in blue; the buttons on his coat shone like rows of little lights: She approached. At the same instant she felt a pair of arms with galloons lift her up as if she were a feather and with a swift movement place her in the room. All was changed. Suddenly a crash was heard, a violent blow that shook the house to its foundations. Neither knew the cause of the noise. They trembled and were silent.

It was the moment in which the dragon had broken the table in the dining-room.

XXV

Unforeseen Events—A Passing Disagreement

The scene changes. We see before us a handsome room, bright, modest, gay, comfortable, and surprisingly clean. A fine matting covers the floor, and the white walls are covered with good prints of saints and some sculptures of doubtful artistic value. The old mahogany of the furniture shines with the polish of many Saturday rubbings, and the altar, on which a magnificent Virgin, dressed in blue and silver, receives domestic worship, is covered with innumerable pretty trifles, half sacred, half profane. There are on it, besides, little pictures in beads, holy-water fonts, a watch-case with an Agnes Dei, a Palm Sunday palm-branch, and not a few odorless artificial flowers. A number of oaken bookshelves contain a rich and choice library, in which Horace, the Epicurean and Sybarite, stands side by side with the tender Virgil, in whose verses we see the heart of the enamored Dido throbbing and melting; Ovid the large-nosed, as sublime as he is obscene and sycophantic, side by side with Martial, the eloquent and witty vagabond; Tibullus the impassioned, with Cicero the grand; the severe Titus Livius with the terrible Tacitus, the scourge of the Cæsars; Lucretius the pantheist; Juvenal, who flayed with his pen; Plautus, who composed the best comedies of antiquity while turning a mill-wheel; Seneca the philosopher, of whom it is said that the noblest act of his life was his death; Quintilian the rhetorician; the immoral Sallust, who speaks so eloquently of virtue; the two Plinys; Suetonius and Varro—in a word, all the Latin letters from the time when they stammered their first word with Livius Andronicus until they exhaled their last sigh with Rutilius.

But while making this unnecessary though rapid enumeration, we have not observed that two women have entered the room. It is very early, but the Orbajosans are early risers. The birds are singing to burst their throats in their cages; the church-bells are ringing for mass, and the goats, going from house to house to be milked, are tinkling their bells gayly.

The two ladies whom we see in the room that we have described have just come from hearing mass. They are dressed in black, and each of them carries in her right hand her little prayer-book, and the rosary twined around her fingers.

"Your uncle cannot delay long now," said one of them. "We left him beginning mass; but he gets through quickly, and by this time he will be in the sacristy, taking off his chasuble. I would have stayed to hear him say mass, but today is a very busy day for me."

"I heard only the prebendary's mass today," said the other, "and he says mass in a twinkling; and I don't think it has done me any good, for I was greatly preoccupied. I could not get the thought of the terrible things that are happening to us out of my head."

"What is to be done? We must only have patience. Let us see what advice your uncle will give us."

"Ah!" exclaimed the other, heaving a deep and pathetic sigh; "I feel my blood on fire."

"God will protect us."

"To think that a person like you should be threatened by a— And he persists in his designs! Last night, Señora Doña Perfecta, I went back to the widow De Cuzco's hotel, as you told me, and asked her for later news. Don Pepito and the brigadier Batalla are always consulting together—ah, my God! consulting about their infernal plans, and emptying bottle after bottle of wine. They are a pair of rakes, a pair of drunkards. No doubt they are plotting some fine piece of villany together. As I take such an interest in you, last night, seeing Don Pepito leaving the hotel while I was there, I followed him—"

"And where did he go?"

"To the Casino; yes, señora, to the Casino," responded the other, with some confusion. "Afterward he went back to his hotel. And how my uncle scolded me because I remained out so late, playing the spy in that way! But I can't help it, and to see a person like you threatened by such dangers makes me wild. For there is no use in talking; I foresee that the day we least expect it those villains will attack the house and carry off Rosarito."

Doña Perfecta, for she it was, bending her eyes on the floor, remained for a long time wrapped in thought. She was pale, and her brows were gathered in a frown. At last she exclaimed:

"Well, I see no way of preventing it!"

"But I see a way," quickly said the other woman, who was the niece of the Penitentiary and Jacinto's mother; "I see a very simple way, that I explained to you, and that you do not like. Ah, señora! you are too good. On occasions like this it is better to be a little less perfect—to lay scruples aside. Why, would that be an offence to God?"

"Maria Remedios," said Doña Perfecta haughtily, "don't talk nonsense."

"Nonsense! You, with all your wisdom, cannot make your nephew do as you wish. What could be simpler than what I propose? Since there is no justice now to protect us, let us do a great act of justice ourselves. Are there not men in your house who are ready for anything? Well, call them and say to them: 'Look, Caballuco, Paso Largo,' or whoever it may be, 'tonight disguise yourself well, so that you may not be recognized; take with you a friend in whom you have confidence, and station yourself at the corner of the Calle de Santa Faz. Wait a while, and when Don José Rey passes through the Calle de la Triperia on his way to the Casino,— for he will certainly go to the Casino, understand me well,—when he is passing you will spring out on him and give him a fright.'"

"Maria Remedios, don't be a fool!" said Doña Perfecta with magisterial dignity.

"Nothing more than a fright, señora; attend well to what I say, a fright. Why! Do you suppose I would advise a crime? Good God! the very idea fills me with horror, and I fancy I can see before my eyes blood and fire! Nothing of the sort, señora. A fright—nothing but a fright, which will make that ruffian understand that we are well protected. He goes alone to the Casino, señora, entirely alone; and there he meets his valiant friends, those of the sabre and the helmet. Imagine that he gets the fright and that he has a few bones broken, in addition—without any serious wounds, of course. Well, in that case, either his courage will fail him and he will leave Orbajosa, or he will be obliged to keep his bed for a fortnight. But they must be told to make the fright a good one. No killing, of course; they must take care of that, but just a good beating."

"Maria," said Doña Perfecta haughtily, "you are incapable of a lofty thought, of a great and saving resolve. What you advise me is an unworthy piece of cowardice."

"Very well, I will be silent. Poor me! what a fool I am!" exclaimed the Penitentiary's niece with humility. "I will keep my follies to console you after you have lost your daughter."

"My daughter! Lose my daughter!" exclaimed Doña Perfecta, with a sudden access of rage. "Only to hear you puts me out of my senses. No, they shall not take her from me! If Rosario does not abhor that ruffian as I wish her to do, she shall abhor him. For a mother's authority must have some weight. We will tear this passion, or rather this caprice, from her heart, as a tender plant is torn out of the ground before it has had time to cast roots. No, this cannot be, Remedios. Come what may, it shall not be! Not even the most infamous means he could employ will avail that madman. Rather than see her my nephew's wife, I would accept any evil that might happen to her, even death!"

"Better dead, better buried and food for worms," affirmed Remedios, clasping her hands as if she were saying a prayer—"than see her in the power of—ah, señora, do not be offended if I say something to you, and that is, that it would be a great weakness to yield merely because Rosarito has had a few secret interviews with that audacious man. The affair of the night before last, as my uncle related it to me, seems to me a vile trick of Don José to obtain his object by means of a scandal. A great many men do that. Ah, Divine Saviour, I don't know how there are women who can look any man in the face unless it be a priest."

"Be silent, be silent!" said Doña Perfecta, with vehemence. "Don't mention the occurrence of the night before last to me. What a horrible affair! Maria Remedios, I understand now how anger can imperil the salvation of a soul. I am burning with rage—unhappy that I am, to see such things and not to be a man! But to speak the truth in regard to the occurrence of the night before last—I still have my doubts. Librada vows and declares that Pinzon was the man who came into the house. My daughter denies everything; my daughter has never told me a lie! I persist in my suspicions. I think that Pinzon is a hypocritical go-between, but nothing more."

"We come back to the same thing—that the author of all the trouble is the blessed mathematician. Ah! my heart did not deceive me when I first saw him. Well, then, señora! resign yourself to see something still more terrible, unless you make up your mind to call Caballuco and say to him, 'Caballuco, I hope that—'"

"The same thing again; what a simpleton you are!"

"Oh, yes! I know I am a great simpleton; but how can I help it if I am not any wiser? I say what comes into my head, without any art."

"What you think of—that silly and vulgar idea of the beating and the fright—is what would occur to anyone. You have not an ounce of brains, Remedios; to solve a serious question you can think of nothing better than a piece of folly like that. I have thought of a means more worthy of noble-minded and well-bred persons. A beating! What stupidity! Besides, I would not on any account have my nephew receive even so much as a scratch by an order of mine. God will send him his punishment through someone of the wonderful ways which he knows how to choose. All we have to do is to work in order that the designs of God may find no obstacle. Maria Remedios, it is necessary in matters of this kind to go directly to the causes of things. But you know nothing about causes—you can see only trifles."

"That may be so," said the priest's niece, with humility. "I wonder why God made me so foolish that I can understand nothing of those sublime ideas!"

"It is necessary to go to the bottom—to the bottom, Remedios. Don't you understand yet?"

"No."

"My nephew is not my nephew, woman; he is blasphemy, sacrilege, atheism, demagogy. Do you know what demagogy is?"

"Something relating to those people who burned Paris with petroleum; and those who pull down the churches and fire on the images. So far I understand very well."

"Well, my nephew is all that! Ah! if he were alone in Orbajosa—but no, child. My nephew, through a series of fatalities, which are the trials, the transitory evils that God permits for our chastisement, is equivalent to an army; is equivalent to the authority of the government; equivalent to the alcalde; equivalent to the judge. My nephew is not my nephew; he is the official nation, Remedios—that second nation composed of the scoundrels who govern in Madrid, and who have made themselves masters of its material strength; of that apparent nation—for the real nation is the one that is silent, that pays and suffers; of that fictitious nation that signs decrees and pronounces discourses and makes a farce of government, and a farce of authority, and a farce of everything. That is what my nephew is today; you must accustom yourself to look under the surface of things. My nephew is the government, the brigadier, the new alcalde, the new judge—for they all protect him, because of the unanimity of their ideas; because they are chips of the same block, birds of a feather. Understand it well; we must defend ourselves against them all, for they are all one, and one is all; we must attack them all together; and not by beating a man as he turns a corner, but as our forefathers attacked the Moors—the Moors, Remedios. Understand this well, child; open your understanding and allow an idea that is not vulgar to enter it—rise above yourself; think lofty thoughts, Remedios!"

Don Inocencio's niece was struck dumb by so much loftiness of soul. She opened her mouth to say something that should be in consonance with so sublime an idea, but she only breathed a sigh.

"Like the Moors," repeated Doña Perfecta. "It is a question of Moors and Christians. And did you suppose that by giving a fright to my nephew all would be ended? How foolish you are! Don't you see that his friends support him? Don't you see that we are at the mercy of that rabble? Don't you see that any little lieutenant can set fire to my house, if he takes it into his head to do so? But don't you know this? Don't you comprehend that it is necessary to go to the bottom of things? Don't you comprehend how vast, how tremendous is the power of my enemy, who is not a man, but a sect? Don't you comprehend that my nephew, as he confronts me today, is not a calamity, but a plague? Against this plague, dear Remedios, we shall have here a battalion sent by God that will annihilate the infernal militia from Madrid. I tell you that this is going be great and glorious."

"If it were at last so!"

"But do you doubt it? Today we shall see terrible things here," said Doña Perfecta, with great impatience. "Today, today! What o'clock is it? Seven? So late, and nothing has happened!"

"Perhaps my uncle has heard something; he is here now, I hear him coming upstairs."

"Thank God!" said Doña Perfecta, rising to receive the Penitentiary. "He will have good news for us."

Don Inocencio entered hastily. His altered countenance showed that his soul, consecrated to religion and to the study of the classics, was not as tranquil as usual.

"Bad news!" he said, laying his hat on a chair and loosening the cords of his cloak.

Doña Perfecta turned pale.

"They are arresting people," added Don Inocencio, lowering his voice, as if there was a soldier hidden under every chair. "They suspect, no doubt, that the people here would not put up with their high-handed measures, and they have gone from house to house, arresting all who have a reputation for bravery."

Doña Perfecta threw herself into an easy chair and clutched its arms convulsively.

"It remains to be seen whether they have allowed themselves to be arrested," observed Remedios.

BENITO PÉREZ GALDÓS

"Many of them have—a great many of them," said Don Inocencio, with an approving look, addressing Doña Perfecta, "have had time to escape, and have gone with arms and horses to Villahorrenda."

"And Ramos?"

"They told me in the cathedral that he is the one they are looking for most eagerly. Oh, my God! to arrest innocent people in that way, who have done nothing yet. Well, I don't know how good Spaniards can have patience under such treatment. Señora Doña Perfecta, when I was telling you about the arrests, I forgot to say that you ought to go home at once."

"Yes, I will go at once. Have those bandits searched my house?"

"It is possible. Señora, we have fallen upon evil days," said Don Inocencio, in solemn and feeling accents. "May God have pity upon us!"

"There are half a dozen well-armed men in my house," responded the lady, greatly agitated. "What iniquity! Would they be capable of wanting to carry them off too?"

"Assuredly Señor Pinzon will not have neglected to denounce them. Señora, I repeat that we have fallen upon evil days. But God will protect the innocent."

"I am going now. Don't fail to stop in at the house."

"Señora, as soon as the lesson is over—though I imagine that with the excitement that there is in the town, all the boys will play truant today— But in any case I will go to the house after class hours. I don't wish you to go out alone, señora. Those vagabond soldiers are strutting about the streets with such insolent airs. Jacinto, Jacinto!"

"It is not necessary. I will go alone."

"Let Jacinto go with you," said the young man's mother. "He must be up by this time."

They heard the hurried footsteps of the little doctor, who was coming down the stairs in the greatest haste. He entered the room with flushed face and panting for breath.

"What is the matter?" asked his uncle.

"In the Troyas' house," said the young man, "in the house of those—those girls—"

"Finish at once!"

"Caballuco is there!"

"Up there? In the house of the Troyas?"

"Yes, señor. He spoke to me from the terrace, and he told me he was afraid they were coming there to arrest him."

"Oh, what a fool! That idiot is going to allow himself to be arrested!" exclaimed Doña Perfecta, tapping the floor impatiently with her foot.

"He wants to come down and let us hide him in the house."

"Here?"

The canon and his niece exchanged a glance.

"Let him come down!" said Doña Perfecta vehemently.

"Here?" repeated Don Inocencio, with a look of ill-humor.

"Here," answered the lady. "I don't know of any house where he would be more secure."

"He can let himself down easily from the window of my room," said Jacinto.

"Well, if it is necessary—"

"Maria Remedios," said Doña Perfecta, "if they take that man, all is lost."

"I am a fool and a simpleton," answered the canon's niece, laying her hand on her breast and stifling the sigh that was doubtless about to escape from it; "but they shall not take him."

Doña Perfecta went out quickly, and shortly afterward the Centaur was making himself comfortable in the arm-chair in which Don Inocencio was accustomed to sit when he was writing his sermons.

We do not know how it reached the ears of Brigadier Batalla, but certain it is that this active soldier had had notice that the Orbajosans had changed their intentions; and on the morning of this day he had ordered the arrest of those whom in our rich insurrectional language we are accustomed to call marked. The great Caballuco escaped by a miracle, taking refuge in the house of the Troyas, but not thinking himself safe there he descended, as we have seen, to the holy and unsuspected mansion of the good canon.

At night the soldiers, established at various points of the town, kept a strict watch on all who came in and went out, but Ramos succeeded in making his escape, cheating or perhaps without cheating the vigilance of the military. This filled the measure of the rage of the Orbajosans, and numbers of people were conspiring in the hamlets near Villahorrenda; meeting at night to disperse in the morning and prepare in this way the arduous business of the insurrection. Ramos scoured the surrounding country, collecting men and arms; and as the flying columns followed the Aceros into the district of Villajuan de Nahara, our chivalrous hero made great progress in a very short time.

At night he ventured boldly into Orbajosa, employing stratagems and perhaps bribery. His popularity and the protection which he received in the town served him, to a certain extent, as a safeguard; and it would not be rash to affirm that the soldiers did not manifest toward this daring leader of the insurrection the same rigor as toward the insignificant men of the place. In Spain, and especially in time of war, which is here always demoralizing, these unworthy considerations toward the great are often seen, while the little are persecuted pitilessly. Favored then by his boldness, by bribery, or by we know not what, Caballuco entered Orbajosa, gained new recruits, and collected arms and money. Either for the greater security of his person or in order to save appearances, he did not set foot in his own house; he entered Doña Perfecta's only for the purpose of treating of important affairs, and he usually supped in the house of some friend, preferring always the respected domicile of some priest, and especially that of Don Inocencio, where he had taken refuge on the fateful morning of the arrests.

Meanwhile Batalla had telegraphed to the Government the information that a plot of the rebels having been discovered its authors had been imprisoned, and the few who had succeeded in escaping had fled in various directions and were being actively pursued by the military.

XXVI

MARIA REMEDIOS

There is nothing more entertaining than to search for the cause of some interesting event which surprises or agitates us, and nothing more satisfactory than to discover it. When, seeing violent passions in open or concealed conflict, and led by the natural intuitive impulse which always accompanies human observation we succeed in discovering the hidden source from which that turbulent river had derived its waters, we experience a sensation very similar to the delight of the explorer or the discoverer of an unknown land.

This delight Providence has now bestowed upon us; for, exploring the hidden recesses of the hearts which beat in this story, we have discovered an event that is assuredly the source of the most important events that we have narrated; a passion which is the first drop of water of the impetuous current whose course we are observing.

Let us go on with our story, then. To do so, let us leave Señora de Polentinos, without concerning ourselves in regard to what may have happened to her on the morning of her conversation with Maria Remedios. Returning to her house, full of anxiety, she found herself obliged to endure the apologies and the civilities of Señor Pinzon, who assured her that while he lived her house should not be searched. Doña Perfecta responded haughtily, without deigning to look at him, for which reason he asked her politely for an explanation of her coldness, to which she replied requesting Señor Pinzon to leave her house, deferring to a future occasion the explanation which she would require from him of his perfidious conduct while in it. Don Cayetano arriving at this moment, words were exchanged between the two gentlemen, as between man and man; but as we are more interested at present in another matter, we will leave the Polentinos and the lieutenant-colonel to settle matters between them as best they can, and proceed to examine the question of the sources above mentioned.

Let us fix our attention on Maria Remedios, an estimable woman, to whom it is indispensably necessary to devote a few words. She was a lady, a real lady—for, notwithstanding her humble origin, the virtues of her uncle, Señor Don Inocencio, also of low origin, but elevated by his learning and his estimable qualities, had shed extraordinary lustre over the whole family.

The love of Remedios for Jacinto was one of the strongest passions of which the maternal heart is capable. She loved him with delirium; her son's welfare was her first earthly consideration; she regarded him as the most perfect type of beauty and talent ever created by God, and to see him happy and great and powerful she would have given her whole life and even a part of the life to come. The maternal sentiment is the only one which, because of its nobility and its sanctity, will admit of exaggeration; the only one which the delirium of passion does not debase. Nevertheless it is a singular phenomenon, frequently observed, that this exaltation of maternal affection, if not accompanied with absolute purity of heart and with perfect uprightness, is apt to become perverted and transformed into a lamentable frenzy, which may lead, like any other ungoverned passion, to great errors and catastrophies.

In Orbajosa Maria Remedios passed for a model of virtue and a model niece—perhaps she was so in reality. She served with affection all who needed her services; she never gave occasion for gossip or for scandal; she never mixed herself up in intrigues. She carried her religion to the extreme of an offensive fanaticism; she practised charity; she managed her uncle's house with the utmost ability; she was well received, admired and kindly treated everywhere, in spite of the almost intolerable annoyance produced by her persistent habit of sighing and speaking always in a complaining voice.

But in Doña Perfecta's house this excellent lady suffered a species of *capitis diminutio*. In times far distant and very bitter for the family of the good Penitentiary, Maria Remedios (since it is the truth, why should it not be told?) had been a laundress in the house of Polentinos. And let it not be supposed that Doña Perfecta looked down upon her on this account—nothing of the kind. She behaved to her without any haughtiness; she felt a real sisterly affection for her; they ate together; they prayed together; they confided their troubles to each other; they aided each other in their charities and in their devotions as well as in domestic matters; but, truth to say, there was always a something, there was always a line, invisible but which could not be crossed, between the improvised lady and the lady by birth and ancestry. Doña Perfecta addressed Maria as "thou," while the latter could never lay aside certain ceremonial forms. Maria Remedios always felt herself so insignificant in the presence of her uncle's friend that her natural humility had acquired through this feeling a strange tinge of sadness. She saw that the good canon was a species of perpetual Aulic councillor in the house; she saw her idolized Jacintillo mingling on terms of almost lover-like familiarity with the young lady, and nevertheless the poor mother and niece visited the house as little as possible. It is to be observed that Maria Remedios' dignity as a lady suffered not a little in Doña Perfecta's house, and this was disagreeable to her; for in this sighing spirit, too, there was, as there is in every living thing, a little pride. To see her son married to Rosarito, to see him rich and powerful; to see him related to Doña Perfecta, to the señora—ah! this was for Maria Remedios earth and heaven, this life and the next, the present and the future, the supreme totality of existence. For years her mind and her heart had been filled by the light of this sweet hope. Because of this hope she was good and she was bad; because of it she was religious and humble, or fierce and daring; because of it she was whatever she was—for without this idea Maria, who was the incarnation of her project, would not exist.

In person, Maria Remedios could not be more insignificant than she was. She was remarkable for a surprising freshness and robustness which made her look much younger than she really was, and she always dressed in mourning, although her widowhood was now of long standing.

Five days had passed since the entrance of Caballuco into the Penitentiary's house. It was evening. Remedios entered her uncle's room with the lighted lamp, which she placed on the table. She then seated herself in front of the old man, who, for a great part of the afternoon, had been sitting motionless and thoughtful in his easy chair. His fingers supported his chin, wrinkling up the brown skin, unshaven for the past three days.

"Did Caballuco say he would come here to supper tonight?" he asked his niece.

"Yes, señor, he will come. It is in a respectable house like this that the poor fellow is most secure."

"Well, I am not altogether easy in my mind, in spite of the respectability of the house," answered the Penitentiary. "How the brave Ramos exposes himself! And I am told that in Villahorrenda and the surrounding country there are a great many men. I don't know how many men— What have you heard?"

"That the soldiers are committing atrocities."

"It is a miracle that those Hottentots have not searched the house!

I declare that if I see one of the red-trousered gentry enter the house, I shall fall down speechless."

"This is a nice condition of things!" said Remedios, exhaling half her soul in a sigh. "I cannot get out of my head the idea of the tribulation in which Señora Doña Perfecta finds herself. Uncle, you ought to go there."

"Go there tonight? The military are parading the streets! Imagine that some insolent soldier should take it into his head to— The señora is well protected. The other day they searched the house and they carried off the six armed men she had there; but afterward they sent them back to her. We have no one to protect us in case of an attack."

"I sent Jacinto to the señora's, to keep her company for a while. If Caballuco comes, we will tell him to stop in there, too. No one can put it out of my head but that those rascals are plotting some piece of villany against our friend. Poor señora, poor Rosarito! When one thinks that this might have been avoided by what I proposed to Doña Perfecta two days ago—"

"My dear niece," said the Penitentiary phlegmatically, "we have done all that it was in human power to do to carry out our virtuous purpose. More we cannot do. Convince yourself of this, and do not be obstinate. Rosarito cannot be the wife of our idolized Jacintillo. Your golden dream, your ideal of happiness, that at one time seemed attainable, and to which, like a good uncle, I devoted all the powers of my understanding, has become chimerical, has vanished into smoke. Serious obstructions, the wickedness of a man, the indubitable love of the girl, and other things, regarding which I am silent, have altered altogether the condition of affairs. We were in a fair way to conquer, and suddenly we are conquered. Ah, niece! convince yourself of one thing. As matters are now, Jacinto deserves something a great deal better than that crazy girl."

"Caprices and obstinate notions!" responded Maria, with an ill-humor that was far from respectful. "That's a pretty thing to say now, uncle! The great minds are outshining themselves, now. Doña Perfecta with her lofty ideas, and you with your doubts and fears—of much use either of you is. It is a pity that God made me such a fool and gave me an understanding of brick and mortar, as the señora says, for if that wasn't the case I would soon settle the question."

"You?"

"If she and you had allowed me, it would be settled already."

"By the beating?"

"There's no occasion for you to be frightened or to open your eyes like that. There is no question of killing anybody. What an idea!"

"Beating," said the canon, smiling, "is like scratching—when one begins one doesn't know when to leave off."

"Bah! say too that I am cruel and bloodthirsty. I wouldn't have the courage to kill a fly; it's not very likely that I should desire the death of a man."

"In fine, child, no matter what objections you may make, Señor Don Pepe Rey will carry off the girl. It is not possible now to prevent it. He is ready to employ every means, including dishonor. If Rosarito—how she deceived us with that demure little face and those heavenly eyes, eh!—if Rosarito, I say, did not herself wish it, then all might be arranged, but alas! she loves him as the sinner loves Satan; she is consumed with a criminal passion; she has fallen, niece, into the snares of the Evil One. Let us be virtuous and upright; let us turn our eyes away from the ignoble pair, and think no more about either of them."

"You know nothing about women, uncle," said Remedios, with flattering hypocrisy; "you are a holy man; you do not understand that Rosario's feeling is only a passing caprice, one of those caprices that are cured by a sound whipping."

"Niece," said Don Inocencio gravely and sententiously, "when serious things have taken place, caprices are not called caprices, but by another name."

"Uncle, you don't know what you are talking about," responded Maria Remedios, her face flushing suddenly. "What! would you be capable of supposing that Rosarito—what an atrocity! I will defend her; yes, I will defend her. She is as pure as an angel. Why, uncle, those things bring a blush to my cheek, and make me indignant with you."

As she spoke the good priest's face was darkened by a cloud of sadness that made him look ten years older.

"My dear Remedios," he said, "we have done all that is humanly possible, and all that in conscience we can or ought to do. Nothing could be more natural than our desire to see Jacintillo connected with that great family, the first in Orbajosa; nothing more natural than our desire to see him master of the seven houses in the town, the meadow of Mundogrande, the three gardens of the upper farm, La Encomienda, and the other lands and houses which that girl owns. Your son has great merit, everyone knows it well. Rosarito liked him, and he liked Rosarito. The matter seemed settled. Doña Perfecta herself, without being very enthusiastic, doubtless on account of our origin, seemed favorably disposed toward it, because of her great esteem and veneration for me, as her confessor and friend. But suddenly this unlucky young man presents himself. The señora tells me that she has given her word to her brother, and that she cannot reject the proposal made by him. A difficult situation! But what do I do in view of all this? Ah, you don't know everything! I will be frank with you. If I had found Señor de Rey to be a man of good principles, calculated to make Rosario happy, I would not have interfered in the matter; but the young man appeared to me to be a wretch, and, as the spiritual director of the house, it was my duty to take a hand in the business, and I took it. You know already that I determined to unmask him. I exposed his vices; I made manifest his atheism; I laid bare to the view of all the rottenness of that materialistic heart, and the señora was convinced that in giving her daughter to him, she would be delivering her up to vice. Ah, what anxieties I endured! The señora vacillated; I strengthened her wavering mind; I advised her concerning the means she might lawfully employ to send her nephew away without scandal. I suggested ingenious ideas to her; and as she often spoke to me of the scruples that troubled her tender conscience, I tranquillized her, pointing out to her how far it was allowable for us to go in our fight against that lawless enemy. Never did I counsel violent or sanguinary measures or base outrages, but always subtle artifices, in which there was no sin. My mind is tranquil, my dear niece. But you know that I struggled hard, that I worked like a negro. Ah! when I used to come home every night and say, 'Mariquilla, we are getting on well, we are getting on very well,' you used to be wild with delight, and you would kiss my hands again and again, and say I was the best man on earth. Why do you fly into a passion now, disfiguring your noble character and peaceable disposition? Why do you scold me? Why do you say that you are indignant, and tell me in plain terms that I am nothing better than an idiot?"

"Because," said the woman, without any diminution of her rage, "because you have grown faint-hearted all of a sudden."

"The thing is that everything is going against us, woman. That confounded engineer, protected as he is by the army, is resolved to dare everything. The girl loves him, the girl—I will say no more. It cannot be; I tell you that it cannot be."

"The army! But do you believe, like Doña Perfecta, that there is going to be a war, and that to drive Don Pepe from the town it will be necessary for one half of the nation to rise up against the other half? The señora has lost her senses, and you are in a fair way to lose yours."

"I believe as she does. In view of the intimate connection of Rey with the soldiers the personal question assumes larger proportions. But, ah, niece! if two days ago I entertained the hope that our valiant townsmen would kick the soldiers out of the town, since I have seen the turn things have taken, since I have seen that most of them have been surprised before fighting, and that Caballuco is in hiding and that the insurrection is going to the devil, I have lost confidence in everything. The good doctrines have not yet acquired sufficient material force to tear in pieces the ministers and the emissaries of error. Ah, niece! resignation, resignation!"

And Don Inocencio, employing the method of expression which characterized his niece, heaved two or three profound sighs. Maria, contrary to what might have been expected, maintained absolute silence. She showed now neither anger nor the superficial sentimentality of her ordinary life; but only a profound and humble grief. Shortly after the good canon had ended his peroration two tears rolled down his niece's rosy cheeks; before long were heard a few half-suppressed sighs, and gradually, as the swell and tumult of a sea that is beginning to be stormy rise higher and higher and become louder and louder, so the surge of Maria Remedios' grief rose and swelled, until it at last broke forth in a flood of tears.

XXVII

A Canon's Torture

R esignation, resignation!" repeated Don Inocencio.
"Resignation, resignation!" repeated his niece, drying her tears.
"If my dear son is doomed to be always a beggar, well, then, be it so.
Lawsuits are becoming scarce; the day will soon come when the practice
of the law will be the same as nothing. What is the use of all his talent?
What is the use of his tiring his brain with so much study? Ah! We are
poor. A day will come, Señor Don Inocencio, when my poor boy will
not have a pillow on which to lay his head."

"Woman!"

"Man! can you deny it? Tell me, then, what inheritance are you going
to leave him when you close your eyes on this world? A couple of rooms,
half a dozen big books, poverty, and nothing more. What times are
before us, uncle; what times! My poor boy is growing very delicate in
his health, and he won't be able to work—it makes him dizzy now to
read a book; he gets a headache and nausea whenever he works at night!
He will have to beg a paltry situation; I shall have to take in sewing, and
who knows, who knows but we may have to beg our bread!"

"Woman!"

"Oh, I know very well what I am talking about! Fine times before us!"
added the excellent woman, forcing still more the lachrymose note in
her diatribe. "My God! What is going to become of us? Ah, it is only
a mother's heart that can feel these things! Only a mother is capable
of suffering so much anxiety about a son's welfare. How should you
understand it? No; it is one thing to have children and to suffer anxiety
on their account and another to sing the *gori gori* in the cathedral and
to teach Latin in the institute. Of great use is it for my son to be your
nephew and to have taken so many honors and to be the pride and
ornament of Orbajosa. He will die of starvation, for we already know
what law brings; or else he will have to ask the deputies for a situation
in Havana, where the yellow fever will kill him."

"But, niece—"

"No, I am not grieving, I am silent now; I won't annoy you anymore.
I am very troublesome, always crying and sighing; and I am not to be

endured because I am a fond mother and I look out for the good of my beloved son. I will die, yes, I will die in silence, and stifle my grief. I will swallow my tears, in order not to annoy his reverence the canon. But my idolized son will comprehend me and he won't put his hands to his ears as you are doing now. Woe is me! Poor Jacinto knows that I would die for him, and that I would purchase his happiness at the sacrifice of my life. Darling child of my soul! To be so deserving and to be forever doomed to mediocrity, to a humble station, for—don't get indignant, uncle—no matter what airs we put on, you will always be the son of Uncle Tinieblas, the sacristan of San Bernardo, and I shall never be anything more than the daughter of Ildefonso Tinieblas, your brother, who used to sell crockery, and my son will be the grandson of the Tinieblas—for obscure we were born, and we shall never emerge from our obscurity, nor own a piece of land of which we can say, 'This is mine'; nor shear a sheep of our own; nor milk a goat of our own; nor shall I ever plunge my arms up to the elbows in a sack of wheat threshed and winnowed on our own threshing-floor—all because of your cowardice, your folly, your soft-heartedness."

"But—but, niece!"

The canon's voice rose higher everytime he repeated this phrase, and, with his hands to his ears, he shook his head from side to side with a look of mingled grief and desperation. The shrill complaint of Maria Remedios grew constantly shriller, and pierced the brain of the unhappy and now dazed priest like an arrow. But all at once the woman's face became transformed; her plaintive wail was changed to a hard, shrill scream; she turned pale, her lips trembled, she clenched her hands, a few locks of her disordered hair fell over her forehead, her eyes glittered, dried by the heat of the anger that glowed in her breast; she rose from her seat and, not like a woman, but like a harpy, cried:

"I am going away from here! I am going away from here with my son! We will go to Madrid; I don't want my son to fret himself to death in this miserable town! I am tired now of seeing that my son, under the protection of the cassock, neither is nor ever will be anything. Do you hear, my reverend uncle? My son and I are going away! You will never see us again—never!"

Don Inocencio had clasped his hands and was receiving the thunderbolts of his niece's wrath with the consternation of a criminal whom the presence of the executioner has deprived of his last hope.

BENITO PÉREZ GALDÓS

"In Heaven's name, Remedios," he murmured, in a pained voice; "in the name of the Holy Virgin—"

These fits of rage of his niece, who was usually so meek, were as violent as they were rare, and five or six years would sometimes pass without Don Inocencio seeing Remedios transformed into a fury.

"I am a mother! I am a mother! and since no one else will look out for my son, I will look out for him myself!" roared the improvised lioness.

"In the name of the Virgin, niece, don't let your passion get the best of you! Remember that you are committing a sin. Let us say the Lord's Prayer and an Ave Maria, and you will see that this will pass away."

As he said this the Penitentiary trembled, and the perspiration stood on his forehead. Poor dove in the talons of the vulture! The furious woman completed his discomfiture with these words:

"You are good for nothing; you are a poltroon! My son and I will go away from this place forever, forever! I will get a position for my son, I will find him a good position, do you understand? Just as I would be willing to sweep the streets with my tongue if I could gain a living for him in no other way, so I will move heaven and earth to find a position for my boy in order that he may rise in the world and be rich, and a person of consequence, and a gentleman, and a lord and great, and all that there is to be—all, all!"

"Heaven protect me!" cried Don Inocencio, sinking into a chair and letting his head fall on his breast.

There was a pause during which the agitated breathing of the furious woman could be heard.

"Niece," said Don Inocencio at last, "you have shortened my life by ten years; you have set my blood on fire; you have put me beside myself. God give me the calmness that I need to bear with you! Lord, patience—patience is what I ask. And you, niece, do me the favor to sigh and cry to your heart's content for the next ten years; for your confounded mania of snivelling, greatly as it annoys me, is preferable to these mad fits of rage. If I did not know that you are good at heart— Well, for one who confessed and received communion this morning you are behaving—"

"Yes, but you are the cause of it—you!"

"Because in the matter of Rosario and Jacinto I say to you, resignation?"

"Because when everything is going on well you turn back and allow Señor de Rey to get possession of Rosario."

"And how am I going to prevent it? Doña Perfecta is right in saying that you have an understanding of brick. Do you want me to go about the town with a sword, and in the twinkling of an eye to make mincemeat of the whole regiment, and then confront Rey and say to him, 'Leave the girl in peace or I will cut your throat'?"

"No, but when I advised the señora to give her nephew a fright, you opposed my advice, instead of supporting it."

"You are crazy with your talk about a fright."

"Because when the dog is dead the madness is at an end."

"I cannot advise what you call a fright, and what might be a terrible thing."

"Yes; because I am a cut-throat, am I not, uncle?"

"You know that practical jokes are vulgar. Besides, do you suppose that man would allow himself to be insulted? And his friends?"

"At night he goes out alone."

"How do you know that?"

"I know everything; he does not take a step that I am not aware of; do you understand? The widow De Cuzco keeps me informed of everything."

"There, don't set me crazy. And who is going to give him that fright? Let us hear."

"Caballuco."

"So that he is disposed—"

"No, but he will be if you command him."

"Come, niece, leave me in peace. I cannot command such an atrocity. A fright! And what is that? Have you spoken to him already?"

"Yes, señor; but he paid no attention to me, or rather he refused. There are only two people in Orbajosa who can make him do what they wish by a simple order—you and Doña Perfecta."

"Let Doña Perfecta order him to do it if she wishes, then. I will never advise the employment of violent and brutal measures. Will you believe that when Caballuco and some of his followers were talking of rising up in arms they could not draw a single word from me inciting them to bloodshed. No, not that. If Doña Perfecta wishes to do it—"

"She will not do it, either. I talked with her for two hours this afternoon and she said that she would preach war, and help it by every means in her power; but that she would not bid one man stab another in the back. She would be right in opposing it if anything serious were intended, but I don't want any wounds; all I want is to give him a fright."

"Well, if Doña Perfecta doesn't want to order a fright to be given to the engineer, I don't either, do you understand? My conscience is before everything."

"Very well," returned his niece. "Tell Caballuco to come with me tonight—that is all you need say to him."

"Are you going out tonight?"

"Yes, señor, I am going out. Why, didn't I go out last night too?"

"Last night? I didn't know it; if I had known it I should have been angry; yes, señora."

"All you have to say to Caballuco is this: 'My dear Ramos, I will be greatly obliged to you if you will accompany my niece on an errand which she has to do tonight, and if you will protect her, if she should chance to be in any danger.'"

"I can do that. To accompany you, to protect you. Ah, rogue! you want to deceive me and make me your accomplice in some piece of villany."

"Of course—what do you suppose?" said Maria Remedios ironically. "Between Ramos and me we are going to slaughter a great many people tonight."

"Don't jest! I tell you again that I will not advise Ramos to do anything that has the appearance of evil—I think he is outside."

A noise at the street-door was heard, then the voice of Caballuco speaking to the servant, and a little later the hero of Orbajosa entered the room.

"What is the news? Give us the news, Señor Ramos," said the priest. "Come! If you don't give us some hope in exchange for your supper and our hospitality— What is going on in Villahorrenda?"

"Something," answered the bravo, seating himself with signs of fatigue. "You shall soon see whether we are good for anything or not."

Like all persons who wish to make themselves appear important, Caballuco made a show of great reserve.

"Tonight, my friend, you shall take with you, if you wish, the money they have given me for—"

"There is good need of it. If the soldiers should get scent of it, however, they won't let me pass," said Ramos, with a brutal laugh.

"Hold your tongue, man. We know already that you pass whenever you please. Why, that would be a pretty thing! The soldiers are not strait-laced gentry, and if they should become troublesome, with a couple of dollars, eh? Come, I see that you are not badly armed. All you want now is an eight-pounder. Pistols, eh? And a dagger too."

"For anything that might happen," said Caballuco, taking the weapon from his belt and displaying its horrible blade.

"In the name of God and of the Virgin!" exclaimed Maria Remedios, closing her eyes and turning away her face in terror, "put away that thing. The very sight of it terrifies me."

"If you won't take it ill of me," said Ramos, shutting the weapon, "let us have supper."

Maria Remedios prepared everything quickly, in order that the hero might not become impatient.

"Listen to me a moment, Señor Ramos," said Don Inocencio to his guest, when they had sat down to supper. "Have you a great deal to do tonight?"

"Something there is to be done," responded the bravo. "This is the last night I shall come to Orbajosa—the last. I have to look up some boys who remained in the town, and we are going to see how we can get possession of the saltpetre and the sulphur that are in the house of Cirujeda."

"I asked you," said the curate amiably, filling his friend's plate, "because my niece wishes you to accompany her a short distance. She has some business or other to attend to, and it is a little late to be out alone."

"Is she going to Doña Perfecta's?" asked Ramos. "I was there a few moments ago, but I did not want to make any delay."

"How is the señora?"

"A little frightened. Tonight I took away the six young men I had in the house."

"Why! don't you think they will be wanted there?" said Remedios, with alarm.

"They are wanted more in Villahorrenda. Brave men chafe at being kept in the house; is it not so, Señor Canon?"

"Señor Ramos, that house ought not to be left unprotected," said the Penitentiary.

"The servants are enough, and more than enough. But do you suppose, Señor Don Inocencio, that the brigadier employs himself in attacking people's houses?"

"Yes, but you know very well that that diabolical engineer—"

"For that—there are not wanting brooms in the house," said Cristobal jovially. "For in the end, there will be no help for it but to marry them. After what has passed—"

"Señor Ramos," said Remedios, with sudden anger, "I imagine that all you know about marrying people is very little."

"I say that because a little while ago, when I was at the house, the mother and daughter seemed to be having a sort of reconciliation. Doña Perfecta was kissing Rosarito over and over again, and there was no end to their caresses and endearments."

"Reconciliation! With all these preparations for the war you have lost your senses. But, finally, are you coming with me or not?"

"It is not to Doña Perfecta's she wants to go," said the priest, "but to the hotel of the widow De Cuzco. She was saying that she does not dare to go alone, because she is afraid of being insulted."

"By whom?"

"It is easily understood. By that infernal engineer. Last night my niece met him there, and she gave him some plain talk; and for that reason she is not altogether easy in her mind tonight. The young fellow is revengeful and insolent."

"I don't know whether I can go," said Caballuco. "As I am in hiding now I cannot measure my strength against Don José Poquita Cosa. If I were not as I am—with half my face hidden, and the other half uncovered—I would have broken his back for him already twenty times over. But what happens if I attack him? He discovers who I am, he falls upon me with the soldiers, and goodbye to Caballuco. As for giving him a treacherous blow, that is something I couldn't do; nor would Doña Perfecta consent to it, either. For a stab in the dark Cristobal Ramos is not the man."

"But are you crazy, man? What are you talking about?" said the Penitentiary, with unmistakable signs of astonishment. "Not even in thought would I advise you to do an injury to that gentleman. I would cut my tongue out before I would advise such a piece of villany. The wicked will fall, it is true; but it is God who will fix the moment, not I. And the question is not to give a beating, either. I would rather receive a hundred blows myself than advise the administration of such a medicine to any Christian. One thing only will I say to you," he ended, looking at the bravo over his spectacles, "and that is, that as my niece is going there; and as it is probable, very probable, is it not, Remedios? that she may have to say a few plain words to that man, I recommend you not to leave her unprotected, in case she should be insulted."

"I have something to do tonight," answered Caballuco, laconically and dryly.

"You hear what he says, Remedios. Leave your business for tomorrow."

"I can't do that. I will go alone."

"No, you shall not go alone, niece. Now let us hear no more about the matter. Señor Ramos has something to do, and he cannot accompany you. Fancy if you were to be insulted by that rude man!"

"Insulted! A lady insulted by that fellow!" exclaimed Caballuco. "Come, that must not be."

"If you had not something to do—bah! I should be quite easy in my mind, then."

"I have something to do," said the Centaur, rising from the table, "but if you wish it—"

There was a pause. The Penitentiary had closed his eyes and was meditating.

"I wish it, Señor Ramos," he said at last.

"There is no more to be said then. Let us go, Señora Doña Maria."

"Now, my dear niece," said Don Inocencio, half seriously, half jestingly, "since we have finished supper bring me the basin."

He gave his niece a penetrating glance, and accompanying it with the corresponding action, pronounced these words:

"I wash my hands of the matter."

XXVIII

FROM PEPE REY TO DON JUAN REY

ORBAJOSA, April 12

MY DEAR FATHER

"Forgive me if for the first time in my life I disobey you in refusing to leave this place or to renounce my project. Your advice and your entreaty are what were to be expected from a kind, good father. My obstinacy is natural in an insensate son; but something strange is taking place within me; obstinacy and honor have become so blended and confounded in my mind that the bare idea of desisting from my purpose makes me ashamed. I have changed greatly. The fits of rage that agitate me now were formerly unknown to me. I regarded the violent acts, the exaggerated expressions of hot-tempered and impetuous men with the same scorn as the brutal actions of the wicked. Nothing of this kind surprises me any longer, for in myself I find at all times a certain terrible capacity for wickedness. I can speak to you as I would speak to God and to my conscience; I can tell you that I am a wretch, for he is a wretch who is wanting in that powerful moral force which enables him to chastise his passions and submit his life to the stern rule of conscience. I have been wanting in the Christian fortitude which exalts the spirit of the man who is offended above the offences which he receives and the enemies from whom he receives them. I have had the weakness to abandon myself to a mad fury, putting myself on a level with my detractors, returning them blow for blow, and endeavoring to confound them by methods learned in their own base school. How deeply I regret that you were not at my side to turn me from this path! It is now too late. The passions will not brook delay. They are impatient, and demand their prey with cries and with the convulsive eagerness of a fierce moral thirst. I have succumbed. I cannot forget what you so often said to me, that anger may be called the worst of the passions, since, suddenly transforming the character, it engenders all the others, and lends to each its own infernal fire.

"But it is not anger alone that has brought me to the state of mind which I have described. A more expansive and noble sentiment— the profound and ardent love which I have for my cousin, has also contributed to it, and this is the one thing that absolves me in my own estimation. But if love had not done so, pity would have impelled me to brave the fury and the intrigues of your terrible sister; for poor Rosario, placed between an irresistible affection and her mother, is at the present moment one of the most unhappy beings on the face of the earth. The love which she has for me, and which responds to mine—does it not give me the right to open, in whatever way I can, the doors of her house and take her out of it; employing the law, as far as the law reaches, and using force at the point where the law ceases to support me? I think that your rigid moral scrupulosity will not give an affirmative answer to this question; but I have ceased to be the upright and methodical character whose conscience was in exact conformity with the dictates of the moral law. I am no longer the man whom an almost perfect education enabled to keep his emotions under strict control. Today I am a man like other men; at a single step I have crossed the line which separates the just and the good from the unjust and the wicked. Prepare yourself to hear of some dreadful act committed by me. I will take care to notify you of all my misdeeds.

"But the confession of my faults will not relieve me from the responsibility of the serious occurrences which have taken place and which are taking place, nor will this responsibility, no matter how much I may argue, fall altogether on your sister. Doña Perfecta's responsibility is certainly very great. What will be the extent of mine! Ah, dear father! believe nothing of what you hear about me; believe only what I shall tell you. If they tell you that I have committed a deliberate piece of villany, answer that it is a lie. It is difficult, very difficult, for me to judge myself, in the state of disquietude in which I am, but I dare assure you that I have not deliberately given cause for scandal. You know well to what extremes passion can lead when circumstances favor its fierce, its all-invading growth.

"What is most bitter to me is the thought of having employed artifice, deceit, and base concealments—I who was truth itself. I am humiliated in my own estimation. But is this the greatest perversity into which the soul can fall? Am I beginning now, or have I ended? I cannot tell. If Rosario with her angelic hand does not take me out of this hell of my conscience, I desire that you should come to take me out of it. My cousin is an angel, and suffering, as she has done, for my sake, she has taught me a great many things that I did not know before.

"Do not be surprised at the incoherence of what I write. Diverse emotions inflame me; thoughts at times assail me truly worthy of my immortal soul; but at times also I fall into a lamentable state of dejection, and I am reminded of the weak and degenerate characters whose baseness you have painted to me in such strong colors, in order that I might abhor them. In the state in which I am today I am ready for good or for evil. God have pity upon me! I already know what prayer is—a solemn and reflexive supplication, so personal that it is not compatible with formulas learned by heart; an expansion of the soul which dares to reach out toward its source; the opposite of remorse, in which the soul, at war with itself, seeks in vain to defend itself against itself by sophisms and concealments. You have taught me many good things, but now I am practising; as we engineers say, I am studying on the ground; and in this way my knowledge will become broadened and confirmed. I begin to imagine now that I am not so wicked as I myself believe. Am I right?

"I end this letter in haste. I must send it with some soldiers who are going in the direction of the station at Villahorrenda, for the post-office of this place is not to be trusted."

April 14

"It would amuse you, dear father, if I could make you understand the ideas of the people of this wretched town. You know already that almost all the country is up in arms. It was a thing to be anticipated, and the politicians are mistaken if they imagine that it will be over in a couple of days. Hostility to us and to the Government is innate in the Orbajosan's mind, and forms a part of it as much as his religious faith. Confining myself to the particular question with my aunt, I will tell you a singular thing—the poor lady, who is penetrated by the spirit of feudalism to the marrow of her bones, has taken it into her head that I am going to attack her house and carry off her daughter, as the gentlemen of the Middle Ages attacked an enemy's castle to consummate some outrage. Don't laugh, for it is the truth—such are the ideas of these people. I need not tell you that she regards me as a monster, as a sort of heretic Moorish king, and of the officers here who are my friends she has no better opinion. In Dona Perfecta's house it is a matter of firm belief that the army and I have formed a diabolical and anti-religious coalition to rob Orbajosa of its treasures, its faith, and its maidens. I am sure that your sister firmly believes that I am going to take her house by assault, and there is not a doubt but that behind the door some barricade has been erected.

"But it could not be otherwise. Here they have the most antiquated ideas respecting society, religion, the state, property. The religious exaltation which impels them to employ force against the Government, to defend a faith which no one has attacked, and which, besides, they do not possess, revives in their mind the feudal sentiment; and as they would settle every question by brute force, with the sword and with fire, killing all who do not think as they do, they believe that no one in the world employs other methods.

"Far from intending to perform quixotic deeds in this lady's house, I have in reality saved her some annoyances from which the rest of the town have not escaped. Owing to my friendship with the brigadier she has not been obliged to present, as was ordered, a list of those of the men in her service who have joined the insurgents; and if her house was searched I have certain knowledge that it was only for form's sake; and if the six men there were disarmed, they have been replaced by six others, and nothing has been done to her. You see to what my hostility to that lady is reduced.

"It is true that I have the support of the military chiefs, but I make use of it solely to escape being insulted or ill-used by these implacable people. The probabilities of my success consist in the fact that the authorities recently appointed by the commander of the brigade are all my friends. I derive from them the moral force which enables me to intimidate these people. I don't know whether I shall find myself compelled to commit some violent action; but don't be alarmed, for the assault and the taking of the house is altogether a wild, feudal idea of your sister. Chance has placed me in an advantageous position. Rage, the passion that burns within me, will impel me to profit by it. I don't know how far I may go."

APRIL 17

"Your letter has given me great consolation. Yes; I can attain my object, employing only the resources of the law, which will be completely effectual for it. I have consulted the authorities of this place, and they all approve of the course you indicate. I am very glad of it. Since I have put into my cousin's mind the idea of disobedience, let it at least be under the protection of the law. I will do what you bid me, that is to say I will renounce the somewhat unworthy collaboration of Pinzon; I will break up the terrorizing solidarity which I established with the soldiers; I will cease to make a display of the power I derived from them; I will have done with adventures, and at the fitting moment I will act with calmness, prudence, and all the benignity possible. It is better so. My coalition, half-serious, half-jesting, with the army, had for its object to protect me against the violence of the Orbajosans and of the servants and the relations of my aunt. For the rest, I have always disapproved of the idea of what we call armed intervention.

"The friend who aided me has been obliged to leave the house; but I am not entirely cut off from communication with my cousin. The poor girl shows heroic valor in the midst of her sufferings, and will obey me blindly.

"Set your mind at rest about my personal safety. For my part, I have no fear and I am quite tranquil."

April 20

"Today I can write only a few lines. I have a great deal to do. All will be ended within two or three days. Don't write to me again to this miserable town. I shall soon have the happiness of embracing you.

Pepe

XXIX

FROM PEPE REY TO ROSARITO POLENTINOS

G ive Estebanillo the key of the garden and charge him to take care about the dog. The boy is mine, body and soul. Fear nothing! I shall be very sorry if you cannot come down stairs as you did the other night. Do all you can to manage it. I will be in the garden a little after midnight. I will then tell you what course I have decided upon, and what you are to do. Tranquillize your mind, my dear girl, for I have abandoned all imprudent or violent expedients. I will tell you everything when I see you. There is much to tell; and it must be spoken, not written. I can picture to myself your terror and anxiety at the thought of my being so near you. But it is a week since I have seen you. I have sworn that this separation from you shall soon be ended, and it will be ended. My heart tells me that I shall see you. I swear that I will see you."

BENITO PÉREZ GALDÓS

XXX

Beating up the Game

A man and a woman entered the hotel of the widow De Cuzco a little after ten o'clock, and left it at half-past eleven.

"Now, Señora Doña Maria," said the man, "I will take you to your house, for I have something to do."

"Wait, Señor Ramos, for the love of God!" she answered. "Why don't we go to the Casino to see if he comes out? You heard just now that Estebanillo, the boy that works in the garden, was talking with him this afternoon."

"But are you looking for Don José?" asked the Centaur, with ill-humor. "What have we to do with him? The courtship with Doña Rosario ended as it was bound to end, and now there is nothing for it but for her mother to marry them. That is my opinion."

"You are a fool!" said Remedios angrily.

"Señora, I am going."

"Why, you rude man, are you going to leave me alone in the street?"

"Yes, señora, unless you go home at once."

"That's right—leave me alone, exposed to be insulted! Listen to me, Señor Ramos. Don José will come out of the Casino in a moment, as usual. I want to see whether he goes into his hotel or goes past it. It is a fancy of mine, only a fancy."

"What I know is that I have something to do, and that it is near twelve o'clock."

"Silence!" said Remedios. "Let us hide ourselves around the corner. A man is coming down the Calle de la Tripería Alta. It is he!"

"Don José! I know him by his walk."

"Let us follow him," said Maria Remedios with anxiety. "Let us follow him at a little distance, Ramos."

"Señora—"

"Only to see if he goes into his hotel."

"Only a minute, then, Doña Remedios. After that I must go."

They walked on about thirty paces, keeping at a moderate distance behind the man they were watching. The Penitentiary's niece stopped then and said:

"He is not going into his hotel."

"He may be going to the brigadier's."

"The brigadier lives up the street, and Don Pepe is going down in the direction of the señora's house."

"Of the señora's house!" exclaimed Caballuco, quickening his steps.

But they were mistaken. The man whom they were watching passed the house of Polentinos and walked on.

"Do you see that you were wrong?"

"Señor Ramos, let us follow him!" said Remedios, pressing the Centaur's hand convulsively. "I have a foreboding."

"We shall soon know, for we are near the end of the town."

"Don't go so fast—he may see us. It is as I thought, Señor Ramos; he is going into the garden by the condemned door."

"Señora, you have lost your senses!"

"Come on, and we shall see."

The night was dark, and the watchers could not tell precisely at what point Señor de Rey had entered; but a grating of rusty hinges which they heard, and the circumstance of not meeting the young man in the whole length of the garden wall, convinced them that he had entered the garden. Caballuco looked at his companion with stupefaction. He seemed bewildered.

"What are you thinking about? Do you still doubt?"

"What ought I to do?" asked the bravo, covered with confusion. "Shall we give him a fright? I don't know what the señora would think about it. I say that because I was at her house this evening, and it seemed to me that the mother and daughter had become reconciled."

"Don't be a fool! Why don't you go in?"

"Now I remember that the armed men are not there; I told them to leave this evening."

"And this block of marble still doubts what he ought to do! Ramos, go into the garden and don't be a coward."

"How can I go in if the door is closed?"

"Get over the wall. What a snail! If I were a man—"

"Well, then, up! There are some broken bricks here where the boys climb over the wall to steal the fruit."

"Up quickly! I will go and knock at the front door to waken the senora, if she should be asleep."

The Centaur climbed up, not without difficulty. He sat astride on the wall for an instant, and then disappeared among the dark foliage of the trees. Maria Remedios ran desperately toward the Calle del Condestable, and, seizing the knocker of the front door, knocked—knocked three times with all her heart and soul.

XXXI

Doña Perfecta

See with what tranquillity Señora Doña Perfecta pursues her occupation of writing. Enter her room, and, notwithstanding the lateness of the hour, you will surprise her busily engaged, her mind divided between meditation and the writing of several long and carefully worded epistles traced with a firm hand, every hair-stroke of every letter in which is correctly formed. The light of the lamp falls full upon her face and bust and hands, its shade leaving the rest of her person and almost the whole of the room in a soft shadow. She seems like a luminous figure evoked by the imagination from amid the vague shadows of fear.

It is strange that we should not have made before this a very important statement, which is that Doña Perfecta was handsome, or rather that she was still handsome, her face preserving the remains of former beauty. The life of the country, her total lack of vanity, her disregard for dress and personal adornment, her hatred of fashion, her contempt for the vanities of the capital, were all causes why her native beauty did not shine or shone very little. The intense sallowness of her complexion, indicating a very bilious constitution, still further impaired her beauty.

Her eyes black and well-opened, her nose finely and delicately shaped, her forehead broad and smooth, she was considered by all who saw her as a finished type of the human figure; but there rested on those features a certain hard and proud expression which excited a feeling of antipathy. As some persons, although ugly, attract; Doña Perfecta repelled. Her glance, even when accompanied by amiable words, placed between herself and those who were strangers to her the impassable distance of a mistrustful respect; but for those of her house—that is to say, for her relations, admirers, and allies—she possessed a singular attraction. She was a mistress in governing, and no one could equal her in the art of adapting her language to the person whom she was addressing.

Her bilious temperament and an excessive association with devout persons and things, which excited her imagination without object or

BENITO PÉREZ GALDÓS

result, had aged her prematurely, and although she was still young she did not seem so. It might be said of her that with her habits and manner of life she had wrought a sort of rind, a stony, insensible covering within which she shut herself, like the snail within his portable house. Doña Perfecta rarely came out of her shell.

Her irreproachable habits, and that outward amiability which we have observed in her from the moment of her appearance in our story, were the causes of the great prestige which she enjoyed in Orbajosa. She kept up relations, besides, with some excellent ladies in Madrid, and it was through their means that she obtained the dismissal of her nephew. At the moment at which we have now arrived in our story, we find her seated at her desk, which is the sole confidant of her plans and the depository of her numerical accounts with the peasants, and of her moral accounts with God and with society. There she wrote the letters which her brother received every three months; there she composed the notes that incited the judge and the notary to embroil Pepe Rey in lawsuits; there she prepared the plot through which the latter lost the confidence of the Government; there she held long conferences with Don Inocencio. To become acquainted with the scene of others of her actions whose effects we have observed, it would be necessary to follow her to the episcopal palace and to the houses of various of her friends.

We do not know what Doña Perfecta would have been, loving. Hating, she had the fiery vehemence of an angel of hatred and discord among men. Such is the effect produced on a character naturally hard, and without inborn goodness, by religious exaltation, when this, instead of drawing its nourishment from conscience and from truth revealed in principles as simple as they are beautiful, seeks its sap in narrow formulas dictated solely by ecclesiastical interests. In order that religious fanaticism should be inoffensive, the heart in which it exists must be very pure. It is true that even in that case it is unproductive of good. But the hearts that have been born without the seraphic purity which establishes a premature Limbo on the earth, are careful not to become greatly inflamed with what they see in retables, in choirs, in locutories and sacristies, unless they have first erected in their own consciences an altar, a pulpit, and a confessional.

Doña Perfecta left her writing from time to time, to go into the adjoining room where her daughter was. Rosarito had been ordered to sleep, but, already precipitated down the precipice of disobedience, she was awake.

"Why don't you sleep?" her mother asked her. "I don't intend to go to bed tonight. You know already that Caballuco has taken away with him the men we had here. Something might happen, and I will keep watch. If I did not watch what would become of us both?"

"What time is it?" asked the girl.

"It will soon be midnight. Perhaps you are not afraid, but I am."

Rosarito was trembling, and everything about her denoted the keenest anxiety. She lifted her eyes to heaven supplicatingly, and then turned them on her mother with a look of the utmost terror.

"Why, what is the matter with you?"

"Did you not say it was midnight?"

"Yes."

"Then— But is it already midnight?"

Rosario made an effort to speak, then shook her head, on which the weight of a world was pressing.

"Something is the matter with you; you have something on your mind," said her mother, fixing on her daughter her penetrating eyes.

"Yes—I wanted to tell you," stammered the girl, "I wanted to say— Nothing, nothing, I will go to sleep."

"Rosario, Rosario! your mother can read your heart like an open book," exclaimed Doña Perfecta with severity. "You are agitated. I have told you already that I am willing to pardon you if you will repent; if you are a good and sensible girl."

"Why, am I not good? Ah, mamma, mamma! I am dying!"

Rosario burst into a flood of bitter and disconsolate tears.

"What are these tears about?" said her mother, embracing her. "If they are tears of repentance, blessed be they."

"I don't repent, I can't repent!" cried the girl, in a burst of sublime despair.

She lifted her head and in her face was depicted a sudden inspired strength. Her hair fell in disorder over her shoulders. Never was there seen a more beautiful image of a rebellious angel.

"What is this? Have you lost your senses?" said Doña Perfecta, laying both her hands on her daughter's shoulders.

"I am going away, I am going away!" said the girl, with the exaltation of delirium.

And she sprang out of bed.

"Rosario, Rosario— My daughter! For God's sake, what is this?"

"Ah, mamma, señora!" exclaimed the girl, embracing her mother; "bind me fast!"

"In truth you would deserve it. What madness is this?"

"Bind me fast! I am going away—I am going away with him!"

Doña Perfecta felt a flood of fire surging from her heart up to her lips. She controlled herself, however, and answered her daughter only with her eyes, blacker than the night.

"Mamma, mamma, I hate all that is not he!" exclaimed Rosario. "Hear my confession, for I wish to confess it to everyone, and to you first of all."

"You are going to kill me; you are killing me!"

"I want to confess it, so that you may pardon me. This weight, this weight that is pressing me down, will not let me live."

"The weight of a sin! Add to it the malediction of God, and see if you can carry that burden about with you, wretched girl! Only I can take it from you."

"No, not you, not you!" cried Rosario, with desperation. "But hear me; I want to confess it all, all! Afterward, turn me out of this house where I was born."

"I turn you out!"

"I will go away, then."

"Still less. I will teach you a daughter's duty, which you have forgotten."

"I will fly, then; he will take me with him!"

"Has he told you to do so? has he counselled you to do that? has he commanded you to do that?" asked the mother, launching these words like thunderbolts against her daughter.

"He has counselled me to do it. We have agreed to be married. We must be married, mamma, dear mamma. I will love you—I know that I ought to love you—I shall be forever lost if I do not love you."

She wrung her hands, and falling on her knees kissed her mother's feet.

"Rosario, Rosario!" cried Doña Perfecta, in a terrible voice, "rise!"

There was a short pause.

"This man—has he written to you?"

"Yes."

"Have you seen him again since that night?"

"Yes."

"And you have written to him!"

"I have written to him also. Oh, señora! why do you look at me in that way? You are not my mother."

"Would to God that I were not! Rejoice in the harm you are doing me. You are killing me; you have given me my death-blow!" cried Doña Perfecta, with indescribable agitation. "You say that that man—"

"Is my husband—I will be his wife, protected by the law. You are not a woman! Why do you look at me in that way? You make me tremble. Mother, mother, do not condemn me!"

"You have already condemned yourself—that is enough. Obey me, and I will forgive you. Answer me—when did you receive letters from that man?"

"Today."

"What treachery! What infamy!" cried her mother, roaring rather than speaking. "Had you appointed a meeting?"

"Yes."

"When?"

"Tonight."

"Where?"

"Here, here! I will confess everything, everything! I know it is a crime. I am a wretch; but you who are my mother will take me out of this hell. Give your consent. Say one word to me, only one word!"

"That man here in my house!" cried Doña Perfecta, springing back several paces from her daughter.

Rosario followed her on her knees. At the same instant three blows were heard, three crashes, three reports. It was the heart of Maria Remedios knocking at the door through the knocker. The house trembled with awful dread. Mother and daughter stood motionless as statues.

A servant went down stairs to open the door, and shortly afterward Maria Remedios, who was not now a woman but a basilisk enveloped in a mantle, entered Doña Perfecta's room. Her face, flushed with anxiety, exhaled fire.

"He is there, he is there!" she said, as she entered. "He got into the garden through the condemned door."

She paused for breath at every syllable.

"I know already," returned Doña Perfecta, with a sort of bellow.

Rosario fell senseless on the floor.

"Let us go down stairs," said Doña Perfecta, without paying any attention to her daughter's swoon.

The two women glided down stairs like two snakes. The maids and the man-servant were in the hall, not knowing what to do. Doña Perfecta passed through the dining-room into the garden, followed by Maria Remedios.

"Fortunately we have Ca-Ca-Ca-balluco there," said the canon's niece.

"Where?"

"In the garden, also. He cli-cli-climbed over the wall."

Doña Perfecta explored the darkness with her wrathful eyes. Rage gave them the singular power of seeing in the dark peculiar to the feline race.

"I see a figure there," she said. "It is going toward the oleanders."

"It is he!" cried Remedios. "But there comes Ramos—Ramos!"

The colossal figure of the Centaur was plainly distinguishable.

"Toward the oleanders, Ramos! Toward the oleanders!"

Doña Perfecta took a few steps forward. Her hoarse voice, vibrating with a terrible accent, hissed forth these words:

"Cristobal, Cristobal—kill him!"

A shot was heard. Then another.

CONCLUSION

From Don Cayetano Polentinos to a friend in Madrid:

ORBAJOSA, April 21

MY DEAR FRIEND

"Send me without delay the edition of 1562 that you say you have picked up at the executor's sale of the books of Corchuelo. I will pay any price for that copy. I have been long searching for it in vain, and I shall esteem myself the most enviable of virtuosos in possessing it. You ought to find in the colophon a helmet with a motto over the word 'Tractado,' and the tail of the X of the date MDLXII ought to be crooked. If your copy agrees with these signs send me a telegraphic despatch at once, for I shall be very anxious until I receive it. But now I remember that, on account of these vexatious and troublesome wars, the telegraph is not working. I shall await your answer by return of mail.

"I shall soon go to Madrid for the purpose of having my long delayed work, the 'Genealogies of Orbajosa,' printed. I appreciate your kindness, my dear friend, but I cannot accept your too flattering expressions. My work does not indeed deserve the high encomiums you bestow upon it; it is a work of patience and study, a rude but solid and massive monument which I shall have erected to the past glories of my beloved country. Plain and humble in its form, it is noble in the idea that inspired it, which was solely to direct the eyes of this proud and unbelieving generation to the marvellous deeds and the pure virtues of our forefathers. Would that the studious youth of our country might take the step to which with all my strength I incite them! Would that the abominable studies and methods of reasoning introduced by philosophic license and erroneous doctrines might be forever cast into oblivion! Would that our learned men might occupy themselves exclusively in the contemplation of those glorious ages, in order that, this generation being penetrated with their essence and their beneficent sap, its insane eagerness for change, and its ridiculous mania for appropriating to itself foreign ideas which conflict with our beautiful national constitution, might disappear. I fear greatly that among the crowd of mad youth who pursue vain Utopias and heathenish novelties, my desires are not destined to be fulfilled, and that the contemplation of the illustrious virtues of the past will remain confined within the same narrow circle as today. What is to be done, my friend? I am afraid that very soon our poor Spain is doomed to be so disfigured that she will not be able to recognize herself, even beholding herself in the bright mirror of her stainless history.

"I do not wish to close this letter without informing you of a disagreeable event—the unfortunate death of an estimable young man, well known in Madrid, the civil engineer Don José de Rey, a nephew of my sister-in-law. This melancholy event occurred last night in the garden of our house, and I have not yet been able to form a correct judgment regarding the causes that may have impelled the unfortunate Rey to this horrible and criminal act. According to what Perfecta told me this morning, on my return from Mundo Grande, Pepe Rey at about twelve o'clock last night entered the garden of the house and shot himself in the right temple, expiring instantly. Imagine the consternation and alarm which such an event would produce in this peaceable and virtuous mansion. Poor Perfecta was so greatly affected that we were for a time alarmed about her; but she is better now, and this afternoon we succeeded in inducing her to take a little broth. We employ every means of consoling her, and as she is a good Christian, she knows how to support with edifying resignation even so great a misfortune as this.

"Between you and me, my friend, I will say here that in young Rey's fatal attempt upon his life, I believe the moving causes to have been an unfortunate attachment, perhaps remorse for his conduct, and the state of hypochondriasm into which he had fallen. I esteemed him greatly; I think he was not lacking in excellent qualities; but he was held in such disrepute here that never once have I heard anyone speak well of him. According to what they say, he made a boast of the most extravagant ideas and opinions; he mocked at religion, entered the church smoking and with his hat on; he respected nothing, and for him there was neither modesty, nor virtue, nor soul, nor ideal, nor faith—nothing but theodolites, squares, rules, engines, pick-axes, and spades. What do you think of that? To be just; I must say that in his conversations with me he always concealed these ideas, doubtless through fear of being utterly routed by the fire of my arguments; but in public innumerable stories are told of his heretical ideas and his stupendous excesses.

"I cannot continue, my dear friend, for at this moment I hear firing. As I have no love for fighting, and as I am not a soldier, my pulse trembles a little. In due time I will give you further particulars of this war.

Yours affectionately, etc., etc.

APRIL 22

MY EVER-REMEMBERED FRIEND

"Today we have had a bloody skirmish on the outskirts of Orbajosa. The large body of men raised in Villahorrenda were attacked by the troops with great fury. There was great loss in killed and wounded on both sides. After the combat the brave guerillas dispersed, but they are greatly encouraged, and it is possible that you may hear of wonderful things. Cristobal Caballuco, the son of the famous Caballuco whom you will remember in the last war, though suffering from a wound in the arm, how or when received is not known, commanded them. The present leader has eminent qualifications for the command; and he is, besides, an honest and simple-hearted man. As we must finally come to a friendly arrangement, I presume that Caballuco will be made a general in the Spanish army, whereby both sides will gain greatly.

"I deplore this war, which is beginning to assume alarming proportions; but I recognize that our valiant peasants are not responsible for it, since they have been provoked to the inhuman conflict by the audacity of the Government, by the demoralization of its sacrilegious delegates; by the systematic fury with which the representatives of the state attack what is most venerated by the people—their religious faith and the national spirit which fortunately still exists in those places that are not yet contaminated by the desolating pestilence. When it is attempted to take away the soul of a people to give it a different one; when it is sought to denationalize a people, so to say, perverting its sentiments, its customs, its ideas—it is natural that this people should defend itself, like the man who is attacked by highwaymen on a solitary road. Let the spirit and the pure and salutiferous substance of my work on the 'Genealogies'—excuse the apparent vanity— once reach the sphere of the Government and there will no longer be wars.

"Today we have had here a very disagreeable question. The clergy, my friend, have refused to allow Rey to be buried in consecrated ground. I interfered in the matter, entreating the bishop to remove this heavy anathema, but without success. Finally, we buried the body of the young man in a grave made in the field of Mundo Grande, where my patient explorations have discovered the archæological treasures of which you know. I spent some very sad hours, and the painful impression which I received has not yet altogether passed away. Don Juan Tafetan and ourselves were the only persons who accompanied the funeral cortège. A little later, strange to say, the girls whom they call here the Troyas went to the field, and prayed for a long time beside the rustic tomb of the mathematician. Although this seemed a ridiculous piece of officiousness it touched me.

"With respect to the death of Rey, the rumor circulates throughout the town that he was assassinated, but by whom is not known. It is asserted that he declared this to be the case, for he lived for about an hour and a half. According to what they say, he refused to reveal the name of his murderer. I repeat this version, without either contradicting or supporting it. Perfecta does not wish this matter to be spoken of, and she becomes greatly distressed whenever I allude to it.

"Poor woman! no sooner had one misfortune occurred than she met with another, which has grieved us all deeply. My friend, the fatal malady that has been for so many generations connatural in our family has now claimed another victim. Poor Rosario, who, thanks to our cares, was improving gradually in her health, has entirely lost her reason. Her incoherent words, her frenzy, her deadly pallor, bring my mother and my sister forcibly to my mind. This is the most serious case that I have witnessed in our family, for the question here is not one of mania but of real insanity. It is sad, terribly sad that out of so many I should be the only one to escape, preserving a sound mind with all my faculties unimpaired and entirely free from any sign of that fatal malady.

"I have not been able to give your remembrances to Don Inocencio, for the poor man has suddenly fallen ill and refuses to see even his most intimate friends. But I am sure that he would return your remembrances, and I do not doubt that he could lay his hand instantly on the translation of the collection of Latin epigrams which you recommend to him. I hear firing again. They say that we shall have a skirmish this afternoon. The troops have just been called out."

BARCELONA, June 1

"I have just arrived here after leaving my niece in San Baudilio de Llobregat. The director of the establishment has assured me that the case is incurable. She will, however, have the greatest care in that cheerful and magnificent sanitarium. My dear friend, if I also should ever succumb, let me be taken to San Baudilio. I hope to find the proofs of the 'Genealogies' awaiting me on my return. I intend to add six pages more, for it would be a great mistake not to publish my reasons for maintaining that Mateo Diez Coronel, author of the 'Métrico Encomio,' is descended, on the mother's side, from the Guevaras, and not from the Burguillos, as the author of the 'Floresta Amena' erroneously maintains.

"I write this letter principally for the purpose of giving you a caution. I have heard several persons here speaking of Pepe Rey's death, and they describe it exactly as it occurred. The secret of the manner of his death, which I learned sometime after the event, I revealed to you in confidence when we met in Madrid. It has appeared strange to me that having told it to no one but yourself, it should be known here in all its details—how he entered the garden; how he fired on Caballuco when the latter attacked him with his dagger; how Ramos then fired on him with so sure an aim that he fell to the ground mortally wounded. In short, my dear friend, in case you should have inadvertently spoken of this to anyone, I will remind you that it is a family secret, and that will be sufficient for a person as prudent and discreet as yourself.

"Joy! joy! I have just read in one of the papers here that Caballuco has defeated Brigadier Batalla."

ORBAJOSA, December 12

I have a sad piece of news to give you. The Penitentiary has ceased to exist for us; not precisely because he has passed to a better life, but because the poor man has been, ever since last April, so grief-stricken, so melancholy, so taciturn that you would not know him. There is no longer in him even a trace of that Attic humor, that decorous and classic joviality which made him so pleasing. He shuns everybody; he shuts himself up in his house and receives no one; he hardly eats anything, and he has broken off all intercourse with the world. If you were to see him now you would not recognize him, for he is reduced to skin and bone. The strangest part of the matter is that he has quarrelled with his niece and lives alone, entirely alone, in a miserable cottage in the suburb of Baidejos. They say now that he will resign his chair in the choir of the cathedral and go to Rome. Ah! Orbajosa will lose much in losing her great Latinist. I imagine that many a year will pass before we shall see such another. Our glorious Spain is falling into decay, declining, dying."

ORBAJOSA, December 23

"The young man who will present to you a letter of introduction from me is the nephew of our dear Penitentiary, a lawyer with some literary ability. Carefully educated by his uncle, he has very sensible ideas. How regrettable it would be if he should become corrupted in that sink of philosophy and incredulity! He is upright, industrious, and a good Catholic, for which reasons I believe that in an office like yours he will rise to distinction in his profession. Perhaps his ambition may lead him (for he has ambition, too) into the political arena, and I think he would not be a bad acquisition to the cause of order and tradition, now that the majority of our young men have become perverted and have joined the ranks of the turbulent and the vicious. He is accompanied by his mother, a commonplace woman without any social polish, but who has an excellent heart, and who is truly pious. Maternal affection takes in her the somewhat extravagant form of worldly ambition, and she declares that her son will one day be Minister. It is quite possible that he may.

"Perfecta desires to be remembered to you. I don't know precisely what is the matter with her; but the fact is, she gives us great uneasiness. She has lost her appetite to an alarming degree, and, unless I am greatly mistaken in my opinion of her case, she shows the first symptoms of jaundice. The house is very sad without Rosarito, who brightened it with her smiles and her angelic goodness. A black cloud seems to rest now over us all. Poor Perfecta speaks frequently of this cloud, which is growing blacker and blacker, while she becomes everyday more yellow. The poor mother finds consolation for her grief in religion and in devotional exercises, which each day she practises with a more exemplary and edifying piety. She passes almost the whole of the day in church, and she spends her large income in novenas and in splendid religious ceremonies. Thanks to her, religious worship has recovered in Orbajosa its former splendor. This is some consolation in the midst of the decay and dissolution of our nationality.

"Tomorrow I will send the proofs. I will add a few pages more, for I have discovered another illustrious Orbajosan—Bernardo Amador de Soto, who was footman to the Duke of Osuna, whom he served during the period of the viceroyalty of Naples; and there is even good reason to believe that he had no complicity whatever in the conspiracy against Venice."

Our story is ended. This is all we have to say for the present concerning persons who seem, but are not good.

THE END

A Note About the Author

Benito Pérez Galdós (1843–1920) was a Spanish novelist. Born in Las Palmas de Gran Canaria, he was the youngest of ten sons born to Lieutenant Colonel Don Sebastián Pérez and Doña Dolores Galdós. Educated at San Agustin school, he travelled to Madrid to study Law but failed to complete his studies. In 1865, Pérez Galdós began publishing articles on politics and the arts in *La Nación*. His literary career began in earnest with his 1868 Spanish translation of Charles Dickens' *Pickwick Papers*. Inspired by the leading realist writers of his time, especially Balzac, Pérez Galdós published his first novel, *La Fontana de Oro* (1870). Over the next several decades, he would write dozens of literary works, totaling 31 fictional novels, 46 historical novels known as the *National Episodes*, 23 plays, and 20 volumes of shorter fiction and journalism. Nominated for the Nobel Prize in Literature five times without winning, Pérez Galdós is considered the preeminent author of nineteenth century Spain and the nation's second greatest novelist after Miguel de Cervantes. *Doña Perfecta* (1876), one of his finest works, has been adapted for film and television several times.

A Note from the Publisher

Spanning many genres, from non-fiction essays to literature classics to children's books and lyric poetry, Mint Edition books showcase the master works of our time in a modern new package. The text is freshly typeset, is clean and easy to read, and features a new note about the author in each volume. Many books also include exclusive new introductory material. Every book boasts a striking new cover, which makes it as appropriate for collecting as it is for gift giving. Mint Edition books are only printed when a reader orders them, so natural resources are not wasted. We're proud that our books are never manufactured in excess and exist only in the exact quantity they need to be read and enjoyed.

bookfinity™

Discover more of your favorite classics with Bookfinity™.

- Track your reading with custom book lists.
- Get great book recommendations for your personalized Reader Type.
- Add reviews for your favorite books.
- AND MUCH MORE!

Visit **bookfinity.com** and take the fun Reader Type quiz to get started.

Enjoy our classic and modern companion pairings!

Classic & Modern

9 781513 290942